FOXING THE GEESE

FOXING THE GEESE

Janet Woods

This first world edition published 2016
in Great Britain and the USA by
SEVERN HOUSE PUBLISHERS LTD of
19 Cedar Road, Sutton, Surrey, England, SM2 5DA.
Trade paperback edition first published
in Great Britain and the USA 2016 by
SEVERN HOUSE PUBLISHERS LTD

British Library Cataloguing in Publication Data

Woods, Janet, 1939- author.
  Foxing the geese.
  1. Great Britain–History–Regency, 1811-1820–Fiction.
  2. Love stories.
  I. Title
  823.9'2-dc23

ISBN-13: 978-0-7278-8582-1 (cased)
ISBN-13: 978-1-84751-690-9 (trade paper)
ISBN-13: 978-1-78010-746-2 (e-book)

All Severn House titles are printed on acid-free paper.

Severn House Publishers support the Forest Stewardship Council™ [FSC™],
the leading international forest certification organisation.
All our titles that are printed on FSC certified paper carry the FSC logo.

Typeset by Palimpsest Book Production Ltd.,
Falkirk, Stirlingshire, Scotland.
Printed and bound in Great Britain by
TJ International, Padstow, Cornwall.

One

Kent, 1812

Vivienne Fox had decided not to get married just for the sake of it. As she told her father at breakfast that morning, a week after he'd informed her of her good fortune: 'I'm twenty-four years old. Until I came into my legacy no man took the slightest interest in me, let alone one with a title.'

'But dear . . .'

'Now they're queuing up at the door . . . men who rejected me year after year and laughed behind my back. It's humiliating. Aunt Edwina intends to trot me out like the family dog on Sunday, all bathed and brushed so I can simper and flutter and wag my tail, and all to gain the attention of a pack of brainless, chinless . . . braying fools!'

'My dear, don't be so angry.'

She waved a handful of invitations in the air. 'Is it because I've suddenly become a more worthy person? Is it because I can dance, play the piano and sing any better than I did last year, or the year before, or all the other years before that? Is it because I've grown to be beautiful?'

She answered her own questions. 'No . . . no . . . no . . . no! It's because Vivienne Fox, eldest daughter of the Reverend Ambrose Fox, has suddenly become endowed with riches beyond her wildest dreams from the ill-gotten gains of a sugar plantation, which was owned by a remote cousin – a cousin we'd never heard of. Moreover, he made the fortune on the sweat of slave labour!'

'Oh, I'd heard of Philip Dubois. I met him shortly after I married your mother. He was considered to be an undesirable relative by her family, but your mother liked the adventurer in him and said he made her laugh. He came to visit you after you were born, and was very taken with you. It was kind of him to leave you his fortune, but then, you're his only blood relative.'

'So although he was considered an undesirable acquaintance, his money does not carry the same stigma, therefore your unmarried and least attractive daughter is suddenly desirable. The whole idea is obscene, and you must promise me that you won't tell anyone of my sudden legacy, especially the size of it.' She scattered the invitations across the carpet. 'There, that's disposed of them. I will not accept any of them!'

Her father smiled at her tirade. 'You're being much too passionate, Vivienne. No man will be interested in having a scold for his wife, whatever the price on her head. You must learn to be a little less forthright, and . . . well, try not to be so *clever*. Ordinarily, men don't like women who can out-think them. It makes them feel foolish.'

'If it does then they are foolish.' She smiled at him. 'You don't expect me to pander to a man's pride by acting like some dizzy miss – not after you taught me to reason and think independently. I don't make you feel foolish, do I?'

'That's different. I'm your father and have different expectations.'

'Then I'll wait for a man who is just like you – one who is extraordinary.'

'And when you meet this perfect gentleman?'

'Because you are so eager to get rid of me, dearest Papa, then I will ask him to marry me and be done with it.'

'You cannot propose to a man!'

She grinned at the shock in her father's eyes. 'Why ever not?'

'It's just not done,' he spluttered.

A lame excuse if ever she'd heard one. 'I will make it *done* if he pleases me. And if I can't find a man I like, then so be it. Instead I will embrace spinsterhood and become a favourite aunt to my sisters' offspring.'

'Just give a suitor a chance. Be pleasant and well-mannered, that's all I ask, Vivienne. Your sisters went through exactly the same thing and without a penny piece between them. Look how well they did in the end.'

Vivienne's annoyance abated. Bethany and Caroline were her younger half-sisters. They had fallen in love at first sight, and married a pair of cousins who adored them. Her brothers-in-law were partners in a legal practice with offices in Yorkshire, and the possessors of comfortable and considerable self-earned fortunes.

But then, her sisters were pretty, sweet and vivacious as well as being younger than her, which was a humiliation in itself. Neither did they possess a mean thought about anyone to share between them, while her own mind created a whole storm at the drop of a hat. Her sisters took after their late mother in looks. Dark-haired, fair-skinned, blue-eyed and dainty; every perfect feature was positioned in just the right place to create a countenance of great beauty.

Vivienne sighed. Her own hair was light brown – her papa described it as honey-brown – with curls that were hard to control, so it never looked quite tidy. She was also a little on the tall side for a woman. Her eyes were several shades, alternating between grey and green, depending on the time of day. Now they sparkled as she gazed at her father. 'Do you never become angry and jealous and have mean thoughts, Papa?'

He smiled. 'Of course I do, but I try to control my temper and see the other person's point of view.'

'What if you can't see it, however much you try?'

He rolled his eyes. 'Then I pray that God will give me the will to impose my own point of view on them before they impose theirs on me.'

She laughed at that. 'Like you're doing now?'

'Exactly as I'm doing now.' He patted her hand. 'It's quite clear, Vivienne, that you need to be loved for your own dear self, and a man with any sense will recognize that. I'm sure it will come to pass if you would but give yourself a chance. But that chance will pass you by if you skulk in your bedchamber and worry about your looks – which, I might add, aren't as plain as you imagine – or seethe about the injustice in the world in a forthright manner that will label you a shrew.'

She kissed the bald spot on the top of his head. 'You are a most unusual man and too manipulative by far. I knew you'd understand, Papa. I have a mercurial nature like yours, and if I had neither the looks nor inclination to become a doting wife before I was wealthy, then obviously I have not had time to acquire pretty manners along with the fortune.'

'On the contrary; judging by those invitations, you're now acceptable to a larger circle of people . . . and from much higher on the social scale, so it stands to reason that the perfect man for you is still in circulation and available.'

'So the news is abroad already?'

Her father offered her a sheepish nod. 'A couple of people are aware of it, but I imagine they will be discreet.'

Vivienne was just as sure that they wouldn't be. 'Couldn't we say it's a rumour, or we've given it to the poor . . . now that's a good idea. If we gave it away the suitors would fade away with it.'

'It will hold you in good stead for your future. With your permission the poor will get a portion but you must be prudent. I was thinking we might visit your uncle, John Howard, who has made a fortune from his own wits. He knows how to invest money and a sum such as yours needs to be managed.'

'When shall we leave?'

'All in good time, my dear. Goodness, I haven't even informed him of the matter yet. I shall have to send a messenger, and I can't spare more than a week.' He took out his watch and consulted it, as if it would sort matters out for him, then placed it back in his waistcoat pocket.

'Would you like me to arrange the visit, Pa? It's several weeks before I need to be in London, and I could go from there.' She had a memory of John Howard, a man who looked stern. He'd told her wonderful stories. He'd also given her some numbers to add together and had told her she had a sharp mind and it was a pity she hadn't been born a boy, because he would have employed her. He'd rewarded her with a silver florin for solving the sum. She still had it.

'I can barely remember my Uncle John, though I have an impression that he was nice in a growly sort of way. He took me to a big house and there was a man with a loud voice who threw me in the air and made me scream with fright, and some rough boys. I think I would like to see my uncle again.'

'And the boys?'

'Certainly not. They said they didn't like girls, and were bad-mannered creatures that teased me and made me cry. The older one threw me into the pigsty. And they all laughed. I can still remember the disgusting smell.' She wasn't about to tell him that the older one had whispered to her when they were alone that he did like her. He'd kissed her on the mouth in a casual sort of way. 'Don't tell anyone,' he'd said. 'It means I'll marry you when I grow up and become an earl.'

For years afterwards she'd expected him to turn up on her doorstep – and although she'd sent him a letter, he hadn't bothered to answer. It was the first time her affections had been rejected, and it still stung.

Her father said, 'I daresay they would have changed by now, don't you? One thing you've forgotten is that your cousin Adelaide is in need of a companion for the London season, and you are to chaperone each other.'

'Such a bore.'

Vivienne hadn't forgotten. Until now Adelaide had always worn a superior air because she had a substantial dowry at her disposal. But the contents of Vivienne's purse now surpassed that of Adelaide's. Looks were a different thing altogether, however. When compared to Vivienne's own nondescript appearance, Adelaide was a beauty, with dark hair, blue eyes and a rosebud mouth. She had a high-pitched voice though, and an unrestrained giggle that could be irritating. Her bosom was ample enough to attract the glances of men, lustful creatures that they were. Their boldly assessing glances tended to wander past Vivienne to rest on Adelaide, who was shameless at flaunting her charms.

From Adelaide's unseemly confidences about men and the physical effects of their wooing on her cousin's body, Vivienne knew her own flights of fancy were as normal as those of any young woman, though she wouldn't stoop so low as to swoon, just to catch the attention of some buck. Her cousin was much too bold in that way.

Vivienne knew she was being prissy. Nevertheless, she did want to marry and she would make somebody a good wife. She just wanted a man who would love her. That was something she hadn't given up on yet – something to look forward to, she supposed.

'Now, gather up those invitations and we'll go through them. I believe I saw a crest or two on the envelopes.'

Her father had made her feel horribly selfish. Yet Vivienne sighed as she thought of the humiliation of being looked over in the marriage stakes once again. True, she did now have a fortune at her disposal to make her a more desirable prospect, despite her indifferent looks. What if she took the first man who asked her? That would put her season of torture to an end before it had begun. No, it might be that silly Freddie Lamington with his derogatory remarks and his loud laugh. Doubtful, since Vivienne suspected that he admired her cousin.

Worse was the lecherous Simon Mortimer, who'd cornered her in an alcove the previous year. He'd told her that her mouth resembled a squashed peach and had tried to kiss her. She shuddered. A squashed peach sounded a bit messy. His mouth had been moist and his breath smelled of brandy. She'd quickly turned her head to one side and his kiss had slid across her face. It had taken all of her strength to push him away and to escape. To make matters worse he'd apologized later for taking such a liberty, saying he'd mistaken her for Elizabeth Carter, who was known for being fast.

What was clear was that her father was determined to get her before the altar with some man, and then eventually provide him with a houseful of grandchildren to dote over . . . just like her sisters were doing.

Vivienne wondered if Jane Bessant had anything to do with it. Her father had been a widower for five years now. Jane was quiet and intelligent, and Vivienne had long thought that Jane would make a perfect match for her father.

Vivienne had told him earlier that she'd propose to a man if she met one she happened to like. She hadn't meant it at the time, but was being provocative, making light of the situation. However the idea had begun to take root in her mind. Why shouldn't she do the proposing? She might meet a man she found presentable . . . one she liked and felt she could rub along with. Then the stupid protocols of husband-catching would be over and done with. It would save having to play games. She wouldn't have to flirt with her eyelashes from behind her fan and make small talk . . . and there wouldn't be large gaps in her dance card. That would be a plus, because she quite liked dancing. Besides, whatever she'd thought or said before about spinsters, she didn't really want to become that most unfortunate of creatures – a tabby.

She determined to keep a book on any man who approached her, and then list their good and bad points before she made her choice. Someone taller than herself would take number one position. Dancing at number two . . . no . . . a sense of humour could go there. Dancing wasn't really important because it could be taught, but she didn't want a miserable man for a husband.

And she wouldn't have anything to do with the men who'd turned their noses up at her before fortune smiled upon her. To confuse matters, she might even start a rumour denying she had a fortune.

When she chuckled at the thought her father turned an enquiring glance her way. 'You're scheming, Vivienne.'

'A little, Papa. Having a fortune has gifted me with a sense of confidence, but there still might be a man out there who is willing to relieve you of your spinster daughter, and without fortune. If that fails, having an extra element to attract suitors might not be too bad after all. At least I'll be able to pick and choose. But I warn you . . . I'm going to be very discriminating.'

'I certainly hope so, Vivienne my dear. I would hate it if you made a hasty decision, because marriage is a lifelong commitment. I love you dearly, and I want you to be happy. Promise me you'll take care.'

'I certainly will. Any man I choose must meet with your approval.'

'I wouldn't expect anything less than that courtesy from you, but in the absence of a mother I must caution you. When love exists between a man and a woman reason is often ignored. Listen to your heart by all means, Vivienne, but remember you will have to live with your decision for the rest of your life. Now pick up those cards and start making arrangements.'

'It will sound more official if you write to my uncle . . . write "urgent" on the outside, and tell him the matter is strictly private. I will ask Jane Bessant to move into the house to keep the cat company while we're away. She would do anything for you.'

A tinge of colour stole into his cheeks and he stuttered, 'That's nonsense.'

'Is it? Jane Bessant would make you a perfect wife, and in case you think your children might not approve, we all like her.'

Kissing him lightly on the cheek, she departed to make arrangements for their visit.

Two

After days of deliberation, Alex LéSayres had made up his mind. 'I must find myself a wealthy woman to wed. Our finances are in a mess and unless I act now we'll have to sell land to pay Father's debts – there's no other choice.'

His brother, Dominic, keeper of the family fortunes, or what remained of them, gazed at Alex, deferring to his elder brother as the earl and the undisputed head of the LéSayres household. 'We could sell Howard the property he wants.'

Alex ignored his brother's grin and dropped his gaze to his scuffed black hessians, wondering when he'd be able to afford a new pair. Eventually he looked up at Dominic. 'If you're referring to the King's Mile, you know what my answer is. John Howard wants to pull down the cottage and erect some damned monstrosity of a house in its place. I'd rather go bare-arsed for life.'

Dominic shrugged. 'That's become a distinct possibility, Alex. Bear in mind that the family owes John Howard a great deal of money, and he's offering a good price for the land.'

They were alike, Alex thought. Olive-skinned, their hair as dark as night. His brother had a quiet if somewhat sinister elegance about him. The difference lay in their eye colour. Alex had inherited the deep blue eyes of his father, while Dominic favoured the calm grey of their mother.

Alex shook his head. 'He can't have the King's Mile. It will have to be something else of value.'

'Name it?'

'The family silver.'

'It's already gone. George Rattattou accepted it in lieu of cash in payment of Pa's promissory note. It would have been melted down by now.'

'The portraits?'

'Nobody but the LéSayres family wants them and we're all

that's left of that. We've been over and over this, Alex. From now on, whether King's Acres estate rises or falls is entirely up to us.'

'Then I must marry . . . and soon. I've quite made up my mind to it.' Alex tried not to let his disappointment show as he contemplated the lack of responsibility their father had displayed towards his two sons. In life, the late Alexander LéSayres had loved them both, and he'd been proud of them. His fault was the need to gamble, and gamble he had, gradually emptying the house of its treasures. By some miracle he'd managed to hold on to the house and land, and he'd been the most understanding of fathers, though strict.

That thought took the edge from Alex's anger as he gazed at Dominic. He heaved a sigh. 'We'll have to sell the LéSayres jewellery if we're to clear John Howard's debt and plant a crop. It must be worth something,' he said into the ensuing silence.

Dominic reminded him of what he'd forgotten. 'We can't. It has to be passed down to the next countess. It's a tradition, and we promised Father.'

They had promised their father a lot when he'd been on his deathbed. He'd been full of remorse for his shortcomings and had expected his two sons to put matters right.

'Promises are made to be broken, as Pa demonstrated on many an occasion, and traditions can be changed.'

Dominic's quick smile took on an ironic edge. 'Marriage it is then.'

Alex's eyes narrowed in on him. 'I don't like that syrupy tone of voice you're using, Dom. You have devious moments that bode me no good, and I think this is going to be one of them.'

'Nonsense, I'm sure my solution to our problem will be perfect for you, especially since you've brought the matter up on several occasions. As the new earl, certain behaviours and duties will be expected of you . . . no more whoring around.'

Devious or not, Dominic did have a good brain for figuring things out, Alex admitted, and although he knew exactly what his brother was going to suggest, he couldn't help but lead him on. 'Go on.'

'We'll pawn the family jewels – which isn't actually selling them. That will scrape us up enough money to fit you out decently.'

A pair of shining new hessians marched across Alex's imagination. 'Why would I want to be fitted out?'

'So you can go to London for the season.'

'A season in London? What am I supposed to do there, dance with a bear in the dung of the market place while the bystanders throw coins into my hat?'

'That's where you'll find yourself a wealthy bride.'

Alex roared with laughter. Then he realized Dom was laughing at him, not with him and his own laughter turned into a growl. 'That might take some time.'

Dominic gave a faint smile. 'We'll have to sacrifice time if we're to save the estate for the future. You must find a willing maid with a fortune as soon as possible.'

'Wait a minute . . . the only person making a sacrifice here is me.'

'You're the only one with aristocratic balls,' Dominic pointed out.

'So because of that you're going to put me out to stud. You want me to sell my freedom and be at the beck and call of some quivering innocent who doesn't know one end of a man from the other?'

'I'm sure it won't take you long to educate her on which end of you does what. Many women would give their all to marry an earl and become the Countess LéSayres. You'd only have to service her once a year to breed a brat in your image,' Dominic pointed out helpfully.

Alex managed a smile. As Dom well knew, the thought of having a family had always appealed to him. But he'd imagined he'd fall in love with a buxom woman of great beauty who would fill the role of Countess LéSayres to perfection, for the family portraits displayed delightfully endowed countesses with satisfied expressions and plump babies clinging to their skirts. The LéSayres men were a lusty-looking lot and the artist had managed to capture the lascivious expressions in their eyes. He sighed. 'I usually sample the wares without the legalities attached.'

'I'm not talking about an easy type of woman, but one who places a value on her worth as a wife. Plenty of the ladies in the church cast long, languishing eyes in your direction.'

'They are either too young and innocent or too old and virtuous.'

Dominic grinned. 'There speaks the voice of experience. What have you been up to with the ladies of the district, brother?'

'Mind your own business.'

'But we are discussing your future nuptials. Apart from money, what quality will you expect from a wife?'

Alex thought for a moment or two. 'I don't want to end up with a spinster who's too plain to attract a man despite having a fortune attached. And neither do I want a dowdy who goes to bed with a lock on her briar patch.'

'To which lock you will hold the key. Have you ever heard the saying, beggars can't be choosers?'

He growled, 'I'm no beggar and I'm aware the more attractive fillies will be encouraged by their mamas to gravitate towards those who can bid the highest for them. She will have to attract me and know her place . . . and she must not be outspoken. She must be sweet and demure . . . and . . . clean. And she must not flirt with other men.'

Dominic chuckled. 'She doesn't sound anything like your usual conquests. Don't underestimate the little ladies on the marriage market. You have good looks, and you're intelligent enough to attract the right type of female. We'll ask Eugenie to teach you how to dance and approach a lady, so you don't need to throw one over your shoulder and carry her off. As for the rest, if your bragging is anything to go by, you certainly know your way round a woman, even a virginal one.'

'I'm frightened of virgins. Their eyes are wide and innocent and you can see their little hearts beating like wings against their bodices at the wickedly delicious thought of being ravished. When it comes down to it I can't bring myself to actually spoil the sweet little creatures . . . then they look all dewy-eyed and disappointed.'

'When did you become such an expert on women, Alex?'

'Since I decided to wed five minutes ago.'

'You knew you were going to have to wed eventually. It might as well be now and at least it's for a good cause.'

Alex knew his smile was smug when he informed his brother, 'Get this through your thick head. I'm not going to play the fool, spout flowery poetry, fawn over a woman and lead her to expect something different than what she'd actually get after the marriage service. As for dancing, I already can. The farmer's wife taught me.'

Dominic managed a thin smile. 'Yes, I noticed that at the harvest supper. One jug of scrumpy cider and you were hopping about like a frog with its bum on a hot skillet. For an earl, you made a complete bumpkin of yourself. No dignity at all. I think you're scared of women.'

'Women are God's gift to men.'

'You've been scared of them since you dumped that relative of John Howard into the pigsty. And called her Princess Piggy. She climbed out stinking to high heaven and almost in flames, then chased after you with a pitchfork to push you into the duck pond.'

'She succeeded.' He grinned as he recalled, 'She was a skinny dab of a creature, too. I underestimated her aggression. I gave her thruppence to take the blame. She told her uncle it wasn't my fault, but Pa gave me a thrashing anyway. I settled the matter with a kiss before she went home, and promised to marry her. She was only about twelve, and the poor little idiot believed me.'

'Perhaps she's still waiting.'

'I hope not. Besides, her father was a parson, I think. He probably hasn't got two beans to rub together.'

'Wealthy and obedient it is then. I don't know any woman like that, but I'll wager my new horse that you can't catch yourself a wealthy wife.'

Alex thought about that. Dominic's horse was an elegant gelding he'd recently won in a card game. It was a glossy black creature standing at sixteen hands and in his prime. 'You're not twitting me?'

'I'm not.'

'All right.' Alex held out a hand. 'Let's shake on it.'

When Dominic took his hand, Alex applied a wrestling throw he'd just learned, and his brother found himself flat on his back.

Alex laughed, but the scowl Dominic offered him was almost admiring as he rose and dusted himself off. He grabbed Alex's shoulders and they pitted their strength against each other.

Attracted by the laughter and grunts, a pair of family lurchers who'd just finished devouring the entrails of a rabbit for breakfast, lobbed in and joined the melee, tails thrashing about, bodies twisting and tongues drooling all over them.

A sudden deluge of cold water intruded into their fun. The dogs ran off yelping towards the kitchen as if they'd been scalded. The LéSayres brothers emerged from the fray as a duet of shabby but well-built and graceful figures. They gazed towards the minstrel's gallery.

Alex shook the excess of liquid from the dark locks of his hair and grinned affectionately at the neat figure in a grey gown with its modest lace-edged fichu. Eugenie had a jug in one hand. She looked personable for fifty and she wore one of her contrite expressions.

'Well aimed, Eugenie, did we wake you?'

'Sorry gentlemen, the water was meant for the dogs.'

Alex didn't believe that for one minute. Eugenie had first been their nurse and then their governess. After their mother died in childbirth Eugenie had become their father's companion. Perhaps she always had been, neither of them knew for certain. What they did know was that their father had loved her. A week before he died, barely two months previously, Eugenie had become Countess LéSayres, for their father had summoned a bishop to his bedside and had refused to die until he'd made an honest woman of her. Eugenie was the nearest thing to a mother they'd ever had, for they couldn't remember their own, and their father had finally got his wish to make her his wife. Now Alex gazed at her with as much deference as if she were their real mother.

She gave a throaty laugh. 'You know very well I'm not still in bed at this time of the morning. Stop grinning in that obnoxious manner, Alex. You're supposed to be getting the carriage hitched to take us to church. We leave in five minutes.'

'It's already hitched, My Lady.' He gave her a sweeping bow and Dominic followed suit.

This time it was Eugenie who grinned, and her voice softened. 'The pair of you go and tidy yourself up. You're a disgrace, especially you, Alex. Remember that you're now the earl and should conduct yourself with dignity if you want to earn respect, especially from that rogue who calls himself your brother.' She bestowed a fond look on Dominic and the brothers exchanged smiles, secure in the knowledge that Eugenie adored them both.

Dominic blew her a kiss before they scattered in opposite directions.

Alex knew how important this day was to Eugenie. Raking the water from his hair with his fingers, he donned his best jacket, and not for the first time wished he had a pair of decent hessians to wear. He smeared soot into the scuffed leather, polishing the boots as best he could before he joined his brother, who was outside astride his horse . . . a beautiful creature that would soon be his, if he found a wealthy wife. He had no trouble attracting women, so it couldn't be too hard.

It was a perfect summer day, the sky blue, the breeze soft and the hedges full of flowers. A song thrush warbled in the trees.

Helping Eugenie into the gig, Alex followed her up and took the reins. They headed sedately towards the church through the winding sun-dappled lanes, his brother, long-legged and lithe, astride his gelding.

Yes, he thought. The time had come when he needed to wed, and his bride must be a wealthy one. It was the right thing to do, for himself, his brother . . . and for the family name.

His gaze travelled over the soft green countryside. 'I'll miss all this when I'm in London,' he said out loud.

Eugenie's brown eyes turned his way. 'You're considering going to London?'

'I've decided the time has come to find myself a wealthy wife.'

'It's not a bad idea. It's about time you were wed, Alex. You need heirs.'

Knowing he was making a last stand, he said, 'Last time I looked I had a perfectly worthy earl presumptive in Dominic.'

'You know very well what I mean. Your father left debts and the estate is nearly bankrupt.'

'Isn't it rather unfair to expect some unsuspecting female to marry a pauper and pay off his debts?'

'No . . . it's not fair, but that's the way things are. Many young women would consider your title worth paying for, and many fathers of means would see the desirability of such a match for his daughter. You're a handsome lad. Both of you are.'

He laughed. 'When will you admit that we're grown men?'

'You were acting like a couple of unruly pups a few minutes ago.'

'We tend to lapse back to childhood on occasion, but I really don't want to be a purchased husband. I want a woman I can feel some affection for.'

'What makes you think you won't fall in love with the woman you wed? You're like your father in that, a born romantic,' she said. 'Find a woman who is honest and who you feel easy with. Treat her with kindness and respect. She will respond to that and you will have a solid foundation to build a future on.'

Alex shrugged and picked up speed as the church bells began to ring. Eugenie had loved his father right until the end. He would like the same regard from a woman.

His brother had surged on ahead and Alex picked up speed when the church bells began to ring.

Eugenie lifted her hand to the crown of the pretty straw hat she wore, anchoring it to her head.

There was a small crowd of people waiting for them to arrive at the church. Alex helped Eugenie down and led her towards the door. There were curtseys bobbed, and murmurs of 'My Lady'.

They came level with John Howard, a man their father owed a considerable amount of money to. 'Good morning, Mr Howard. It's a fine day.'

'Indeed it is.' There was a pause in which John Howard nudged his wife.

'Good morning, My Lord.' Mary's gaze raked over Eugenie. Her lips pressed together in a thin line. 'My Lady.'

Howard took a step to one side. 'May I present the Reverend Ambrose Fox and his daughter, Miss Fox.'

A pair of jade eyes engaged his directly. 'I believe the earl and I have met before, Uncle.'

They had? Alex's brow wrinkled as he wracked his memory.

'Have you forgotten so easily?'

The little touch of mockery in her voice was annoying, but then she had one of those faces that appeared unremarkable. She smiled, and now he saw that her mouth curved in just the right places, her eyes were wide and beautiful with their long lashes, and all was set in a face of flawless complexion. A pity about the straw bonnet; it didn't suit her.

He found himself floundering for words. 'Really . . . you have me at a disadvantage, Miss Fox. I'm afraid I cannot recall . . .'

'Perhaps I should jog your memory a little, My Lord. It was

about twelve years ago when you dubbed me the princess of pigs. The ceremony took place in a pigsty.' More softly she said, 'Or was it a duck pond?'

Alex nodded, made uncomfortable by her grin, and even more discomforted by the fact he'd been thinking of her just two days before, and now she'd appeared to haunt him like a witch on a broomstick.

'I believe we were children at the time, Miss Fox.'

'Ah yes . . . now you remember.'

'Only just . . . I tend to put childish things behind me, Miss Fox. Perhaps you should do the same.'

After a short pause into which his careless reprimand sank, her face heated with embarrassment – or was it anger?

She murmured, 'I feel it would be a convenient action for both of us to adopt at this moment.' A twinge of guilt trickled through him when she took her father's arm. 'Shall we go in, Papa?'

Alex's family and the Howards lingered in the porch for a few moments more while a business meeting with the financier was arranged.

Of more interest to Alex was Eugenie's reception. Their stepmother's position had been acknowledged. The brothers grinned at each other, and ranging either side of her they proceeded down the aisle. Their backs would not absorb the imaginary daggers as keenly as Eugenie's would feel them though.

John Howard and his wife followed after and the two parties separated to the left and right at their designated pews. Alex was satisfied with the small amount of respect paid to his stepmother by the leading light in the district. She had not been snubbed by the Howard family, as he'd feared she might be.

When fortune was restored to the LéSayres name he intended to play the role of earl to the hilt in a way his father never had, and gain respect for the family name in the process. To that end he would call on John Howard in a day or two to discuss his father's debt. With Dominic's guidance he intended to renegotiate the accumulated interest, which now amounted to several times the original loan.

As they took their place in the family pew, Alex gently squeezed Eugenie's hand and she gave him a warm and grateful smile.

When he glanced across the aisle his eyes tangled with the jade depths of Howard's niece, Miss Fox, who had positioned herself as far away from him as she could get. A silky lock of reddish brown hair escaped from under her bonnet.

He must apologize for his churlish remark after the service, he thought.

He offered her a smile, one that had softened many a female heart in the past.

She ignored his overture and stared at him with disinterest, as if she was viewing a beetle in a specimen case, all prim and proper and keeping her distance. Her gloved hands rested one on top of the other in her lap, as if guarding her femininity. It was a typical spinster pose.

He remembered her in the pigsty, a girl all shining and bright in her visiting clothes with the sun turning her hair to gold. She'd been rightfully aggrieved by the trick he'd played on her and she'd stood there with tears tracking down her dirty face and a coin in her pocket. She'd lied so convincingly in defence of her thrupenny piece that she'd nearly convinced him that he was innocent too. Unfortunately it hadn't convinced his father . . . nor hers. A huff of laughter left him.

She stuck her nose in the air and turned away, her stupid bonnet shielding her profile from his sight.

He missed her after church too, intercepted by the rector. He got outside just as the Howard carriage was about to move off. There was a second when she gazed at him through the glass, and he could have sworn she stuck out the pink tip of her tongue at him. Then she was gone.

Three

The main offices of John Howard were situated in the High Street in Poole, but the man spread his net wide, Alex thought.

The port town was a bustling place, the harbour filled with shipping and the quay littered with goods being loaded or unloaded. There were stalls too, smoked eels and pickled cockles for sale, fancy women in fancy dresses, giggling and flirting as they eyed the seamen.

Howard also had loan offices in Dorchester, Southampton and London, if the gold lettering on the door was to be believed. The place looked impregnable; the windows were securely barred and the door had stout bolts with padlocks. In the thirty years since he'd moved into town John Howard had acquired several properties in lieu of debt and was reputed to be the wealthiest man in the district. Alex would not allow him to help himself to the family seat, whatever the debt.

John Howard rose and came round the desk, a professional smile set in place as he indicated a chair apiece. He was as tall as Alex, long in the jaw and immaculately dressed. 'Good day, My Lord . . . Mr LéSayres. To what do I owe the pleasure of this visit?'

'You know damned well,' Alex growled.

Dominic placed a hand on his arm. 'We are here to make a payment off my father's debt.'

'My clerk will deal with that.'

'And our intention is to negotiate a lesser rate of interest.'

Howard's smile faded and he put the desk between them. 'That's impossible, I'm afraid. The late earl agreed to my terms and he signed the agreement, which is legally binding.'

'The principal sum advanced to our father has already been repaid by us. We expected to pay his debts and a reasonable amount of interest, but the amount you charged our father is on par with rates offered by the moneylender. He must have been inebriated when he signed that IOU, and you took advantage of that.'

'Be that as it may, Mr LéSayres, he did sign it. His signature was witnessed by my clerk, and by another man named Thomas Gould who is employed as a customs officer. Gould cautioned your father against it, but he wouldn't listen to reason. He was a man who insisted on his own way, as you know. Perhaps you'd reconsider selling me the King's Mile. It would cover the debt with a little to spare.' His smile was that of a man who thought he had them backed into a corner.

Dominic put that notion to rest. 'Definitely not, Mr Howard . . . besides, we have received a better offer for it.'

Alex gave his brother a hard look as he wondered what Dom was up to.

Howard made a platform of his hands and settled his chin on his entwined fingers, completely relaxed. The expression in his eyes was clearly disbelieving. 'Really, My Lord, may I ask from whom?'

There was a long moment of silence, and then Dom kicked his ankle. Obviously his brother expected him to go along with this farce.

Alex examined his fingernails as he scrambled for an answer that didn't sound too much of a lie. What did Dom expect him to say? He opened his mouth and a gem fell out of it without being prompted. 'That information is confidential as well as irrelevant. I will not sell the King's Mile because it was a gift from the crown. To sell it would cause insult to the throne.'

'How can the sale of a small slice of land cause insult to the crown? I doubt if King George even knows it exists.'

Dom shrugged as he drawled, 'I've examined the deed, and there's nothing to say it can't be sold, Alex. Perhaps I should point out that the land is worth far more than Mr Howard has offered as a settlement of the interest on our father's private debt. If we sold the land to the latest bidder, then the debt would be covered with money to spare. The interest is far too high. I will not allow the estate to be fleeced in such a manner. It's outright greed.'

'You might find yourself in debtors' prison, My Lord,' Howard said, leaning forward to peer over his glasses at them.

Did Howard think they were stupid? Alex raised an eyebrow. 'Are you threatening me or trying to frighten me?'

Dominic informed Howard, 'I imagine we're all aware that peers of the realm do not go to debtors' prison, and the debt wasn't ours. It was a private agreement between yourself and our father.'

Alex thought of something useful to add to the conversation. 'I could place the claim before the House of Lords, where it's possible you would be proclaimed a "cent-per-cent" and the debt cancelled. Also, may I remind you that the premises you rent belong to the LéSayres estate.'

'And may I remind *you* that the lease is for my lifetime.'

Alex felt his blood rise. 'Which doesn't come with a guarantee of longevity.'

'Are you threatening me, My Lord?'

Dom's expression was one of supreme smugness as he took a purse from his satchel and bounced it in his hand. 'The earl is not disposed towards violence, but you must admit that your agreement with our father was blatantly unfair. Gentlemen, this is a negotiation, so let us not quarrel. Allow me to put it this way, Mr Howard. We are prepared to pay the normal interest on the loan, as is fair and right – but not one penny more. If you will accept that, taking into account that it will be all you will get out of us, the debt can be cleared here and now.'

It was on the tip of Alex's tongue to ask Dom where the money had come from, but he desisted. No doubt his brother would explain when it suited him.

Howard's gaze followed the purse as it spun in the air and was recaptured in Dominic's palm with a solid thud. 'And if I refuse?'

'You mentioned your lease, I believe. Perhaps I should inform you that I was just about to review the rents.'

Colour mottled Howard's face and the wind seemed to go out of him. 'Setting them high enough to cover the interest on your father's loans if I'm reading this conversation correctly. Can we stop sparring? We all know it's a farce.'

'By all means . . . do unto others, etcetera.' Dominic threw the purse up again.

Howard caught the purse in mid-air, then gave a heavy sigh. 'Before I answer I have a proposition I would like you to consider, My Lord.'

'Which is?'

'You've met my niece through my connection with the Dubois

family. The Dubois were sugar planters, and her great-uncle was the black sheep. He had a cousin called Jeanne Dubois, and she was Vivienne Fox's mother.'

Alex shot to his feet so fast he thought he might have left his breeches behind in the chair. So that was what the crafty sod was after. He had a plan to plant his niece in the LéSayres family to give himself legitimate access to the aristocracy via his offspring. 'Definitely not! Besides, I'm leaving for London in a day or two.'

'Oh, that's no problem, because the girl will be in London with her cousin and aunt, which is why I mentioned it. The girl has neither looks nor fortune and has sworn never to marry . . . or so her father informed me in his last letter. She is my only female relative, and is more intelligent than most. I'm of a mind to do something for her, settle an annuity of some sort on her.'

'It would be a kind gesture.'

'I wouldn't like to think she'd be forced to suffered hardship in her later years. I was about to ask you to call on her, and sign her dance card perhaps. I would also appreciate an opinion before I act.'

'As long as you don't expect me to wed her. We have met twice, and both times was a disaster.'

Howard laughed. 'As to that . . . it's up to you. However, I have a proposition for you . . . a wager if you like.'

'What is it?' Dom said suspiciously.

'Quite simply, if your brother returns with a suitable wife, one who is endowed with grace and good fortune, I will cancel the interest. If you don't, then I'll double it.'

'Either way you stand to lose nothing, except perhaps the interest,' Dom said.

Howard sighed. 'And neither should I gentlemen, for the debt is yours.'

'If we lose the wager it's doubled, interest upon interest. I didn't take you for a gambling man, Mr Howard.'

'Didn't you? Lending money is a gamble in itself.'

Which was the truth. Alex exchanged a look with Dom. 'It shouldn't be too hard to get myself a wife.'

'You're not thinking of accepting the wager, Alex?'

He nodded and held out his hand to Howard. 'Why not, when we've already decided on the same course of action? You're on.'

'Good. With your permission I'll furnish you with letters of introduction. You will find that a money connection opens doors in the most unlikely places of power. It will certainly get you an invitation into Almack's for the Wednesday ball. In fact I can almost guarantee the invitation will be waiting there for you.'

Dominic sniffed the air like a terrier after a rat, as if he suspected something.

Alex narrowed his eyes. 'I don't suppose it will do any harm, as long as the young woman is not given any false expectations.'

John Howard smiled. 'Vivienne Fox is of an age where she has no real expectations left. A pity, since Vivienne is an intelligent girl, I believe. Had she been born a male I would have offered her a position in my counting house.'

'What does being male have to do with it when females are cheaper to employ?' Dominic said. 'Besides, any lady worth her mettle could accurately calculate the earl's wealth with one look, right down to the last starving moth in his pocket.'

Alex grinned expansively at Dominic. 'My brother is a great admirer of the fairer sex. Perhaps he should dance with your spinster relative instead. Is she still here?'

'Miss Fox is out and about. She likes the countryside and she likes to walk. I believe she said she was going to walk along the cliff top. She leaves with her father tomorrow . . . she needs to prepare her wardrobe for the London season, when she usually acts as chaperone to her cousin.'

A spark of alarm registered on Dominic's face. 'Ordinarily I would have been delighted to offer your relative my arm, but since I won't be going to London I'm sure you can count on the earl doing the gentlemanly thing.'

'I had no doubt. Thank you, My Lord. If you would allow, sir, I have a suite of rooms I could put at your disposal. I use them when I'm in London on business.'

When Alex exchanged a grin with Dominic, John Howard shrugged. 'I advise you not to jump to hasty conclusions, gentlemen. I own the building.'

'What's the girl's disposition?'

'I'm given to believe she's well tutored and is inclined towards debate rather than social chit-chat.'

'You mean that she's argumentative and opinionated.'

'I mean that not at all. Generally I find females of that ilk seem to pride themselves on being informed when they're merely being tiresome. Vivienne Fox is different. Reverend Fox is indeed blessed with his daughter. She is a credit to him.'

John looked from one to another, then smiled and said to the clerk who answered the bell, 'Bring me the LéSayres file, I've decided to write off the interest, on paper at least.'

After it was done Howard offered them his hand. 'I have made this a gentleman's agreement. I'm not one to hold a grudge and I believe you will act with honour in this instance. Shall we shake on it, My Lord?'

'My pleasure,' Alex said, which wasn't exactly the truth, but he knew it was better to maintain an acquaintanceship than create enemies. Due to Dominic's quick thinking they had won the battle and he could afford to be gracious. All he had to do was attract the right kind of woman, and he'd never had any trouble wooing the fairer sex.

When they got outside, Alex said with more than a hint of admiration in his voice, '*That* was a surprise! Well done, Dom, you're a conniving bastard when you need to be. Where did you get the money from?'

'I thought you'd ask.' His brother laughed and spurred his horse into a canter.

'Well . . .?' Alex said, catching him up.

Dominic slowed to accommodate a wagon coming from the opposite direction and patted his horse's elegant neck. 'I entered Nick here in a few races on the tavern circuit and he won easily. He seems to like the chase. That got me half of it.'

'I'm looking forward to when he belongs to me.'

'He's not an easy ride. He doesn't like strangers on his back and will corkscrew and toss you off until he gets used to you. The rest of the money came from the sweat of my brow. It's the accumulation of my life savings. When you've found yourself a wealthy bride I'll expect it to be repaid.' He thought for a moment. 'It all seems so easy. All you've got to do is find yourself a suitable wife. Do you think John Howard has a hidden agenda regarding this female relative of his?'

'I wouldn't be surprised, but I can't imagine what. He's already said she has no fortune and doesn't stand a chance on the marriage market. Besides, he hardly knows her. She didn't impress me in the slightest.'

'And you made it clear you're not interested in her as a bride, Alex. All you've got to do is dance with her and listen to her prattle for a bit. If you manage to give her a kiss as well it will keep her warm in her old age and you can leave her dreaming while you hunt down more exciting prey.'

Alex felt a twinge of conscience, for it went against his grain as a gentleman to target a woman because of age, looks or fortune. He felt sorry for John Howard's niece. It must be hell to be measured up against women who were younger, prettier, wealthier, probably wittier, and generally more accomplished. It was just as bad for a man, except a title went a long way and he had more scope to escape, as long as he hadn't declared himself in any way.

They parted company at the crossroads, Dominic heading towards his place of work, and Alex for his home, his horse at a canter.

He slowed to an amble when he spied Vivienne Fox in the distance. She was on the cliff top. Seated on a flat stone she gazed out over the water to where a fishing boat leaned heavily to one side as its crew hauled the nets ashore. Mist rose from water that was as calm and shining as a length of dark blue silk rippled with star shine. The gentle shush of water against the shore sounded like a mother calming her infant. It was a rare day.

He dismounted and walked towards her, saying her name so she wouldn't take fright. She turned towards him, the expression in her eyes soft and still filled with the remnants of her daydream. Her bonnet was tied to her wrist by its ribbons, lest an errant puff of wind should carry it off. Her hair was glorious in its golden brown torrent, her eyes enigmatic . . . yesterday they'd been jade, today they were turning the dark and wary colour of pine needles as her dreaming turned into reality.

She scrambled to her feet when she recognized him. 'My Lord! I had not thought to see you on the cliff top.'

'Why not, when this land is part of my estate?'

'I'm sorry . . . I had not sought to trespass.'

'You were dreaming, Miss Fox. I'm sorry I've disturbed you.'

'You haven't.'

'I was looking for you. Your uncle said you might be here.'

Her head slanted to one side and she seemed almost alarmed

by the thought. 'You've been to see my uncle. Did he say anything about me?'

'Should he have?'

'No . . . of course not . . . your pardon, My Lord.'

'Actually, he did mention you . . . he spoke very highly of you in fact. He said you were intelligent and a credit to your father.'

'He's my uncle. I imagine he was indulging in a little exaggeration.'

Alex chuckled. 'More likely he was telling the truth, since he doesn't strike me as a man who is less than totally honest.'

She picked up her sketching block. 'Will you excuse me, My Lord.'

'Not yet, since I've only just found you.'

'You were looking for me . . . why?'

How straightforward she was. He was equally straight in his answer. 'I wanted to apologize for my behaviour at the church. It was unforgivable of me, and I know your feelings were hurt.'

'I recovered easily enough. Old grudges are best forgotten and I reminded you of it unfairly. We were children, after all.'

'You were. I was a young man who should have known better.'

'You're still a young man, but you are not quite so brash.' She laughed. 'Every time I see a pig I remember how awful I smelled.'

'And every time I pass the duck pond, the ducks tell me off.'

'You must have very old ducks.'

'I imagine they pass the story down from mother duck to her ducklings. The cautionary tale of the princess with the pitchfork.'

A giggle rippled from her.

The cool breath of a breeze slid from the surface of the sea and surrounded them. He watched goose pimples run up her arms, and picking up her shawl, she drew it around her shoulders.

The smell of honeysuckle drifted from her. 'You've changed, Vivienne Fox. You're quite the graceful young lady now. With your permission I'd like to call on you when we're in London. You'll be the only person I know there.'

'Will you be there for the season?'

'I can only afford to stay a few weeks, so if you know any wealthy young ladies looking for a titled gentleman to wed, please put a word in for me. You'll be the only person I know there, and as we are both as poor as church mice, we could possibly be of use to one another.'

Their eyes met. She didn't look entirely enamoured by the prospect since her lip curled – and a very nice curl it was. Then she nodded. 'I suppose I can fit you in somewhere. It's not as if I'm in great demand, except at the beck and call of my aunt and cousin.'

Alex was not used to being treated in such an off-hand manner. Vivienne Fox deserved to have her arse smacked. He thought of a better plan, reminding her, 'A penny for a kiss?'

Before her mind had time to assimilate his words he closed the gap between them. For a moment her expression was one of surprise, then indignation, and then surprisingly, she yielded. His mouth settled on hers like a fish catching a dragonfly for its supper.

This time it was worth more than a penny. Her mouth was soft, tender and compliant . . . and there was a moment when he felt the passion come awake inside her.

So did she, for her body stiffened and she took a hasty step back. 'What must you think of me?'

'That you have a sweet mouth and I'd like to kiss you again.'

'Oh! How dare you be so familiar, My Lord.' She turned and ran, her hair flying.

Alex began to laugh. Poor or not, she amused him, and he intended to continue this interesting relationship in London.

Four

London

After being frugal all her life Vivienne felt a twinge of guilt at spending so much money on her appearance.

She'd tried to keep her acquisition of wealth private but word had gone before her and rumour had won the day. Establishments in which she'd once been obliged to queue for a length of ribbon now invited her into the private cubicles, the assistants offering her fawning smiles. Or a consultant came to the house and expertly milked her for information. Vivienne avoided answering while she was being respectfully measured and advised about fabrics and colours.

She would neither confirm nor deny any mention of fortune, knowing that the gossipmongers would eventually find some other hapless victim to prattle about. And she didn't need much advice. Her own sense of style and modesty drew her towards unfussy, elegant gowns that didn't expose her to unwanted stares. Jane Bessant had advised her on accessories such as lace collars and dancing slippers.

So it was a well-equipped young lady who was delivered to the house that her Aunt Edwina had rented in London for the season. Although small, the residence was situated in a smart part of town and came complete with servants.

Her cousin Adelaide pounced on her like an enthusiastic puppy, her eyes wide and shining with excitement. 'I've been dying for you to arrive, Vivienne. You'll never guess. Mother has hired us a personal maid for the month we are here, and you shall share her. We must get her to do something with your hair. I've heard that a vinegar rinse makes it shine.' Her glance travelled past her to where the coach driver was bringing in her second trunk. 'Goodness, you have two trunks this year. I'd heard that you'd been the recipient of a legacy? I've been seething with curiosity ever since. You must tell me all about it.'

Vivienne shrugged. 'It's true. I was remembered in a relative's will. On the strength of it I was able to buy myself a decent wardrobe. Papa has consulted with my uncle on the best way to invest what's left for my future.'

Adelaide's laughter was off-hand but relieved. 'Oh, is that all. I heard it was a fortune. I had visions of every aristocrat in town knocking at the door with the intention of wedding and bedding you for your sack of sovereigns. Poor Vivienne, without a decent dowry there will be nobody to love you.'

Forgetting that she'd condemned all men in a previous outburst to her father, and giving only a fleeting thought of how it would feel to be wed and bedded to a stranger, Vivienne said, 'Pray do not judge all men by the actions of a few. Men, even those wealthy and titled, are capable of loving a pauper.'

Adelaide shrugged. 'But they rarely marry them. It would be unfortunate if both of us were attracted to the same man and he had to choose the one with the biggest dowry.'

'Yes . . . I suppose it would.' And especially if he ignored what his heart told him and offered for her cousin, Vivienne thought, rather unexpectedly making herself the heroine of the situation. For the first time she confronted the fact that having a fortune might indeed give her an advantage. But talking about a man in the abstract and then facing the reality of becoming his wife, with all the intimacies of the marriage bed, brought a tremor of fright to salt her throat. 'It would be even more unfortunate if one of us fell in love with such a mercenary creature.'

'Oh, I shan't do that,' Adelaide said. 'Love has nothing to do with marriage, which is a business arrangement.' She lowered her voice and giggled. 'I shall save that for my lovers once I'm married.'

Feeling slightly shocked, Vivienne said, 'Have you ever been in love, Adelaide?'

'Loving one's husband would be the same as loving your parents, I imagine. And when I have babies I shall love them, no doubt, though I don't really like children much. They are horrible, dribbly little creatures that kick up a din for the smallest of reasons. I shall have nursemaids for mine.'

Must it be like that? Vivienne wondered. When she thought of being in love the tumultuous yearnings stirred up in her were nothing like the love and respect she felt towards her father. As for children, she was sure she would love being an aunt to her sisters' infants, even if they did dribble.

'We must make sure not to fall for the same man then. At least you won't be obliged to wear your shabby gowns this year. We already have several invitations. Viscount Statham has just arrived from his estate in Scotland and is considering taking a wife – even one without a dowry. He's as rich as Midas and is a widower in his forties. Apparently he's looking for a woman young enough to bear him children, and old enough to be sensible. He might suit you, though I have heard that he resembles a goat.'

Vivienne removed her bonnet, while the footmen, who were part of the lease contract of the house, carried her trunks upstairs.

Poor Viscount Statham to have to stoop so low because he resembled a goat. Was love no longer part of the equation of family? Was it all bricks and mortar and the production of children one by one, like eggs being hatched by so many clucking hens into an expensive nest.

Adelaide was nineteen, and on her mother's advice had already turned down two offers of marriage to much older men, one when she was barely sixteen. She didn't seem to have gained much sense in the three years since.

'Come and say hello to Mama. She has a headache and is resting, but asked me to tell her when you arrived.'

Her Aunt Edwina offered her a wan smile. 'Ah . . . Vivienne, my dear. How lovely to see you again. Was the journey tedious?'

'It was a little tiring, Aunt, but I travelled with Mr and Mrs Parker, who are Papa's parishioners, so I had interesting company. Despite having to stop and change the horses the weather was clement and we made good time. After all, Maidstone is only thirty or so miles away.'

'How is your dear papa?'

'He sends his best wishes and said he is looking forward to some peace and quiet while I'm away. He said you must send a messenger if he is needed.'

'I'm sure he didn't mean it for you are as quiet as a mouse, and you're such a sensible young lady . . . not like Adelaide, who is full of bounce. I'm hoping she will find someone suitable this year and settle down. Would you go and ask the cook to provide some refreshment in the drawing room in half-an-hour, my dear? I should be better by then and we can talk and make plans.'

Vivienne ignored the niggle of resentment she experienced. The notion that she was there to fetch and carry for her aunt and her cousin was plainly still embedded in them.

What would they do if she refused? After all, she was wallowing in wealth now and could have a house filled with servants at her beck and call, if that was what she wanted. She reminded herself that she'd rather make herself useful than sit and gossip about fashions or men all day. However, her aunt meant well and had taken her under her wing for the occasion of husband-hunting on several occasions. If Vivienne hadn't resisted strongly she might have been married to one of several men by now.

She would make her own choice in her own time.

Adelaide kissed her mother. 'In the meantime I'll go and supervise the maid and help her to unpack Vivienne's trunks. I'm dying to see her new wardrobe. And Mama, there is no truth in the rumour that Vivienne has acquired great wealth. She only inherited enough to buy herself a new wardrobe.'

Aunt Edwina's eyes flew open and Vivienne wondered if her aunt would swallow the lie as easily as it had slid off her tongue . . . though she hadn't actually lied, just evaded the truth a little. Perhaps her father had already sent a message and informed her of the legacy.

'Never mind, my dear. More's the pity since wealth attracts wealth. People shouldn't start these unkind rumours when they encourage falsehood. We will just have to work harder at attracting a man who is worthy of you and suitable to your station in life. I'm sure you'd be happy as the wife of a country doctor, or a cleric like your father. You've had plenty of experience helping out in your father's parish so you would be an asset to any clergyman.'

'Yes, I would be happy with that, as long as I loved him.'

It was as though she'd never spoken. 'I'll ask around.'

He aunt seemed determined to marry her off this year. A little desperately, Vivienne said, 'I'd rather you didn't.'

'Nonsense dear, it will be my pleasure.'

Adelaide said, 'Perhaps Viscount Statham would suit her.'

'There's him, of course. He lives rather a long way away, and

Scotland is so cold in the winter. Also, the Scottish dialect is quite unintelligible, and the men wear skirts, or so I've been told.'

'A goat in a skirt, how priceless,' Adelaide whispered, and giggled.

'Then again . . . he's twenty years older than you and not in robust health, I believe, so he would reasonably be expected to die before you, leaving you a fortune – which would be a blessing.'

'Vivienne is waiting for true love to come her way, not widowhood. Perhaps you should marry the Scottish viscount yourself, Mama. You're still young enough to give him a child.'

Abandoning her headache, Edwina aimed a frown at her daughter. 'Which is not so far-fetched as you seem to think because I have heard that the viscount is a very nice man. You really must get out of the habit of giggling and making silly remarks, Adelaide. You're no longer sixteen and it's irritating. Try and be sensible and level-headed, like Vivienne.'

Adelaide's face flushed from the reprimand, 'It hasn't got her very far.'

'But it will. Some men are impressed by a woman's ability to converse on any subject, and this year we'll be successful in finding her a husband. I feel it in my bones. Off you go now, you two. I shall see you in half an hour and we will go through the engagement book.'

Adelaide turned to leave the room first, her mouth in a sullen pout. To cheer her cousin up Vivienne handed her the keys to her trunk. 'Your mother didn't mean it; her headache is troubling her. Go and open my trunks while I talk to the cook. I've bought you a gift.'

'What is it?'

'Wait and see.'

When she returned, Adelaide exclaimed over the blue paisley stole that Vivienne had paid a fortune for, then threw it on a chair and watched as the maid unpacked her cousin's gowns. She couldn't help but criticize. 'How plain your gowns are; you should have bought something with frills on.'

'Frills don't suit me.'

'Is that one of your ballgowns?'

The maid shook it out and the silvery white diaphanous overskirt drifted down over a petticoat of embroidered roses. 'Such an elegant gown, Miss Fox,' she said.

Adelaide sniffed. 'I think it's disappointing. The neckline is too high to be fashionable. Have you brought stays? You didn't bring them last year. Not that it mattered because you had nothing to show off. I fancy you've gained a little flesh at the top since.' Looking in the long mirror Adelaide cupped her breasts in her hands and lifted them. 'See . . . if you have an asset you should draw attention to it, not hide it. I've heard that men find a lady's bosom attractive.'

Vivienne wasn't about to cater to a man's like or dislike of her bosom. There was a fichu in the same diaphanous material for the gown in question, one with pleats to conceal as well as tease while leaving much to the imagination – if the designer of the gown was to be believed. A corsage of silk roses for her wrist matched the double band for her hair.

'Leave them, Maria. I can unpack the trunks myself,' Vivienne said when the bell rang to summon the maid to attend her aunt.

Vivienne pushed the trunks to the end of the bed. There they could serve as a repository for her shoes and accessories. The gowns were spread on trays in an old-fashioned wardrobe that smelled fragrantly of the bags of pot pourri hidden here and there.

Adelaide prowled around the room looking discontented while Vivienne changed from her travelling clothes into a pale green day gown. 'I'll be glad when the weekend comes. We have been invited to a ball given by the parents of Miss Elizabeth Beauchamp, who has recently made her debut. Her father is a baron, and her brother is a navy man. He looks handsome in his uniform, I'm told, and will inherit the title.'

The maid knocked at the door. 'Madam has gone down to the drawing room and requests your presence. Would you like me to tidy your hair, Miss Fox? It will only take a minute.'

'Thank you.'

A few minutes later she was in the drawing room and her aunt was scrutinizing her. 'Ah, there you are, how nice you look. Is that a new gown, it looks expensive?'

'Yes, Aunt.' Vivienne handed over the gift for her aunt, a shawl similar to the one she'd bought for Adelaide except it was the colour of claret.

'How sweet of you to think of me . . . and what's this? More invitations, where did they come from?'

'They were delivered to my home before I left.'

'So I see. The gossips have been busy. Well, we shall sift through the invitations together by and by. Pour the tea, would you, Vivienne dear.' Her eyes went to the invitations and she said, 'Lord LéSayres wishes to call on us. Have you met him before?'

Her face heated at the sound of his name. 'On a couple of occasions. He is a neighbour of John Howard, who is my uncle. Lord LéSayres is an earl, and I think his Christian name is Alexander. Apparently he has no fortune and he'll be in London to see if he can attract a wealthy wife; in that aim he wishes to take advantage of our acquaintance.'

'Hmmm . . . I shall make enquiries first, though I don't recognize his crest. I must ask the housekeeper if they have a copy of *Debrett's* in the library. If he proves genuine, and suitable, I shall then invite him to tea. But an earl – that sounds most promising and will be a feather in my cap, since if he has no acquaintances in town he will be available to escort us around. You shall wear your best gown for our titled gentleman, Adelaide, the one that makes the most of your figure.'

Our titled gentleman? Lord LéSayres was coming to see her, not her aunt and her cousin. He was *her* titled gentleman and Vivienne felt a fierce sense of possession.

What the devil was the matter with her? Previously, she'd found the season yawningly boring. Now she was in competition with someone six years younger, and over an earl neither had the pedigree to attract. The whole thing was ridiculous. She wouldn't bow and scrape to any man, and would treat the blue-blooded creature as if he were ordinary . . . only a bit more respectfully perhaps, in case his highness pouted. And if he kissed her again she would bite his roving tongue off!

Once Adelaide was married off Aunt Edwina would have no further use for her, Vivienne thought. Then she'd pine away in Maidstone, meeting no men at all except worthies of the church and of her father's acquaintance, who were intelligent and sometimes fun to argue with, but usually too old, too earnest, too religious, too married or just too patronizing towards women.

And she'd become one of those querulous women who regarded all men as unworthy, which would be wrong and judgmental of her. After all, everyone grew old, and most people, including herself, held firm opinions. As for women being patronized – she had a passing thought that it was because they allowed themselves to be.

Another thought hit her. Her father wouldn't marry until she was settled, and this unknown earl might be her last chance to be rescued from the monster called spinsterhood.

He might fall in love with her!

Oh yes. Most likely the handsome earl will arrive on his white charger and carry you off, a tiny voice inside her mocked.

She came down to earth with a thud. It was possible he could simply be like her, one of those people who wanted to wed only for love. But how could he fall in love with her when she'd be measured against Adelaide?

She could kill her cousin, push her in the Thames or suffocate her with a pillow while she slept. Her sigh nearly deflated her. This earl had already turned her into a murderess and was fast becoming a nuisance. In any case, it took two people to fall in love, and that seemed rather remote, since Adelaide was secretly in love with Freddie Lamington.

'Oh, my goodness, Vivienne . . . what did I say to bring that sigh from you?'

'Nothing, Aunt, I'm just a little tired after the journey.'

'Then you must go and rest for an hour or two, else you'll be dull company at dinner tonight.'

A little while later Vivienne kicked off her shoes and took out a writing block and her pen and ink. On the page she wrote:

Alexander LéSayres

Rank: Earl.

Home county: Dorset.

Age: About twenty-eight.

After that she wrote: *Attributes: Sense of humour, intelligence, appearance, manners, disposition* and ticked all but one, since he had them in abundance.

Her pen hovered over the inkwell. An earl! She'd never expected someone so elevated in position to call on her. Goodness, she was reading more into his manners than they deserved. He was an acquaintance of her Dorset relative, John Howard, who was well off by all accounts and was many times removed in the matriarchal Dubois family.

But then, so was she well off . . . extremely so. A pit opened up in her stomach and her hand began to tremble as she remembered exactly how well off she was. A blot fell from the nib of her pen, landed, and then spread into a perfect heart shape complete with arrow shaft and haft, and right next to *disposition*. She had been going to write 'Provocative creature' there. 'An omen perhaps, and who am I to argue with fate,' she murmured.

When she'd finished her chart she smiled encouragingly at the blot and murmured, 'There you are, My Lord. Cupid must be hiding in my inkwell and you are not so ordinary after all. You are a man with a good heart, albeit a black one.'

Five

Had Alex known he'd already appeared on somebody's list of possible husbands, he would have been astonished. He made his way from the coach terminal at the Black Bull in Bishopsgate, striding through the dirty, crowded streets to his accommodation.

It had been a while since he'd been in London and he noted that the city still had an air of excitement and bustle, and it still stank, especially now with the tide out. Exposed was a length of sour mud that choked on the detritus it was forced to absorb. Despite that he enjoyed the walk after the cramped condition in the coach.

The rooms were part of a gentleman's boarding house. The landlady was named Mrs Crawford, and a surprise. About forty-five, she was graceful, and well dressed in rustling grey taffeta. She was also nicely spoken.

The entrance from the hall to the day room revealed a leather armchair at each side of the fireplace with a table between. Up a step and through the door, the bed looked comfortable. There was a washstand and a dresser with mirror. The rooms were clean and he complimented Mrs Crawford on her superior housekeeping.

'I have servants to keep my house clean and tidy, otherwise it would attract the wrong type of gentlemen. Usually I cater for business gentlemen and then only by recommendation, since other classes often find it inconvenient to pay their debts. Mr Howard retains these rooms for his own use and they're apart from the other tenants. May I know your name, sir?'

Alex nodded. He was not about to expose his title until he'd looked over the merchandise on offer. After all, it was his only asset. 'It's Alexander LéSayres.'

'And your profession?'

When the information she'd fished for wasn't forthcoming, she said, 'I can see you're a gentleman. There are no rules, sir, but I don't like rowdy, drunken behaviour or too much cussing. As for lady friends, if you are discreet I mind my own business.'

'I doubt if I will entertain. I'm here to seek a wife.'

'Ah yes.' She looked him up and down, making him aware of his untidy state. 'One who has run away from you or one you have yet to catch?'

He laughed at her unexpected sense of humour. 'It's the latter, I'm afraid. My home needs a woman and children in it.'

'And the woman needs to be fair of face and sound of mind and limb.'

He shrugged. 'I'm certainly not looking for a new hound, the pair I have at home are enough trouble.'

'You'd like your chosen bride to have a fortune at her disposal, I take it.'

He shrugged. 'That would be the ideal, though it seems rather cold-blooded in the light of day. I would not like her to think I married her simply for her fortune.'

'Why not, if it's true? Pretending you're in love when you're not is cruel. Business arrangements have their merit, though sometimes love tends to override logic when least expected. Good luck with your search. Mr Howard has vouched for you and he's a truthful gentleman altogether, very polite and obliging . . . and as clever as they come.'

Such a compliment stated about John Howard surprised Alex.

'If you don't mind me saying so, sir, you look a little down at heel for the gentleman you so obviously are. It so happens that I have a suit of clothes that was left in lieu of rent. You can buy them if you wish, and since the previous owner went into the navy, nobody but us will know.'

Alex was wearing his dittos, black trousers and frock coat, and a hat with a curled rim. 'My funds are extremely limited.'

She sighed. 'The garments are no good to me and they include a pair of hessians that look as though they might be a good fit. You will be assessed by your appearance. The garments are hardly worn and you can owe the money to me.'

The woman was handsome and had a fine figure. She reminded Alex of Eugenie. 'You would trust me with them when we've only just met?'

'It seems so.'

'I promised myself I wouldn't fall into debt.'

'If you are low in funds you could do some work for me

instead. One or two tiles in the porch need fixing and the carpet on the stair is loose. The upstairs windows are grimy and the garden beds need weeding.'

'I'll be happy to help you with a few tasks in exchange, even if the clothes don't fit.'

The woman smiled. 'They will fit, My Lord. I promise.'

He laughed. 'I have not given you my rank, so how did you guess?'

'Easily. The way you talk, your manners and by the signature ring on your little finger. Besides, John Howard wrote of an earl named Alexander LéSayres who would be occupying his rooms, and asked me to expend every courtesy to you. I thought you'd be an older man.'

'I share the same name with my late father. He died a couple of months ago. He did some business with Howard, I believe.'

'And came off the worst for it if you lack funds. John is an astute man who knows how to pursue an advantage when he senses one. He will just as quickly let it go if he doesn't smell a profit.'

As he did when they'd tackled him over his father's debt. That success had been down to Dominic's devious mind. John Howard had obviously recognized a kindred spirit when he'd seen one in his brother. All Alex had to do was find a wealthy wife and his father's debt would be covered, and he'd also be riding Dominic's fine horse.

Mrs Crawford brought the clothing up. 'I will leave you to try these on at your leisure, and then perhaps you'll join me for tea. You will need some sustenance after your long journey.'

The blue double-breasted cutaway jacket, grey breeches and the dashing striped waistcoat of silvery grey brocade fitted him beautifully. There was enough room in the seat for comfort and it was taut, but not tight, across the shoulders. The shirtfront was pleated – no ruffles, he was pleased to note. Alex had brought with him several cravats that had belonged to his father. They'd been boiled and starched by the housekeeper.

He hung his finery on the back of a chair and unpacked his bag, folding the contents neatly into the dresser drawer before changing back into his dittos again. He kept the best until last, trying on the shining boots and thinking, new hessians . . . such a luxury. His smile was blissful as the soft leather boots with their little side tassels captured his calf muscles in a hug. He decided to wear them.

'I wasn't being serious about you working for me,' she said when he went down to join her.

'In a household of two men and a stepmother who does the best she can, and with barely enough money to pay the house-keeper, who also does what she can, we have learned to shift for ourselves. I'm not too proud to dirty my hands and I'll be happy to help out with any tasks you care to give me, Mrs Crawford.'

'You most certainly will not . . . an earl cleaning my windows? That would be a fine thing to entertain the gossips with. At least it would get you noticed, and you'd be laughed out of London – and that would defeat the object of your visit.'

'You are right of course. The first thing I must do is pay a duty visit to Mr Howard's relations,' he told her. 'Do you know of Mrs Goodman and her daughter?'

'I do . . . that would be Edwina Goodman. The daughter is named Adelaide. The girl is a pretty, pert young woman with a reasonable dowry, I believe.'

'That doesn't sound like the young woman I was introduced to before. John Howard said her given name was Vivienne.'

'Oh yes, I'd quite forgotten about Miss Fox. She's John's blood relative. She comes from a respectable home and is the daughter of the Reverend Ambrose Fox of Maidstone. She acts as a chap-erone to Miss Goodman, I believe.

'We've not met, but a friend pointed her out to me in the market place last year. I thought her looks to be fair and her carriage elegant. She was a little shabby and had a make-do air to her. I used to be a lady's maid before my marriage to the late Mr Crawford, so do speak from some experience. I've been given to understand Miss Fox has a superior mind and is able to converse about many things. However she pales into insignificance when next to the cousin, who is a beauty.'

A twinge of pity for Vivienne touched a soft spot in his heart. It would be bad enough being a parson's daughter; being poor as well as insignificant must be demoralizing for a woman. He decided he would be nicer to her. 'I'll invite her to dance.'

'Then I'll see what there is for you to wear, because first

impressions count. In the absence of your manservant I could trim your hair to a more fashionable length, perhaps?'

He ran his fingers through it and laughed. 'I have no manservant. Do I resemble the complete hayseed?'

'If you will forgive me for being personal, you look more like the romantic, poetical type.' She sighed. 'No . . . we will not trim it, unless you intend to wear your cravat extremely high like a dandy. The longer length suits you.'

He was embarrassed by her casual observation. 'Then since I'm used to it I'll keep it this length. However, I would like some hot water so I can shave before I go out.' He hoped his embarrassment wasn't reflected in his eyes. He wasn't used to flattery from women and resorted to clumsy humour. 'If you ever meet my brother, don't tell him I favour a poetical look, else I'll never hear the last of it.'

She went to place a hand on his arm and then quickly withdrew it when he gazed at it. 'I do believe my banter has embarrassed you, My Lord. You must get used to flirting in London. The ladies will expect it.'

While the atmosphere was still cordial he drew a firm line. 'Thank you for your advice, I will take heed of it.'

She inclined her head. 'Of course, My Lord, and I must stop chattering. I have better things to do with my time and so do you. My pardon for any embarrassment I caused you.'

'You are making too much of it, Mrs Crawford.'

She bobbed a little curtsey and was gone, her tread hardly registering on the floorboards.

It was a short but interesting walk to the residence of Mrs Goodman. The soft June evening was balmy and Alex took his time, taking in the sights and sounds. The carts that had been laden with loaves of bread, fruit and fish earlier in the day were almost empty and heading back in the direction they'd come from, leaving rotting fruit and fish behind in the gutters for scavenging children, dogs and rats to sift through.

The space they'd taken up was now beginning to accommodate different fare. Beggars sat with hands cupped, a young girl sang, her plaintive voice high pitched. Around the next corner a woman of the night flirted her skirt at him as she adjusted a stocking.

The tide was in, the river high, the stink hardly noticeable now. Perhaps he'd grown used to it.

By the time he arrived on Mrs Goodman's doorstep some twenty minutes later the smell hardly registered at all.

A muscular footman answered the door and led him into a small reception room. The man took his card and his hat and gloves. 'Please be seated, My Lord. I'll inform Mrs Goodman.'

Instead, Alex went to look through the window, so he wouldn't have to go to the effort of standing up again when the ladies finally sorted themselves out. The servant had left the door slightly ajar. He crossed the room to close it, overheard the sound of slippered feet running hither and thither and a whispered conversation in which his name was mentioned.

He should have closed the door, but didn't when he heard a high-pitched giggle and, 'You must go and ask the maid to arrange your hair, Vivienne.'

The reply was softly spoken but vehement. 'Damn my hair. Lord LéSayres won't even notice me let alone examine every hair on my head. Do we have to go through all this fudge every time a man calls at the house?'

'If you want to catch a husband—'

'Catch . . .? How mercenary. At the mention of marriage we would run in different directions. And since the earl will be able to run faster than me I would have expended my energy for nothing, and he would have caught nothing of use.'

For that remark alone Miss Fox endeared herself to him.

More footsteps, then a breathless, 'Oh there you are, my dear girls. Adelaide, will you stop grinning. As for you, Vivienne, pinch your cheeks . . . you are much too pale. You're not going to faint are you?'

The one called Adelaide giggled. 'Oh what fun if you swooned into his arms. Perhaps you should loosen your stays. Or perhaps he will loosen them for you.'

'I'm not the swooning type, and if he makes an attempt to loosen my stays I shall strangle him with them and hang him from the nearest tree as a warning to others.'

Alex grinned broadly because he'd almost heard the sigh she repressed. Who would have thought his arrival could cause such a hubbub in a household. He quickly closed the door and headed for the nearest chair, had barely got his rear on the cushion when the door opened and he was obliged to stand again when two young women entered, swept along before an older one.

'Mrs Goodman.' He kissed the older woman's hand.

She was handsome, though well powdered.

The hand he'd kissed fluttered to her cheek and she said, 'May I introduce my daughter, Adelaide.'

Like mother like daughter. Adelaide Goodman giggled and bobbed a curtsey when he kissed her hand too. She was a pert and petite little miss who had a doll-like appearance, and who took after her mother for looks.

'And you have met Miss Fox before, I'm given to understand.'

He bowed a little and murmured, 'We had a mutual interest in pigs, I recall.'

Mrs Goodman's voice lifted an octave. 'How very odd.'

Vivienne Fox slid her hands behind her back and stabbed him with a challenging glance. 'My Lord . . . we meet again. I'm so honoured.'

'The honour is all mine, Miss Fox. Your uncle sends his felicitations with a fervent hope that you're keeping well.'

Her eyes narrowed a fraction and she moved to a chair next to her aunt. 'How kind of him to remember me. You'll be able to tell him I'm in perfect health. Do be seated, My Lord.'

He moved to the settee opposite her and examined this slightly aggressive wallflower more closely. Her modest blue gown fitted her figure perfectly. A wide mouth had a natural pout to the bottom lip that invited a kiss, and she was tall and graceful. For certain she wasn't a flirty little chit, and thank goodness for that. She didn't look all that plain to him either, but interesting . . . more the classic type of woman with her high cheekbones.

He decided to test her mettle. 'You most certainly seem to be healthy, Miss Fox, though you look a little pale to me—'

Mrs Goodman pounced on that with gleeful satisfaction. 'There, I said you looked sickly.'

'I didn't mean it in that sense, Mrs Goodman. I was about to refer to the rustic tan most of my acquaintances acquire at this time of year. It has been a hot summer has it not? Miss Fox has a fine, unblemished complexion, one that must be the envy of every other woman of her acquaintance.'

His victim's eyes flew open, an unusual shade of green and grey, and the expression on her face battled between anger, embarrassment and amusement.

He smiled at her. 'You're more striking than I recall from our recent meeting.'

Amusement won, and she laughed, coming back with, 'Be careful I don't take it upon myself to prove just how striking I can be.'

'Vivienne! Lord LéSayres did not come here to be insulted. You must apologize at once, and stop monopolizing the conversation.'

Heat bloomed in her cheeks, but it was defiance rather than anything more. She had taken a stand and didn't know how to gracefully change it. 'I'm sorry, My Lord. I forgot my manners.'

She didn't look in the slightest bit sorry and took a quick glance at her aunt before saying, 'I haven't seen my uncle for a while. Is he well?'

'I didn't ask him, but he looked well enough'

Mrs Goodman said, 'Vivienne! What on earth has come over you? To ask a guest for his opinion of your relative is undignified. What sort of impression are you having on our visitor?'

'My pardon.' She fell silent for a moment then choked on a laugh as she engaged his eyes again. 'As for the latter, I don't know what impression I have on him. Only he can answer that . . . My Lord?'

He'd begun to feel sorry for the young woman, who was past the age where she should be chastised in the company of a guest. Now she'd turned the tables and had him on the run.

He capitulated with, 'The prongs of a pitchfork should dig so deeply.'

As sweet as sugar, Adelaide slid into the conversation. 'Please excuse my cousin, My Lord, she isn't usually so talkative. She's still tired after her journey.' Adelaide came between them, moving from her chair to the vacant end of the settee he was seated on. She flirted her eyelashes. 'Are you staying in town for long, My Lord?'

'A month . . . or less if I'm lucky.'

Adelaide looked taken aback. 'Don't you like London?'

'I prefer the country to the town.'

'Oh . . . isn't that a little boring?'

'Not at all, we make our own amusements.'

Adelaide and her mother began to prattle about the assemblies and dances they attended, and the information that Adelaide had a dowry was carefully slid into the conversation, as was the cousin's lack of a significant one.

'Such a disappointment! A rumour has circulated that Vivienne recently inherited a fortune. Alas, it was a false one; my niece only inherited enough money to buy a decent gown or two. Poor Vivienne, not only does she lack in looks, disposition and wealth, and now in fashion sense. We despair that she'll ever marry. I understand you have neither wife nor family, My Lord?'

He could almost hear *poor Vivienne's* teeth grind at the reminder of her situation.

He told Mrs Goodman what she wanted to know. 'I live in hope, but I have no fortune at my disposal. I'm basically a farmer whose livelihood depends on what the land produces.'

'Oh, I see . . .' He could feel the calculations going on inside Mrs Goodman's head. She would be picturing him wearing a shepherd's smock with a crook in his hand and a dog at his heels.

'There's the title of course, and the house and the estate . . .' He threw them into her mental abacus.

'Is it a large estate, My Lord?'

'Large enough to require a great deal of my time; unfortunately it has been neglected over the past few years.'

Now the Goodman females had got the information they'd been after, Alex felt their interest in him wane a little.

He glanced at Vivienne, who was gazing down at her hands. After a while she chanced to look at him, offering a brief, apologetic glance through her lashes. The little smile she gave was so wounded he wanted to hug her.

He noted again that her eyes were extraordinary and her voice had been low and soft, so unlikely to grate on a man's ears. He'd like to spend some time alone with her – get to know her better.

He took out his watch to gaze at it. 'I must not keep you any longer, but before I leave . . . if you are going to the Beauchamps' ball at the assembly rooms on Saturday, perhaps you'd allow me the first dance, Miss Fox.'

'Me?'

'Is there another Miss Fox in the room?'

'I suppose not. Thank you, My Lord, but I'm not a good dancer, I'm afraid.'

'Neither am I. We can be not-very-good together.'

Hesitantly, she asked him, 'Did my uncle tell you to partner me?'

The smoothest of evasions slid from his lips. 'It would be fair to say that your uncle does not dictate my life in any way, Miss Fox, and I do have a mind of my own.'

'Of course you do, sir. My pardon, I meant you no disrespect.'

He leaned on her a little, for his patience was wearing thin. 'Will you dance the first dance with me or not? I must warn you though, I'll regard it as an insult if you refuse.'

'In the face of that threat, I will dance with you, since pistols at dawn hold no appeal.'

He nodded and turned to the cousin. 'Miss Goodman, perhaps you'll allow me the pleasure of the second dance.'

Adelaide offered him an offended smile that told him he'd done something wrong. 'I know all the dances well, sir.'

'One dance will be sufficient, Miss Goodman. I don't want to monopolize your time and deprive the other gentlemen of your delightful company.'

'As is right and proper.' Mrs Goodman turned as she opened the door and frowned, tossing the last lightning bolt at her hapless niece. 'Adelaide has her cousin to chaperone her. You will have to excuse Vivienne. Usually she is a well-mannered, sensible girl who can be trusted implicitly.'

'I've seen nothing in your niece's demeanor to suggest otherwise. The young lady's self-discipline does her credit, Mrs Goodman, as does your indulgence with any foibles of character she may possess. We have, after all, been acquainted since childhood, which explains, or excuses, any familiarity that passes between us.'

'One can only try,' his hostess said, her hand pressed against her bosom to match her heartfelt sigh.

He saw Vivienne's eyes narrow.

The thought crept into Alex's head – Vivienne Fox was just what his estate needed. It was a pity she was as poor as a church mouse.

'Since you are unfamiliar with London society you may escort us to the ball tomorrow, if you wish, My Lord. I can then introduce you. The assembly hall is only a short distance from the house. We can walk from here with your good self and the footman as escort.'

No doubt he would be acquainted with one or two men at the assembly, men he'd studied at Cambridge with. It would be a feather in Mrs Goodman's cap to be associated with an earl when they were announced, even an impoverished one. 'I'd be delighted.'

'*Foibles, hah!*' Vivienne hissed as he moved past her.

He grinned . . . he'd got her to bite.

Six

When she got upstairs Vivienne went to the window and watched the earl depart. Twilight had faded the sky to a dusky purple hue and the night people were beginning to appear from goodness-knew-where, like rats from their holes.

The earl lifted his hat to an old woman waiting to cross the road and offered her his arm. Carrying her flower basket in his free hand, and sure-footed, he tackled the crowded street and guided her through the wheeling horses and carriages. When they reached the other side she offered him a flower.

The cries of the night vendors were loud and raucous. An organ grinder went past with a monkey clinging to his shoulder, the creature gibbering nervously.

There was the smell of cooking in the air and her stomach rattled.

When the earl was out of sight she took her book from the drawer and wrote next to Appearance: *A tall man with pleasing features, striking blue eyes and a long stride.* Disposition: *Consult ink blot. Also, he's self-possessed, but impatient.* Fortune: *Not a penny to his name but he doesn't allow it to bother him.*

She knew how humiliating it could be to be without funds, yet required to keep to a standard. Her father had told her there was no shame in being poor, but it must be doubly shaming when you were an aristocrat and dismissed as undesirable because of lack of wealth.

She closed the book and placed it back in the drawer when she heard Adelaide coming up the stairs, then when the door flew open she turned, saying quietly, 'I do wish you'd pay me the courtesy of knocking first.'

'And I do wish you wouldn't keep correcting me. You sound like my grandmother sometimes.'

Adelaide's disposition became more assertive every season. Vivienne turned to challenge her. 'If you have something to say, then say it.'

Adelaide berated her with, 'How could you, Vivienne? You're a guest in my mother's residence and should have allowed me to take precedence.'

'Over what?'

'You know very well over what – and it's whom. You should keep your place when we have visitors.'

'Like a servant, you mean?'

'Of course you're not a servant, though I should point out that you're living here on my mother's good will,' she said with some exasperation. 'You're just being difficult.'

'If I'm not a servant then it means I'm a guest . . . but I understand my father pays for the hospitality I receive.'

'Oh, don't twist things. We all know what your function is, to be a companion and chaperone to me. You should have refused Lord LéSayres invitation to partner you in the first dance in favour of me.'

'So that's what this is all about. Have you been sitting in your room fuming over it for all this time? If you recall, the earl called on me, not on you. I had very little choice but to accept.'

'You're jealous because he paid more attention to me.'

'Did he? I didn't notice. The earl was just doing a duty call. Oh, do stop being childish, Adelaide. You know your mother wouldn't consider him for you. He's a farmer and a man without fortune. Aunt Edwina has only taken him up because of the title.'

'But I liked him, and he's so handsome,' Adelaide wailed, like a child about to have a tantrum over being denied a favourite toy.

The earl certainly was handsome, and charismatic if one overlooked the nuances of impatience in his manner, Vivienne thought. He was a man unused to drawing room niceties. 'No doubt you'll see him again, and there will be other handsome men at the ball tomorrow to distract you. What about Freddie Lamington? He seemed very fond of you last year. Now tell me, what are you going to wear?'

Adelaide turned here and there, admiring her reflection in the long mirror. 'Dear Freddie, he makes me laugh so. I shall wear my pale blue gown with the puffed sleeves and the low neckline that dips to a point. I have heard that French women rouge their breasts to attract men . . . how scandalous. I think

I will do the same. Freddie has come into his title now, but if he doesn't offer for me this year I shall look for someone else. I don't want to end up old and unmarried like you. Mama said you'll probably end up taking the veil.'

'What nonsense!' Did she need to put up with these barbs every year in the quest of finding a husband for Adelaide? No . . . she did not. She felt like shaking her cousin until her brains rattled, except Adelaide didn't have many to spare. She counted to ten before answering, hating herself for being so mean. 'I could think of worse things to be . . . in a loveless marriage to start with, or being bred with a man who's a complete stranger like a . . . a cow to a stud bull.'

Adelaide giggled. 'You say such shocking things sometimes, Vivienne. Mama would have a fit if she heard you. One word from me and she'd send you home in disgrace, on the grounds that you're an unsuitable companion . . .'

'Is that a threat or a promise? Perhaps you should bear in mind that chaperoning you is a chore and returning home would be a pleasure. In fact, I might even do so rather than face the endlessly boring tea parties and dances, and all the chatter and gossip that goes with it. I don't suppose it's occurred to you that you might end up a spinster too.'

Adelaide laughed. 'No fear of that, and you won't abandon me because this is probably your last chance to find yourself a husband.'

This would be a perfect time to tell Adelaide about her fortune and rub her nose in it. She was weary of the whole thing. All the same, she must bear in mind that she wanted a man who loved her for herself. She adjusted that condition to *liked*. She'd begun to doubt in love after she'd overheard a man she'd once admired describe her as a penniless dowdy.

'Do you take pleasure in my single state, Adelaide . . . is that why you keep mentioning it?'

Adelaide avoided her eyes. 'I don't know what you mean.'

'Then I'll tell you in simple language. You're using the fact that I'm unmarried as an insult. I don't like it, especially when we're in company. It does you no favour.'

'Oh, don't let us argue, cousin.' Adelaide kissed her on the cheek. 'There, I'm sorry if I've upset you . . . please forgive me.

You're different this year, much more serious and not so much fun. Mother said it was because your chances of being settled were diminishing . . .'

Vivienne did forgive her, knowing it would happen again and they would argue again.

Opening the door, Adelaide peered outside, and then closed it and lowered her voice. 'Don't tell my mother, but two days ago I consulted with a fortune-teller who promised me I'd meet the man of my dreams this season.'

'Fortune-tellers are everywhere. It's an easy way to make money from the gullible.'

'This one was recommended by Prudence Duffeney. The teller read her sister's palm two years ago and everything came true. She married and gave birth to a baby a year later, just like the woman said.'

'It was a guess, since that's what usually happens. What else did she tell you?'

'She said a man who was dark and handsome would knock at the door and a marriage would take place. All this time I've been waiting for Freddie Lamington to propose, as he said he would when he came into his title, and he has come into it now.'

'Freddie's dark and handsome.'

'But he's not as handsome as the earl. It was so exciting when he arrived. What if he's the man the gypsy told me about? He certainly looks like he might be. I felt odd when I first saw him, as though my stomach was churning and my heart was about to leap from my chest like a frog. My knees were so trembling and weak that I wanted to swoon into his arms. I didn't because he wasn't close enough to catch me, and I would have made a fool of myself by falling on the floor.'

Vivienne would have laughed if her own response to the earl hadn't been similar to Adelaide's, except she'd never swooned in her life, especially over a man. She rationalized: of course, the feelings she'd experienced could quite easily have been caused by hunger. 'You must stop believing the lies of such people. Dark handsome men are knocking at doors all day and night over London. Some of them deliver coal and some are chimney sweeps, and like Lord LéSayres said, rustic gentlemen have skin darkened by the summer sun. All those fortune-tellers do is relieve the gullible of their money and tell you what you want to hear. London is full of fortune-tellers, and filled with tall, dark and handsome aristocrats at the moment.' She smiled to take the sting from her words. 'You must remember that the earl is penniless.'

Adelaide snorted. 'You haven't got a romantic bone in your body, have you? I feel as though I'm being preached at from all directions sometimes. Perhaps I will wed Freddie and take the earl for my lover.'

Not if Vivienne had anything to do with it, because such an event would be blamed on her own lack of vigilance. 'Your mother is just trying to present you to society well, so as to attract a good match for you. She has your welfare at heart.'

'And yours, Vivienne. I overheard her say to Mrs Barlow that she was going to ask your father if she could take you on as her companion once I'm settled.'

Although Vivienne liked her aunt to a certain extent, becoming her fetch-and-carry wasn't the most appealing of occupations. Surely her father wouldn't agree to such a request. Her heart plunged. He might, if her aunt convinced him that a woman's influence would be beneficial to her future.

She had the means to live independently, but could she with her father taking a hand in managing her fortune? Without a by-your-leave he had consulted with John Howard, who managed monetary estates such as hers. Although she had enjoyed the visit, nobody had asked her opinion on where her fortune should be invested. Once it had been sorted out to the men's satisfaction, she'd be urged to marry the highest bidder and only a small amount of her inheritance would actually land in her palm – in the shape of an allowance, no doubt.

Not that she was extravagant, but she liked value for money and did have a yearning for pretty things sometimes – a chemise edged in lace, a scarlet petticoat, a gown of silk and the softest of shawls.

Adelaide broke into her reverie. 'The maid has promised to enhance my complexion with rice powder and put vermillion on my lips and face. You should try it.'

'I have some Rose Salve.'

Adelaide tossed her head. 'Everyone uses Rose Salve. It's so pale as to not signify.' She opened one of the trunks and idly looked through it. 'May I borrow this purse? It's so sweet and it matches my gown.'

It matched each one of Vivienne's four dance gowns, which was why she'd bought such an expensive frippery. 'You'll look after it, won't you?'

'Of course I will.' She opened a jewellery box and gazed down at a pearl necklace with a dangling jade stone, and some matching earrings. 'Where did you get these?'

'Papa gave them to me. They used to belong to my mother.' She took the box from Adelaide's hands, closed it and placed it back in the trunk. 'And before you ask, no, you cannot wear them. Papa bought them for my mother and they're precious to me. The jade is the same colour as my eyes, he said.'

'You can be really mean sometimes, Vivienne.'

'Bear that in mind because I'm having second thoughts about lending you the purse at this moment.'

Adelaide ran off, clutching it against her chest.

The next day was spent preparing for the ball. Baths were filled and hair washed. Warm water was bliss and Vivienne's bath was scented with rose oil. She could have relaxed completely had it not been for the querulous voices of mother and daughter demanding this and that as they sent the maid dashing back and forth.

When she returned home she would buy a house and live by herself, she thought. She would paint and write stories, learn to ride a horse and have dogs and cats to keep her company. Perhaps she would hire a maid to help her.

Her mind moved on. Since she'd have no husband or children to worry about, her sisters and their children would visit and chat about their lives, offering her a small sliver of family life, like a silver sardine lying on a sea of dry brown toast. Her house would be filled with grey ghosts of what might have been. Perhaps she should buy a house further north, to make visiting easier.

She drifted off, only to wake when the water had cooled. Shivering a little she dried herself, pulled on her robe and applied a brush to the long strands of her hair.

Ten minutes later the maid came in, looking flustered. 'I'm sorry, Miss Fox, I couldn't get away and I nearly forgot you.

That's because you're so quiet and polite and no trouble. You should have rung the bell.'

'I fell asleep in the bath. It was very relaxing. Where are my aunt and cousin now?'

'Resting. They wanted a massage and now they're both sleeping, so they won't be tired later.'

Vivienne was the last on the list for the maid, who scurried back and forth, shaking out gowns and inspecting them.

'No repairs are needed. Slow down, Maria, you're tiring yourself out. I usually do everything for myself except tighten my stays on the occasions when I wear them. So if you will assist with those I can manage the rest.'

'What about your hair, Miss Fox?'

'I can wear it in a bun.'

'And have it fall down when you dance?'

Vivienne remembered previous balls. 'I doubt if I'll dance much.'

'I heard that Lord LéSayres has booked the first dance. You're lucky Miss, you've got a classical face that will still be lovely when you grow old. I know how to create a simple Grecian style with little curls at the back. I'm not sending you out looking anything less than elegant because I'm hoping to find a permanent place as a lady's maid and you're a good showcase for my skills.'

It was the first time anyone had complimented her on her looks, and although Vivienne didn't know quite whether to believe her or not she felt a warm glow. 'If I hear of someone who needs a maid I'll suggest you. Perhaps myself, if circumstances change.'

'Thank you, Miss Fox. I'll fetch you some refreshment, and then I'll get on with repairing the frill on Miss Goodman's gown. She trod on it when she tried it on.'

'Place a cup and saucer and extra food on the tray for yourself, Maria. You might not get the chance later on.'

'That's very kind of you, Miss Fox. Thank you.'

Four hours later and Maria was putting the finishing touches to Vivienne's hair when Adelaide came in. 'Mama's in a froth because the tongs have frizzled her hair. The earl has arrived and she wants you to go down and entertain him, Vivienne.' Her cousin stared at her. 'What on earth have you done to your hair, it looks odd.'

'Odd?'

'Well . . . different anyway, in an old-fashioned way.'

Vivienne's hairstyle, with which she'd been thrilled until then, sank in her estimation. 'Maria gave me a new hairstyle.'

'Maria, you must remember who is paying you for your services. If there is to be a new hairstyle it should be fashioned on me first. You must create one for me in exactly the same way. It's a lovely style and wasted on my cousin.'

A worm of stubbornness surfaced in Vivienne. 'On the contrary, Adelaide, it is not wasted on me and it's about time you realized it. It would also be bad manners to keep the earl waiting while your hair is restyled in the meantime. Maria has been rushed off her feet as it is.'

'Will you hurry up, Maria?' Adelaide said crossly. 'My stays need adjusting.'

Maria closed the catch on the pearl and jade necklace. 'There, you look lovely, Miss Fox.' She had yet to don her second glove but she could do that downstairs.

Adelaide reminded the maid sharply, 'You still have my rouge to apply.'

Vivienne gave the maid a quick smile of thanks as she moved past her.

The earl was waiting in the hall. He watched her descend, his eyes never wavering from hers. She wondered what he'd do if she jumped astride the banister and slid down to the bottom. Would he step forward and catch her?

When she reached halfway he smiled, as though he'd read her thoughts.

She was sure she was grinning like an idiot when she reached him. 'I'm sorry we're keeping you waiting.'

'You are certainly well worth the wait, Miss Fox.' He took her ungloved hand, turned it over and kissed her wrist, saying softly, 'Exquisite . . . just exquisite.'

He was such a good liar she nearly believed him.

'Your cloak, Miss.'

'Allow me.' The earl took the cloak from the footman and placed it around her shoulders.

His proximity was disturbing enough to make her feel less in control of herself than was wise, or seemly. He was taller than her so she had to look up to him. A smile trembled on her lips, and then her cheeks warmed.

He was doing this on purpose and she was cross with him. 'I should remind you, sir, that despite any rumours to the contrary, I have no dowry, and flirting makes no impression on me.'

He looked surprised. 'Then why are you blushing?'

'I'm not. It's a warm night, that's all.'

'It will get warmer, I imagine.' She didn't quite know how to take that. 'With regards to your dowry, your uncle has already informed me of your lack of one.'

'Then why are you paying me attention?'

'You want me to be honest?'

'Of course.'

'It's because I like you and find you easy to be with. Can we put our previous skirmishes behind us and be friends?' Her heart leapt, and then crashed when he said, 'I'm charged by my brother with finding myself a wealthy wife, one who will restore the LéSayres family fortune. In return I can offer her a home and my title. Will you help me find that suitable wife, Miss Fox?'

'Why me?'

'You are both sensible and intelligent. Also, you are mature in your thinking and will not, hopefully, flutter your eyelashes and make me feel as though I'm being pursued.'

'I thought that's what the aim of this seasonable charade was for.' The children he'd father would be beautiful, inheriting his blue eyes and dark hair. 'You forgot to mention love?' she murmured. 'Do you not want to marry for love?'

He began to tie the ribbons of her cloak and those eyes of his were gazing into hers now. They were intense. 'If I could find a woman to love, one who would love me in return, then that would be all that mattered.'

'And the fortune you need?'

'A sad fact of life and nothing to do with love, though in fact I hope it will come about. So will you advise me . . . you could regard me as a brother if you wish?'

A brother? What was wrong with her that he couldn't see her as a woman? When she nodded he leaned forward and his mouth touched against her forehead in a brotherly kiss. 'Thank you, Miss Fox. In return I'll advise you on men who are suitable for you, and men who are not.'

'And I'll tweak your brotherly nose if you dare stick it where it's not wanted, My Lord. Over the past few years I've not met one man I consider to be suitable, which has stood me in good stead.'

'You're a coward, Miss Fox, but a challenge nevertheless. Perhaps your luck will turn this year in the form of a hero on a black horse who will come to steal your heart away.'

'Black horses always look so fierce. I'd prefer a white one.'

'They show the mud. Would brown be suitable . . . I think so. Now we're kin of sorts you may address me as Alex when we're alone if you wish. May I call you Vivienne?'

'I do not wish – and no, you may not address me in such a familiar manner. Notwithstanding our peculiar relationship, you are being much too forward on such a short acquaintance.'

'I have very little time in which to achieve my goal, and I don't like idling my time away when there's an estate awaiting my attention.'

'You expect some woman to place her fortune and her . . . *person* in your hands without bothering with the effort required in wooing her?'

The corners of his lips twitched. 'Would she expect me to lie then?'

'I imagine she'd appreciate being treated with respect, especially if you considered her worthy of the honour of becoming Lady LéSayres.'

'Now you are being sarcastic, my dove.'

'I am not your dove, and I refuse to argue with you anymore, since you are amusing yourself by provoking me.'

He gave a little huff of laughter. 'Forgive me and let's be friends.'

'There is nothing to forgive, My Lord. I allowed my temper to get the better of me. It's for you to forgive me.'

'Then we will forgive each other.'

He was very attractive, his mouth a firm curve, and the thought of him sweeping her off her feet and kissing her senseless was still active in her mind. As for the nose she'd threatened to tweak, a stray thought placed a kiss on the end of it to soothe it. No man had affected her like this before. There must be something wrong with her. Did all spinsters have such vigorous spurts of imagination?

She sighed. Perhaps she should consult with Adelaide's fortune-teller.

Surely you're not that desperate.

Yes I am! Why else am I hoping he'll kiss me in such a disgusting but thrilling manner?

She was acting like a schoolgirl.

The footman coughed. The earl moved a step or two back as there came the patter of feet. Adelaide and her mother trod lightly down the stair, fluttering their hands and swishing their skirts. They looked lovely and wore similar gowns. Edwina tripped forward. 'Ah . . . my dear Lord LéSayres, how wonderful to see you again. We're so sorry to keep you waiting. Vivienne, you may walk behind us with the footman.'

The earl lifted Aunt Edwina's hand to his mouth. 'Mrs Goodman . . . Miss Goodman . . . you resemble sisters rather than mother and daughter.'

They gazed at each other and tittered in tune.

The earl had kissed her on the forehead! Vivienne must correct him about such familiar behaviour. That might be all right in the country but it was not acceptable here. Not that she'd expect a friendly kiss to lead to anything, but some ladies might get the wrong impression altogether. She wondered what his mouth would feel like against hers and she touched her bottom lip with a fingertip.

Edwina squawked like a fairground parrot. 'For goodness sake, Vivienne, do stop daydreaming. The evening will be over before we get there.'

Seven

Dressed in pale rose satin, and the plumes on her headband waving with every toss of her head, Vivienne's aunt fussily arranged their small procession to the assembly room to attend the Beauchamps' ball. She issued final instructions.

'You must allow me to introduce you to those of my acquaintance at the ball, My Lord,' Edwina said, her smile ingratiating as she gathered them all together on the doorstep like a mother goose with her goslings.

It was as if they were the main players in a wedding, Vivienne thought. Aunt Edwina took possession of Alex's right arm and Adelaide attached herself to his left, so he couldn't escape even if he wanted to.

'You bring up the rear with the footman, Vivienne. Keep a look out for footpads.'

'How will I know one if I see one?'

Mother and daughter turned similar frowns her way, and her aunt chided, 'Don't be facetious dear, it's so unbecoming.'

Manacled as he was by mother and daughter, Alex managed to turn his head and wink at her.

'Do you have something in your eye, My Lord?' Edwina trilled.

'Definitely,' he said, and without further explanation, 'shall we go?'

Vivienne smothered her laughter.

The evening air was cool and satiny against her face as she trailed invisibly behind them with the footman. His name was Matthew, she remembered. She imagined she was walking with a prince in a scented garden, instead of a dirty street full of unfortunate beggars, pickpockets and ladies of the night – those much maligned creatures that lacked the skill to earn enough money to keep body and soul together. No doubt the stocky young footman would be amused at the thought of his rapid elevation to the peerage.

She was tired of being Adelaide's shadow and wondered how

people would react if she danced down the street braying like a donkey. 'Hee-haw,' she whispered, which was as close to it as she could get.

The footman's glance slipped her way. 'I beg your pardon, Miss Fox, did you say something?'

'Nothing of importance . . . I neighed.'

His mouth slipped into a grin. 'As one is obliged to on occasion.'

'Do you have a family, Matthew?'

He looked surprised at being addressed by his name, and then smiled. 'No, Miss Fox. I was married once but my wife passed away due to a fever.'

'I'm so sorry to hear it.'

'Cease your gossiping with the servant, Vivienne, it's so lower class,' her aunt said sharply.

Vivienne gazed apologetically at Matthew, who raised a wry eyebrow. She moved her gaze to the more refined backs of her companions. Alex looked just as handsome from behind as he did from the front, she mused. His suit was a snug fit. She loved the way his hair curled against his neck, and the taut rolling movements of the muscles under the tail of his jacket as he moved with the strength that powered him.

She had no time to admire him further because they were soon at their destination. Matthew relieved them of their cloaks.

'Lord *LéSayres* . . . *Mrs Goodman* . . . *Miss Goodman* . . . *and Miss Fox.*'

Vivienne was pleased the announcer had remembered her name this year, due no doubt to the rumours of her good fortune. Last year she'd been announced as Miss Frocks, and people had called her that all evening.

The lawyer, Simon Mortimer, stood next to Freddie Lamington. He eyed her up and down, his expression bold, and then bowed from the waist. She ignored him.

Freddie's gaze went to Adelaide, and when her cousin glanced over her fan at him and giggled, he smiled expansively.

The crowd had fallen silent when they'd been announced and Vivienne could almost hear the collective heartbeat of the women present, and feel the draught from the fluttering eyelashes as the ladies set eyes on the earl. Then the hubbub resumed, but at a higher level, and it wasn't all about the earl as snatches came her way.

'The poor relative looks well this year. Do you think there's any truth in the rumour that she's inherited a fortune?'

'Ask the chit with her . . . it's not something she'd be able to keep to herself. Her mother has a smug look though, I thought LéSayres . . . have you met him before?'

'Not that I recall. Miss Goodman is a pretty little filly, isn't she? Freddie has been after her since she came out. Now he's a baron I'd wager my money on him getting her to the altar this year.'

'I wouldn't be so sure. Is anything going on there with LéSayres, d'you think?'

'I've heard he's without funds and is sponsored by the broker, John Howard. Not a bad friend to have if one needs to raise the wind, not so if you can't repay the interest. Howard is after a title, I believe, so it doesn't hurt him to have friends amongst the aristocracy. Not that LéSayres has any influence there. He's a farmer, here to find a wife with a fortune to spare. As for Mrs Goodman, she won't accept anything below an annual ten thousand for her daughter, and the girl has a purse of five thousand a year, I'm given to understand.'

'That much . . . I might make a bid for her myself.'

'You'd better be quick because the mother might decide to settle for a title instead now she's got a live earl on her arm.'

'Money talks with her. I'm given to understand LéSayres hasn't got a feather to fly on, which is why I'm curious as to Howard's sponsorship of him.'

'There is a connection between Miss Fox and John Howard; I believe she's a distant relative. If Howard has an ambition to join the ranks of the aristocrats then he might marry his relative into the LéSayres family. The girl is attractive in a quiet sort of way, and she has a sense of quality about her. She's certainly not full of bounce, like her cousin.'

'Money certainly talks in such cases, but I doubt if our country gentleman has any influence in the matter.'

They moved off, leaving Vivienne pink with the pleasure of overhearing the compliment.

Vivienne wasn't sure how much she was supposed to be worth.

She had owned a total of five shillings before the inheritance. Her father didn't know for certain either, though he'd waved the letter in the air muttering the vague and immeasurable sum of £500,000 – a figure with so many noughts it was much too vast to absorb.

They had stared at each other while the sum registered in their minds, looked at the letter again, and had then danced around the room together, laughing at the ridiculousness of such wealth. When they were out of breath her father had said doubtfully, 'Perhaps the clerk put the comma in the wrong place and added a couple of zeroes by mistake,' which seemed the most likely. This had lessened their merriment a little, until the letter was followed up by a visit from a lawyer.

She was jerked out of her reverie when the earl moved closer to her and said, 'It seems we're going to be the topic of the evening.'

'People like to gossip, that's what the London season is all about. It's because you're a new face. They will pick on someone else once they learn what they want to know.'

'Which is?'

'Every detail of your family background and fortune, I expect. If you'd like to inform me of your circumstances now it will save me finding out when it's been enhanced by somebody's imagination.'

'That shouldn't take long then. Apart from myself I have a stepmother, two dogs and a brother, all of whom eat like horses.'

She ignored the impulse to giggle. 'Are oats and hay so very expensive then?'

He grinned. 'As for the fortune . . . I'm carrying it in my pocket.' He took a coin from his waistcoat and spun it in the air before returning it to its hiding place with a huff of self-deprecating laughter that she found endearing.

Her aunt came between them. 'Do stop your monopoly of the earl, Vivienne. He's here to meet people, and I was about to introduce him to some of my friends and acquaintances.'

'You still can, Mrs Goodman, but the evening is young and monopoly is too strong a word when I'm enjoying Miss Fox's company. Besides, I promised your niece the first dance. Vivienne is, after all, the relative of a neighbour of mine, so is one of the people I came here to acquaint myself with.'

How beautifully the earl put her aunt in her place, and he'd made Vivienne feel important to him in the process. But Edwina wasn't beaten yet.

'I don't suppose she'd fret if you changed your mind, would you, Vivienne?' Without waiting for an answer her aunt turned to the earl and took him by the cuff. 'Vivienne is one of those docile creatures. She's such a dear.'

He smiled but there was a glint of irritation in his eyes. He gave a sharp tug and her aunt had no choice but to let go when the cuff came free. 'Your niece is an absolute treasure, although she doesn't strike me as being as docile as you suggest. How could she be when you need her to chaperone your own daughter, whose nature could be described as . . . lively. What do you think, Miss Fox?'

She thought that she could throw her arms around him and kiss him for defending her, if it were not for the fact that it would only make matters worse for her. 'I think that you are teasing, My Lord. What is obvious to me is that you're keeping my aunt waiting. When she has finished her introductions then you may approach me to claim your dance.'

He gave a little smile and bowed. 'Your wish is my command.'

Her hackles rose at the thought that he might be mocking her. 'I doubt it, since you don't strike me as being a man who is that easily managed. Excuse me if you would, My Lord.' She bobbed him a curtsey and turned to her cousin, who was gazing from one to the other with her mouth almost hanging open. 'Come Adelaide, we must go and greet Mrs Carter and her daughter.'

'I'll look forward to our dance together,' the earl said as he walked away.

You'll have to find me first, she thought, but doubted he'd bother after her rudeness towards him.

But the earl did find her, even though she'd hidden herself in the most unexpected of places – seated in an alcove behind a palm tree in a pot. She'd left Adelaide with her friends. Her cousin would spend much of her time here in the public gaze, dancing, laughing at silly jokes and competing for the attention of men. She would laugh too much and for much too long . . . and tomorrow she would be tired and on edge.

The earl pulled the palm fronds aside and held out his hand. 'I've come to claim my dance.'

'How did you know I was here?'

'I saw you go in.'

She gazed at him, curious. 'After the way I spoke to you I'm surprised you still want to dance with me.'

'I'm sure I deserved the reprimand.'

She gazed down at her hands and said in a low voice, 'You know you didn't and now you're making me feel guilty.'

'Look at me, Vivienne.'

She gazed at him – at a face that bore faint creases scored there by hours in the open air, and by laughter. His eyes were as blue and smoky as the evening sky as it darkened into night.

'Tell me . . . is there any way I can please you?' he asked.

She was quite sure he'd be able to please her in a thousand different ways if he put his mind to it. She liked him – liked him more than she'd ever liked any man. 'I don't know why you are paying me so much attention.'

'I thought we'd agreed that we were to be friends.'

His hand was still outstretched and she placed her own in it. 'Yes, we did. Thank you . . . *Alex*.'

'See, that wasn't so hard, was it?'

Her hand enclosed by his was warm and comfortable. 'We have yet to discover if we can dance together.'

'Or if I can dance at all without making a fool of myself.'

'This is a *Contredance Anglais*, and there will be a caller to begin with. If we place ourselves in the middle of the row you will be able to follow the other dancers without too much trouble.'

And so it was. Vivienne enjoyed the dance. She had a popular partner in Alex and the other ladies flirted with him. As promised, his second dance was with Adelaide. She was dainty, like a butterfly, easily one of the best dancers there. She drew the eyes of the men, including Freddie Lamington, who had informed her aunt that he'd just inherited a baronetcy and intended to call on Adelaide – with her mama's permission.

While he had not got it then – since Aunt Edwina was disinclined to offer him that liberty before she'd made the proper enquiries – Freddie and Adelaide exchanged long flirtatious looks.

Aunt Edwina was seated with two of her friends and looked on Freddie with a certain amount of speculation in her eyes.

The music changed and a waltz was announced. The scandalized gasp from the older people in the hall went almost unheard under the spontaneous burst of excited chatter and clapping from the younger members.

Freddie Lamington relieved Alex of her cousin and escorted Adelaide on to the floor. A pair of soldiers in colourful uniform joined them with ladies on their arms and the music began. The merry-makers were thin on the floor to begin with, but gradually the more daring joined in and the dance floor became a whirl of flaring skirts while the perfumed air rang with their laughter.

After a short while Alex raised an eyebrow. 'This dance doesn't look too difficult. One-two-three, one-two-three, tread on your partner's toes, two-three. Shall we try it?'

A niggle told her she might appear to be fast, and then contradicted itself by suggesting she was being too prissy for words. So what would happen if her actions were out of character? There would be plenty of time to do what was generally expected of her – to sit and look disapproving – when she was twenty years older and set into spinsterhood like a fly in amber. She might never be asked to dance again, especially so scandalous a dance as a waltz. So she stepped into Alex's arms and was soon whirling gracefully around the floor with him. For a big man he was light on his feet and Vivienne felt secure in his arms.

As they circled and dipped, Adelaide and Freddie danced past. They slowed and the two men danced their partners around each other in a neat manoeuvre. Adelaide said, 'I've been avoiding you, Vivienne, I didn't expect to see you waltzing away the night on the dance floor.'

'Why not?'

Adelaide shrugged. 'You don't usually. I'm having so much fun, aren't you? Be careful Mama doesn't see us, cousin. Lord, we'll get such a roasting if she does.'

Idly fanning her face, Aunt Edwina wasn't watching the dancing, but was engaged in an earnest conversation with Viscount Statham.

Vivienne swooped in a breath when Alex took her by the

waist and spun her in the air, then laughed as he set her lightly on her feet again.

And as Freddie twirled Adelaide away she left a breathless burst of laughter in her wake.

It would be awful if Adelaide were pushed into marrying Viscount Statham. She was so young and shouldn't be hidden away to languish in a cold castle and be used for breeding purposes. Someone like Freddie Lamington would be a much better prospect, especially now he'd become a baron. He'd long been an admirer of Adelaide, and Vivienne hoped his persistence in the matter would pay off. Now he had a title and estate he would need to marry and get himself an heir.'

The music ended with a flourish amid a buzz of laughter and a spattering of applause from the onlookers.

Uneasiness touched her as they walked from the floor. What if the conversation with Viscount Statham wasn't about Adelaide? What if her aunt was trying to arrange a match for herself with the Scottish peer?

Vivienne shook the thought off. She wasn't in a position where she'd have to accept him.

'You look flushed, Vivienne. I'll fetch us some refreshment to drink and we can cool off in the garden for a while.'

She looked around and located Adelaide by her laugh. Her cousin was in the middle of a group of young hopefuls who were pairing off and forming long lines for the next dance.

'She won't come to any harm for the next fifteen minutes,' Alex said quietly.

The garden was decorated with flickering candles in coloured glass lanterns. A table on the terrace served punch, lemonade and ginger ale. He brought her lemonade and ginger ale for himself. They wandered round the garden, and finding a vacant bench in an alcove, took possession of it.

'We must be careful people don't get the wrong idea about us,' she said, putting some space between them.

'Yes . . . I suppose my attention towards you could be misconstrued, and that might be of concern to you. Someone might think I'm your lover rather than your brotherly advisor.'

Shock tore through her at the thought he'd voiced, but it wasn't entirely unpleasant, rather it was a shivery feeling that sent tiny, glittering ice shards skittering up her spine. 'Tell me, what do you know about the pretty Miss Stephens?'

'She's only sixteen and has just come out. Her father is a lawyer. Surely you are not considering her . . . she is much too young for you, Alex.'

He laughed. 'Believe it or not her youth and shyness is half her charm. She will soon be snapped up, I imagine.'

'I misunderstood . . . I thought . . .'

'You jumped to a conclusion. I'm not taken in that easily. The young lady is well trained, wealthy and will go to the highest bidder, as is expected of her. I'm not one of them.'

'I didn't jump . . . you led me there by asking my opinion, and now you're being unkind as well as a little mercenary. You make it sound like a horse sale.'

Quietly, he said, 'Isn't that what the marriage market is all about, value for money as regards to breeding, property and fortune, but there's very little value in the way it's acquired. People are judged by what they have to barter with. The first attraction would be appearance, and that's deceptive.'

'How?'

He shrugged. 'Here we both are, wearing our finery but with our pockets empty. What would we do if we were attracted to one another, but circumstance forced us to wed another?'

'Ah yes . . . but people learn to love after marriage, surely.'

'Do they?' He gazed at her, the candlelight flickering on the surface of his eyes. 'Is it emotional love you're referring to or physical love?'

She was thankful he couldn't see her blush. 'It's not a subject I'm familiar with since I've never been in love. Besides, I'm uncomfortable at the thought of discussing the subject with you.'

'My pardon, Vivienne.' He took her hand in his and changed the subject. 'Tell me about your mother. Can you remember her?'

She shook her head. 'Sometimes I can picture her . . . or think I can. I was too young to remember her properly, a child of about four years, and I get her mixed up with Pa's second wife. Five years later she passed away too. My sister Caroline had just celebrated her first birthday when my stepmother died giving birth to Bethany. We never lacked for mothering though because Grandmother Fox moved in to care for us.'

'And your father never married again?'

'No . . . though I think he's reached a stage where he'd like to. When my grandmother died I was old enough to take responsibility for the house and the welfare of my sisters. Papa was always there for me when I needed him, but he found the presence of three young girls in the house a little overwhelming at times . . . especially when we needed to be disciplined. We grew up with a comfortable roof over our heads, but we've always had to economize. It became a little easier when Bethany and Caroline wed.'

He gave the little huff of laughter that seemed to be peculiarly his. 'Hopefully they made a good match.'

'Yes . . . they're very happy. They married cousins who are partners in a law office and moved north.'

They both fell quiet and she smiled at him. 'My apologies, I've been talking far too much.'

'I prefer hearing you talk than listening to the empty-headed prattle going on inside. You have a voice that's pleasant to listen to.'

'Thank you.' She finished her lemonade. 'We'd better go back in. I'm supposed to be looking out for my cousin.'

'I've enjoyed tonight. Thank you for your company, Vivienne, and forgive me.'

'For what?'

'For this.' He took her face between his hands and kissed her gently on the mouth. The moon and stars seemed to be stirred by an invisible spoon, for they circled all around her.

When he was through kissing her she gazed at him. 'As this is the first time you've attended a season in London I should inform you that a kiss generally represents an intention or a promise. This time I'll overlook it, but you should bear it in mind if you intend to kiss any more women else you'll end up with more wives than you bargained for. Beware, Lord LéSayres.'

'The thing is, Vivienne . . . did you enjoy being kissed?'

'Enormously. It was unexpected.'

'The best kisses usually are.'

'Are you an expert on kissing then?'

'Could be.' He took her shawl and draped it around her shoulders. 'Let's go in. It must be nearing supper time.'

After supper came more dancing, and this time Vivienne didn't lack for partners. She danced the night away until the crowd began to thin out.

Dawn was breaking when they left for home. The air felt raw and sooty. Her aunt was weary and complaining. Adelaide had a fit of the sulks when Freddie's set went in a different direction and she was forbidden to go with them. Alex joined her at the back of their little procession and Vivienne smiled when he drew her hand into his, while Matthew led the Goodman ladies. It was as if Aunt Edwina had made the grand gesture of arriving with an earl, and as there was nobody to see them depart, so the need to repeat the gesture was superfluous.

'May I call on you the day after tomorrow, ladies?' Alex said. 'With your permission I thought we might go and listen to the band in Hyde Park.'

'Viscount Statham is calling on Vivienne at eleven.'

Dismayed, Vivienne said, 'I wished you'd asked me first, Aunt.'

'Beggars can't be choosers, my girl, and you have no other serious prospects. Besides, I couldn't find you to ask your permission. You were whirling around in that dreadful dance with your skirts flying like a hussy. That's what comes of growing up without a mother. Thank goodness my Adelaide has better sense than to flaunt convention.' When Vivienne opened her mouth to speak, her aunt hissed, 'It's no good denying it, I saw you. Then you were gone.'

She hadn't gone, she'd been kissing Alex in the alcove . . . rather, he'd been kissing her. She flicked him a glance and he grinned and said, 'Miss Fox was in safe hands with me. We joined a party of people admiring the gardens. It was very pretty with all the candles flickering in the trees, and quite informative.'

Vivienne turned to him. 'Your company and your attention was appreciated, My Lord. Do feel free to call at eleven-thirty. Perhaps Viscount Statham would enjoy the music too and will come to listen to the band with us. I'll ask the staff to pack us a picnic basket.'

They said goodnight and left him on the doorstep.

As soon as Vivienne reached her room she looked out of the window and blew the back of his head a kiss as he turned the corner. Taking out her book she wrote a note. *The earl kissed me on the mouth. It was a proper kiss, like a man would kiss his lover. I will never forget how wonderful he made me feel . . . I think I'm in love.*

She gazed at what she'd written for a few seconds then scored through ~~think~~ and ended with a flourish – *I know I'm in love!*

Eight

Alex strode through the night contemplating the situation he was in. So far, he hadn't met a woman who was entirely suitable for his purpose. Those with money didn't attract him . . . the one exception was a young woman he liked, who had a sense of humour as well as good sense. The sad thing was, she was as poor as he.

He wondered if John Howard would provide her with a dowry, because it was obvious the broker had planned for them to meet. What would he stand to gain from the union though – control perhaps? He thought further. Howard was a forward planner. Vivienne's children would be blood kin to Howard as well as the LéSayres family if they married. Their firstborn son would inherit the title of earl on his own death. Howard had no children to pass his considerable fortune on to, so it would be likely to merge with the LéSayres estate.

That bore some thinking about but it was all supposition. The man supported many charities and would leave them well provided for. It was doubtful that Howard would live long enough to see Alex's son become the earl, but he was the type of man who planned well in advance, leaving very little to chance. Alex appreciated the fact that Howard hadn't placed any pressure on him. The man had been generous with accommodation, and Alex was beginning to suspect the suit of clothes Mrs Crawford had offered him had come from Howard's pocket. The quality was too fine to belong to a man of business, unless he was a very wealthy one.

The faded crescent of white moon was leaning against a chimney top, the night hawkers had gone with their carts, and a few street women were still advertising their charms to rapidly disappearing customers. Two cats were swearing like fiends at each other.

A woman smiled and beckoned. 'All alone dear? I can lift my skirt and offer you ten minutes of my time for sixpence. I was deloused this morning, so I'm clean, and I have a certificate from the boneshaker saying I'm free of disease.'

The certificate had probably cost her a penny. 'No thank you.' Nothing would tempt Alex to stray from his purpose. Street trollops were notoriously unclean in their habits, and diseased. The thought of going home to a wife, who was calm, soft and sensible – one he could love and laugh with – was suddenly appealing. A woman like . . . well, Vivienne Fox was a good example. He liked the way her eyes challenged him when she was vexed, and danced with amusement when she was pleased. He liked the way she walked with a subtle sway of her hips . . . the smell of her . . . the soft rise of her breast under her bodice . . . She would be friend and foe as well as lover.

His breeches tightened and he cursed. His estate would fall down around his ears if the maintenance was left much longer, and he needed some money for seed and livestock. Vivienne Fox had no fortune to bring into his life. He'd be better off marrying her cousin. Adelaide Goodman was a tasty morsel, if a little too obvious. She whined like a sulky child when she couldn't get her own way, and he doubted if either Edwina Goodman or her daughter would get on with Eugenie. Adelaide would be bored in Dorset. She'd want to entertain all the time and more than likely flirt with his brother and cause trouble. He needed someone Dominic and Eugenie could respect, too.

He quickened his step when a roll of fog suffused the distant buildings, successfully leaving the problem of Adelaide Goodman behind. He didn't want to lose his way. The vanguard of the approaching fog had long tendrils that reached out and clung to him. It smelled of smoke, decomposing meat, soot and the slime of river mud. He held his handkerchief to his nose, longing for a deep lungful of Dorset sea air.

'Christ!' he said, his heart leaping when a pair of cats exploded from under his feet and streaked across the road. There they formed a spitting, clawing ball of yowling black and orange fur. They parted and the orange tabby fled into the invisibility of the mist with the black chasing after it, leaving behind the acidic smell of urine.

Alex's heart settled back to a steady thump and his thoughts returned to Vivienne. She would fit into his life perfectly . . . if only she had wealth to spare.

He found the boarding house exactly where he'd left it, and

just before it was enveloped by the foul, mustard-yellow fog, and slid his fingers into the small pocket in his waistcoat where he'd placed the door key. As he fished it out his fingers encountered a piece of folded paper. It was a five-pound note. After he'd let himself into his rooms he placed it on the dresser in his bedroom and began to undress, gazing at it now and again as though it were something alien. He hadn't seen one for a long time. He would deal with it later.

The clock told him it was five a.m.. The fog pressed against the window, keeping the outside at bay. He undressed and, slipping between the sheets, placed his head on the pillow. His yawn nearly unhinged his jaw. He wasn't used to being awake at this hour and although he was tired he also felt unsettled.

He needed a woman in his bed. Not any woman, but the prim and proper Miss Vivienne Fox. She had a look to her. Under that calm demeanor was a woman whose body would embrace his in lust if she would allow it to. He could see it in her eyes, and had felt it in the trembling response of her mouth when he'd kissed her.

He shouldn't have taken that liberty, and he wondered if she'd allow herself to be seduced outside of marriage. No . . . her father was a parson. In his eyes, and in her own, she'd be damned for the rest of her life and he didn't want that on his conscience. Her confidence in herself was fragile, and she'd suffer if he crushed her trust in him. No, there was nothing for it. He'd have to wed her if he wanted her in his bed.

Shock jolted through him at such a thought. *Her father is a clergyman, and a poor one, at that.*

Yes, yes . . . I know, but it seems the sensible course to take, with me craving a particular woman, and to hell with the cost to my estate. Besides, once we're wed she'll become my countess. If marrying a commoner was good enough for my father, then it's good enough for me.

The day after tomorrow seemed a long time to wait before he saw Vivienne again. He would think about his problem in the meantime.

His logical side butted into his thoughts again, reinforcing what he already knew. *Excuse me, My Lord, may I just point out that London is full of women you've yet to meet?*

True . . . therefore I must be certain I capture the heart of the right one. That's where Vivienne comes in, as my advisor, for of course it would not be sensible for me to actually wed an impoverished commoner.

That settled he snuggled his head into the pillow, not believing a word he'd just thought.

Her breath drifted to him, low and purring, and her body stretched against his, naked and sinuous as a cat. He imagined her tongue, warm, moist and erotic, as she delicately licked the lobe of his ear and whispered into it, 'Sweet dreams, Alex.'

He imagined his own tongue gliding against her flesh . . . He groaned. That wasn't a good idea – not when he was just going to sleep.

A knock at the door woke Alex. He rolled out of bed and dragged on a robe he'd found hanging on a hook behind the bedroom door. His morning erection rode high and proud. He secured the robe tightly around his waist, for he was naked underneath, then picked up a towel and held it modestly in front of him. The clock told him it was noon.

'Who is it?' he said foggily against the door panel.

'Mrs Crawford. I've brought you some refreshment.'

He would be at a disadvantage if he opened the door when he was practically naked. 'I'm dressed only in a robe. Give me a moment or two.' He scrambled into his trousers and a shirt and opened the door to the welcome sight of his landlady carrying a tray with breakfast and a pot of tea.

Following her in was a lad, one not yet grown into his muscles, but on the verge and still with the bloom of youth on his face. He placed a jug of hot water next to the basin.

'This is Ned, my son. He can shave you if you like, or run errands. He's clever like his father was, and can even read and write.'

He searched the youth's face and saw a passing resemblance to her. The lad's face was flushed, uncomfortable at being in the presence of a peer of the realm, no doubt, and that coupled with his mother's obvious pride in him.

'I'm used to shaving myself, but thank you, Ned.'

She set the food on the table. 'I thought you'd be ready for something to eat by now. Is there anything else you require, My Lord?'

'There's something I'd like to know. I found some money in the waistcoat pocket of that suit you gave me.'

'Did you now? How very fortunate.'

'Mrs Crawford, you don't strike me as the type of woman who would have overlooked that amount of money. Did you place it there?'

'Do I look like a woman who would ignore the presence of a five-pound note? It's your suit therefore it stands to reason that it's your money. Would there be anything else, My Lord?'

'Since the rooms are usually kept by John Howard, perhaps I should ask him where it came from.'

'As you wish, My Lord, though seeing that he's not here that might prove to be a little difficult.'

He sighed, he wasn't going to get much information out of Mrs Crawford. The woman was as closed as an oyster. God only knew, he needed the money. 'Do you know where I can get the note changed into coin?'

'If you'll trust me with it I'll see to it on your behalf, since the previous owner of the suit is long gone.'

If a previous owner existed in the first place, since the garments hadn't shown any sign of wear. Alex nodded. He was as sure of that as he was also sure she'd been trusted with placing the money where it had been found – in the waistcoat pocket. He had nothing to lose. Mrs Crawford would only need to go downstairs to her strongbox to fulfill his request.

'There's a message for you on the tray and some invitations, My Lord. Fresh blood in town is always popular.' Her head slanted to one side and her eyes slid up to engage his. 'Will you be accepting visitors today? You're welcome to make use of my drawing room if you like. Between four and six would be convenient and I'd be happy to provide refreshments. Most of my gentlemen conduct their business there, and on Saturday there's a social evening with a card game or two. Low stakes, of course. You might like to attend that if you're free. Lady Luck has provided you with a stake . . . perhaps she'll be present to help you increase it.'

So she ran a card game to supplement her earnings, and from her last few words he suspected it might not be an honest one.

Mrs Crawford was nothing if not enterprising. No doubt she would harvest any information she might glean and pass it on to John Howard. He was a man who collected and stored snippets of information in case they proved to be useful at a later date.

All the same, Alex didn't feel the need to rob others of their hard-earned shillings. 'That's kind of you, Mrs Crawford, but I think not. I've received several invitations so will be out for most of the day.'

During the afternoon he visited his father's club and introduced himself. Early evening found him at St James, where he tested the Lady Luck theory by gambling with a sovereign. He won a tidy sum rolling the dice in a Hazard game, lost a little, and then gained it back with more besides. Halfway through the evening he discovered his pockets to be considerably heavier than when he'd started out. He cashed in his winnings while they were still modest and unlikely to raise the ire of the serious gamblers.

The venue was already noisy. People argued with each other or shouted out greetings. Some were already inebriated, and reckless, and he was tempted to stay longer. He understood now why gambling was such an addiction for his father, especially since he and his brother had grown up under the dark side of it. His respect for his stepmother increased two-fold. Despite his father's faults she had been a constant and affectionate presence in their lives, and had shielded them from the worst of his excesses or the urge to follow in his footsteps.

Although he was tempted to stay and consolidate on his winning streak, that thought alone stopped him gambling any more of what he'd gained so far. He'd won enough to pay for what he considered to be his immediate debts, the suit of clothes and the cash in the pocket, and with a surplus left over to see him through the month – if he was careful.

He withdrew from the gambling room and headed for the Covent Garden Theatre.

The flower seller smiled at him and held out a posy. 'Violets for your lady love, sir.'

'Unfortunately, I have no lady love as yet.' He bought them anyway and pinned them to his lapel, for they masked the smell of the streets and reminded him of Eugenie's garden, a sunny spot full of every kind of fragrant flowering plant.

He bought a ticket and took a seat in the stalls to watch a variety of acts, which were followed by a satire. The audience was loud, booing every time the villain appeared and blowing kisses at a buxom, bandy-legged milkmaid, obviously male, and with a grotesque leer on his face. The milkmaid didn't look a day younger than fifty and sang in a deep baritone while the villain warbled in a high-pitched soprano. Alex could hardly stop laughing.

The theatre was soon filled with smoke. This wasn't finding himself a wife, he thought. He caught a glimpse of Mrs Goodman and Adelaide, who were seated in a box either side of an older man with bushy grey eyebrows. He wondered if the man might be Viscount Statham, whom they'd mentioned on occasion. Obviously Mrs Goodman liked to display her trophies.

He couldn't see Vivienne. Was she ill? During the interval he made his way to the box and tapped at the door.

Mrs Goodman looked surprised to see him. 'Lord LéSayres. I wasn't expecting to see you tonight. Are you acquainted with Lord Statham?'

The man was verging on middle age, of wiry build and well-muscled. Alex glanced at the empty chair. 'Is Miss Fox not with you tonight?'

Her aunt answered. 'Vivienne is indisposed. She developed a slight headache, just after the viscount had called and surprised us with tickets for the theatre. Most women endure such minor nuisances without complaint.'

'Perhaps if she stays home quietly for the evening her affliction will abate.'

'Nonsense, one does not give in to such peccadilloes.' Edwina sounded personally insulted as well as aggrieved.

Adelaide offered him a flirtatious smile. 'We have a spare chair . . . will you stay and keep us company, My Lord? The acts tonight are so boring.'

'I thought they were quite amusing. Much as I'd like to I'm afraid I have an appointment. I must say you look charming tonight, Miss Goodman. You as well, Mrs Goodman.'

The ladies smiled at each other and the older woman said coyly, 'Is it anyone we know . . . an assignation with a lady perhaps?'

He must make the lie sound convincing. 'Nothing so exciting,

I'm afraid. It's with a friend of my father, who is only in town for the night. May I send one of the ushers up with some refreshment for you on my way out?'

'I've already ordered for the ladies,' Statham said, bristling fiercely as he thrust out his hand.

Alex found his hand pumped up and down while the man uttered a few deep and unintelligible gargling noises from his throat. He sounded like a whale wallowing on the bottom of a pot of pea soup.

Alex didn't want to spend the rest of the evening fending off the advances of Adelaide and her mother; neither did he want to clash antlers with the Scottish gentleman escorting them. He bade them goodnight and left the theatre.

His footsteps carried him to Portland Place. A light was burning in a window and he gazed at it, wondering if Vivienne occupied the room. He picked up a small pebble and threw it at the glass. Nothing . . . He picked up a second one, a little larger. It pinged against the glass.

A shadow came between him and the light and the curtain was held aside. The window opened a chink and Vivienne whispered, 'Who is it?'

'Alex.'

The window was slid up. 'What are you doing here? My aunt and my cousin are not at home.'

'I've just come from the theatre. Your aunt told me you were ill, and I came to see how you were.'

'It was a headache, and it's gone now.'

He remembered the violets in his lapel and unpinned them. 'I've brought you a posy of violets.'

Her voice lowered. 'That's sweet of you, My Lord. Leave them on the doorstep and I'll ask one of the servants to bring them to me.'

'You won't come down yourself, then?'

'I think not.'

'Before you go, promise me you will not accept Lord Statham if he proposes.'

She laughed. 'I will make no such promise. Goodnight, Alex, I will see you tomorrow.' The window was pulled down, the curtain adjusted.

He waited in the shadows for a few moments then the door opened. A maid stooped to pick up the posy and briefly held it to her nose before closing the door again.

For ten minutes he watched the shadows on Vivienne's curtains move around, and then the light was extinguished.

Nine

Although her aunt and cousin had disturbed her sleep in the night with banging doors, heavy footsteps on the stair and their loud voices, Vivienne had managed to get back to sleep without too much trouble.

She woke to the thought that Lord Statham intended to call on her at eleven, and her heart sank. Of course she wouldn't accept the viscount, though she felt sorry for him, living alone in his great big castle.

The first thing she saw when she opened her eyes was the posy of delicate violets in a vase on her dressing table.

A smile spread across her face as the fragrance reached her in elusive drifts. She lay back on her pillow for a few moments, listening to the clank and rumble of carts going past and people shouting greetings at one another. Finally she rose, washed, and dressed in a summery cream day dress with panels of pink and yellow honeysuckle in a twisting vine. There was a small straw bonnet decorated with matching flowers and ribbons to wear with it, and she would take her parasol to protect her from the sun.

Maria fashioned some curls.

She breakfasted alone, her aunt and cousin not yet awake, and returned to her bedroom.

Plucking the two best violets from the vase, she inhaled the scent as she pressed the flowers between blotting paper then carefully laid them between the pages of a copy of Samuel Johnson's dictionary she'd taken earlier from the library.

She pulled her London journal from the drawer.

Yesterday evening Alex called to enquire if my headache still pained me, and presented me with a small posy of violets. He didn't ring the bell, but stood under my window and threw small stones at the glass to attract my attention. I thought it to be an odd, but romantic gesture, though I declined to spend a short time in his company. I always feel reckless when I'm alone with him, as if I could dance the waltz through the streets of London in his arms and cause a huge scandal. I'm so looking forward to his company at the picnic this afternoon.

Her aunt and cousin still hadn't completed their toilette when Lord Statham arrived, nearly an hour early. The maid was told to put him in the drawing room.

'How tedious of him,' her aunt said. 'I do hope he's not going to make a nuisance of himself by turning up at odd times. Make sure you're polite to him, Vivienne. Keep in mind that he has a fortune at his disposal.'

It strengthened her resolve to know she had her own fortune.

He stood when she entered, and she noted he was shorter than her. He looked to be in his middle years. She mentally wrote on his page, even though it was unfair of her to judge a man by his appearance: *not tall enough and too old.*

He gave a little bow. 'Miss Fox.'

'I understand you wish to speak to me in private, My Lord.' She seated herself and waved him back to his chair.

He remained standing and cleared his throat. 'Miss Fox . . . I am looking for a wife.'

She tried him with a little gentle humour to lessen the tension. 'Do you have a description of her?'

He gazed at her, a wrinkle pleating his forehead. 'You do understand I've never been married.'

No sense of humour.

'I was teasing, My Lord.'

'Ah yes . . . I don't find the matter one of amusement. I imagine you would like to know what I have to offer you.'

Definitely no sense of humour!

'There's no need to go on, My Lord. You are practically a stranger to me, and I have no intention of marrying you.'

'But your aunt said—'

'Mrs Goodman has no say in the matter. I'm sorry you were put to the embarrassment of presenting your petition, and thank you for your consideration.'

'Aye well, I won't be fobbed off that easily, lassie. At least let me have my say, otherwise you'll be sorry you turned me down. It's not as though you have anything of substance to bring to a marriage, or a string of admirers waiting in a queue . . . except that penniless nere-do-well LéSayres, who has drunk and gambled his way through a fortune, or so I've been told.'

'You do the earl a disservice, My Lord. I believe you are mistaking him for one of his relations.'

'Be that as it may, that sort of behaviour is bred in the blood.' His colour rose. 'Och . . . but now I see you up close, lassie, you don't look the type of woman who would breed easily.'

She bit back a gasp at his vulgarity, though she would have rather sunk her teeth into his leg. This man was certainly no gentleman . . . but he hadn't finished.

'Your aunt said you might be difficult, and indicated she was eager to be rid of you since she expects to announce her daughter's engagement any day.' He held up a hand when she opened her mouth to protest. 'Kindly allow me to finish.'

'You have finished as far as I'm concerned.'

He raised his voice. 'Your aunt informed me you have an argumentative disposition. Behaviour can be modified by discipline though, so I'm willing to take you off her hands. You're a bonnie lass in your own way, and we can be wed by special licence and be on our way to Scotland by Sunday. I'm not one to dilly-dally so make up your mind quickly, girl.'

Lord Statham would probably expect her to breed once a year, until she'd produced enough children to form a bagpipe band. And how on earth had Alex got into the conversation?

She bit down on the outrage that welled up inside her. The whole proposal had been ludicrous. Argumentative? He didn't know how argumentative she could be. Laughter trickled stealthily into her mind to blend with her anger. It had a hysterical edge and it took all of her effort to keep it at bay.

She crossed to the bell pull and gave it such a jerk that she mentally apologized to the bell at the other end.

To her relief, the footman, Matthew, appeared just as she was saying to Statham, 'I find your manner to be objectionable and your choice of conversation inappropriate. Let me put you right about one thing, since you saw fit to raise the subject – Lord LéSayres presents himself as the true gentleman he is, one who is of modest habit as well as means.'

She turned to Matthew. 'Show Viscount Statham out before . . . well, before I *strike* him.'

'Yes, Miss Fox, should I use force?'

'If he resists.'

Matthew opened the door, surprising Vivienne's aunt who had her ear to the keyhole and who staggered backwards and only just regained her balance. 'I dropped my handkerchief and stooped to pick it up,' she said.

The expression on Matthew's face told the Scottish lord he'd welcome the chance to kick him in the rear. 'This way, sir.'

'I know the way,' Statham growled. After a moment of hesitation he picked up his hat and coat and departed.

'Oh, my goodness,' Aunt Edwina gasped, one hand clutching the newel post for support, the other fluttering against her chest. 'Whatever did you say to him, Vivienne?'

'I told him he was being objectionable and his conversation was inappropriate.'

'How could you?'

'Quite easily, especially after he'd insulted me several times.' She turned to Matthew. 'My thanks.'

'It was a pleasure, Miss Fox.' He bowed and headed towards the servants' quarters.

'We must talk, Vivienne. I can't have you insulting guests in my establishment, especially guests of honourable intent.'

'I will not discuss what took place with you, since there was no honour attached to it. However, I understand you took it upon yourself to discuss my circumstances with him.'

'But—'

'I also object to the fact that you told him I was argumentative, and you couldn't wait to get rid of me. He told me discipline would modify my faults.'

'Oh, what a to-do,' Adelaide said from the top of the stairs. 'I wish I'd been there to watch you see him off. I can see you are quite put about, Vivienne, but there, I placed a wager with Freddie Lamington and I'll share the prize money with you. Freddie bamboozled Statham by telling him you were pining with love for him and he should propose.' Her laughter sounded forced. 'I told him you'd turn the man down.'

'Are you telling me that you and Freddie Lamington brought this mockery about?'

'And his friend Simon Mortimer as well. He's such a wit. It was only fun, Vivienne.'

'Fun for whom? It's not fun to single out a man and make a fool out of him. He came here with the right intention, an intention that had been bolstered by your falsehoods, and he left here horridly embarrassed. Worse . . . he will think I was involved in your silly game. You have caused animosity where previously there was none. I shall have to write an apology to him and explain the circumstances.'

'Oh, I shouldn't bother. It will be all over town within the hour and I will beg his pardon myself, and in person. He likes me; he said so. It's because I'm shorter than him. He finds your height intimidating. Goodness, Vivienne, what has come over you? You used to be such fun, but you've turned into a stodgy old maid.'

'While you're still acting like a child.'

'Enough, Vivienne,' her aunt cried out. 'This is such a carry-on over what can only be described as a silly prank. Perhaps I should remind you that it's not your duty to chastise my daughter. Goodness, you are giving me such a headache. I shall not attend the picnic after all, and I doubt if Lord Statham will join us now.'

'I hope not,' Adelaide said irreverently. 'He's a vulgar old man who can't remove his gaze from my bosom, and he leers.' She shuddered. 'I'm not sorry I played that trick on him, but I am sorry if I caused you embarrassment, Vivienne.' Adelaide threw her arms around her. 'Say you'll forgive me.'

Vivienne nodded, knowing it would be churlish not to forgive her cousin after such a genuinely offered plea.

Aunt Edwina sighed. 'Despite the situation, you have turned your back on a perfectly good suitor, Vivienne. I despair of you. I suspect you have no intention of entering the state of wedlock, and shall not encourage any more suitors to call on you. As for the viscount's hurt feelings, I will send him a note explaining the matter myself and apologize on your behalf.'

'Pray do not, for I have no intention of doing so. The proposal of marriage and my response to it was a private matter.'

'Very well, my proud missy, I shall write to your father regarding your lack of respect towards your elders and your odd behaviour in general.'

'As you wish, Aunt.'

'Hah! It's not what I wish . . . it's not what I wish at all,' she said. 'It's my duty. Now go to your room, for I don't want to see you for the rest of the day. I will tell the earl that the picnic is cancelled.'

Adelaide almost flung herself at her mother. 'No, Mama . . . please! You mustn't. I've been so looking forward to it, and besides, I've arranged for Lord Lamington, and Mr Mortimer and his sister, to meet our party in the park. They are much in demand, and such fun . . . especially Freddie Lamington. He's a baron now.'

Adelaide collected a sharp look from her mother. 'Am I to take it that the baron is taking a serious interest in you, when he seems to be too shallow and flippant to be serious about his pursuit of you?'

'Oh . . . but he is serious, he just seems to be that way to people who don't know him. We love each other.'

'Very well, Adelaide, since there is safety in numbers, I suppose it can still go ahead. Vivienne, until the earl arrives you must stay in your room and reflect on what has taken place. After that you can resume your chaperone duties for the day. By that time I hope your disposition will have improved. There is nothing more irritating to a man as a petulant woman.'

She swept past her daughter. 'Adelaide, follow me into the drawing room. You will tell me all about the two gentlemen you've just mentioned.'

Alone in her bedroom, Vivienne supposed her behaviour had been less than ladylike and she'd been more outspoken than she should have been. She just wished her aunt would stop harping on about her lack of suitors. How could she attract a husband when her aunt told them she had a temper like a viper?

Vivienne drew out her London journal and wrote on Lord Statham's page: *Wealthy: Yes. Looks are indifferent. He has no manners or sense of humour. This is a gentleman in name only. He's a dour, self-opinionated and rough little man and there is a hectoring tone to his voice that warns me he might be a bully. A thousand times, no.*

She turned to Alex's page and ran her finger over his name.

Alex arrived in a horse and carriage hired for the afternoon, just as the clock chimed eleven. She beat Matthew to the door and the smile Alex offered her bathed her in warmth, so any tension still left in her body from the earlier argument fled before its onslaught.

His gaze lingered on her face. 'Are you sure you're recovered from your headache? You look a little strained.'

'I'm fine, really. The flowers you sent me are so pretty. I've pressed a couple to keep for when I'm old and need pleasant memories to sustain me.'

After a quick look around he kissed her on the forehead then said softly, 'You look delightful, my dear.'

'So do you.' He was wearing his dittos. Black suited him. It made him look slightly sinister, and she trembled with pleasure at the thought of spending the afternoon with him.

'Lord Statham and my aunt will not be in attendance, so there are only three of us left, though some friends of my cousin may join us there. You have probably heard of Freddie Lamington. There will also be Freddie's friend, Simon Mortimer, and his sister, Miss Mortimer. Are you still happy to escort us? You're under no obligation.'

'Most definitely . . . unless your wish is to be in the company of younger men?'

Surely he didn't mean that, and she looked at him, uncertain. 'Certainly not, I value your friendship and your companionship highly. It would be fair to say I feel I can trust you, Alex, and besides, you couldn't be described as old.'

His chuckle tickled up her spine. 'Neither could you, and as for the declaration of trust . . . that's a blatant attempt to gain access to my finer feelings.'

'It certainly was not . . . do you have any finer feelings?' She laughed with him. 'I hadn't realized you were so conceited, Alex LéSayres.'

'You also haven't realized what a flirt you are becoming. It's very enticing.' He stooped to kiss her, but on the mouth this time.

Surely their mouths must have been specially created to cling together so lovingly, she thought, even while knowing she shouldn't encourage his attention. All the same, she hadn't meant to fall in love with him, it had just happened. She returned his kiss.

They were driven apart by the sound of a footfall on the stair above. For the space between a heartbeat their gazes deepened and clung and she was drawn into the naked depths of his thoughts.

She murmured his name, a tiny whisper that would have been audible only to him. 'I should not have allowed that.'

'You're a baggage.'

She didn't know whether to laugh or scold him at the tease.

He rescued her with a smile. 'I'm not going to apologize because I enjoyed every second.'

'So did I.' It had been a beautifully intimate start to the day. She could have him if she wanted. All she need do was tell him of the fortune she possessed.

She argued with her conscience.

Purchase him, do you mean? What happened to your noble intention to love and be loved?

I do love him. Look, he's kissed me twice, and he's brought me flowers so I think he likes me.

Think? You need to be sure if you want to be happy. Too many women have fallen into the trap of thinking a man was in love with them and lived to regret it. Have the courage of your convictions.

She wavered. Must I? What will I do if in the meantime Alex meets a woman who has everything he needs in a wife? Languish in my room for the rest of my life, or die of a broken heart?

She had no answer to that. The first solution was too melodramatic to be anything but laughable, the second too morbid to contemplate. She stiffened her resolve. She would not perish over a man, even if his kiss did rob her of common sense.

Maria came down the stairs carrying rugs to spread on the grass. The food hampers were brought up from the kitchen, along with a rug and pillows for the ladies to seat themselves on. Matthew also brought a small folding table to act as a servery, and everything was placed in a donkey cart.

The three of them seated themselves in the carriage. They were about to set off when her aunt hurried out of the house, looking flustered. 'I've decided to come after all. It's no good moping at home when the day is so pleasant.'

Adelaide sucked in an annoyed breath.

'Allow me.' Alex helped Edwina into the carriage.

It was a bright afternoon and they found a shady spot under a tree, and not far from the bandstand. The bandsmen looked smart in their blue uniforms with red trouser stripes, gold braid and a black and red hat with a jaunty red pom-pom. Military marches were played and small boys marched up and down, saluting each other as they passed.

Adelaide's gaze roved over the crowds, her mouth pulled tight and down at the corners. Just as the food was being served she underwent a sudden metamorphosis. She smiled, then waved, calling out, 'Here we are, Freddie.'

There were introductions all round. Miss Mortimer resembled her brother with eyes as dark as her hair. She was exquisitely gowned in pale green with white lace, with matching parasol. Graceful, and with a tinkling smile, her glance swept over the party in acknowledgement, then settled on Alex, who'd offered her his spot on the blanket.

'How sweet of you,' she cooed, and detained him with a silk-gloved hand when he stood. 'I'm sure there's room for two of us.'

Simon Mortimer sat between Vivienne and his sister. He said, 'I have caught up with you at last, Miss Fox. I do think you've been avoiding me.'

'I assure you I haven't, for I have no reason to.'

'You're looking well this year. One can almost believe the rumour that you've inherited a fortune in the form of a West Indian sugar plantation.'

So Simon had managed to scratch the source of her supposed fortune out of the dirt? She recalled that he was an attorney-at-law, and he might have learned of it through his colleagues. He was reputed to be quite wealthy, and was exceedingly handsome.

'Really? How amusing, Mr Mortimer. Pray, do tell me all about it.'

'Oh no . . . please do not,' Aunt Edwina begged. 'The suggestion is preposterous. My niece is tired of the subject and so am I.'

Simon ignored Aunt Edwina's remark and his amused eyes gazed into Vivienne's. 'My sources are very reliable. Either you're a very good liar, Miss Fox . . . or I have been misled?'

'A liar . . . misled? Some might find your remarks objection-able, Mr Mortimer,' Vivienne warned, but lightly.

'Fox by name and Foxy by nature. Can it be that the lady is also a little vixen? Be careful of her, Simon, she might bite.' Freddie laughed at his own wit, and Adelaide, along with her mother, dutifully tittered.

'Well?' Simon said, giving a chuckle. 'Are you going to tell us?'

'Tell you what, that I received a legacy? Yes, I did. There, I've admitted it.'

Adelaide laughed. 'Don't get your hopes up, Simon, My cousin inherited enough money to refurbish her wardrobe . . . though I don't admire her taste in fashion.'

'Some men prefer modesty in a woman,' Alex said.

'Except in private,' Simon suggested.

His sister gave a tinkling laugh. 'Her gown is of excellent quality and cut and it seems to me that Miss Fox makes the best of her appearance – what do you think, Simon?'

He patted his sister's hand then turned to Vivienne. 'I would certainly agree with that, Sophia. Tell me though, is it true, Miss Fox . . . did you squander all your inheritance on new gowns?'

'Not all of it. I purchased what I needed and I do have an amount put aside.'

His eyes flicked over her, faintly dismissive. 'That gown wouldn't make much of a dent in say . . . fifty pounds.' His eyes snapped up to hers, as if to catch her unaware.

She gazed at him, hoping her expression was incredulous enough to fool him. 'Considering your profession, I would have thought you'd rely on facts rather than rumour, Mr Mortimer. Besides, the cost of my wardrobe is nobody's business but mine and I have no intention of discussing the cost of my apparel with you.'

'You should perhaps reveal the sum of your dowry. It would stop the conjecture.'

'As I told you, Mr Mortimer, I'm not very good at calcula-tions, but I'll tell you all a secret,' and she gazed round at them all and lowered her voice. 'It fills my father's study from floor to ceiling. There is so much money there that we can hardly open the door to get in or out.'

The room dissolved into laughter, except for Simon. 'You are quite the wit, Miss Fox. Anyone would think you don't want to wed.'

'Oh, I do, but only to the right man. One who is kind and respects me. The sad thing is you haven't seemed to grasp the concept of confidentiality within your profession. Had I inherited such a fortune, and had I been foolish enough to trust you with the matter, I would now be questioning your integrity since you appear as a wolf in sheep's clothing.'

Freddie gave a high-pitched giggle when Simon scowled. 'I told you she would bite.'

Aunt Edwina gasped. 'Vivienne! You are ruining the day with your snappish behaviour. Apologize at once.'

'Certainly not.'

'Vivienne . . . I insist.'

Her stubborn streak surfaced and she pressed her lips together. She'd rather die than apologize to Simon Mortimer.

With a pretty gesture Miss Mortimer said, 'Pray do not blame Miss Fox, when my brother was the one being provocative, Mrs Goodman. Let us enjoy the company and the day. Simon, you must take the blame.'

'We were just having a little fun.'

Leaning forward Alex offered Simon a warning look. 'We were not . . . you were, and at Miss Fox's expense. Apologize to the lady for being offensive, Mortimer . . . and now if you please.'

'Far be it for me to argue with you, My Lord. I'd be delighted.' He took Vivienne's hand in his and kissed it. 'Forgive me, I beg of you, Miss Fox.'

She wanted to slap him. She turned to Alex only to find Miss Mortimer gazing up at him, her eyelashes all of a flutter. Miss Mortimer's smile would have attracted gentlemen crocodiles for dinner and had them snapping at her ankles, but it seemed to make no impression on Alex. He offered Vivienne a wry smile and lifted an eyebrow slightly.

Then the woman leaned forward so her cleavage was on display under a scanty arrangement of lace. Her voice was a low purr. 'My Lord, I have been so longing to meet you. Tell me about your estate, and do call me Sophia.' When she spread her fan and gazed at him over its spread, Alex grinned in the way men did when they liked what they saw.

It felt as though the sun had lost its shine. Nothing was

going right for her today, Vivienne thought, and now might be a good time to swoon – if only she knew how to do it without making a complete idiot of herself. She was simply not the fainting type.

Ten

It was the worst day of Vivienne's life. She'd been proposed to twice . . . but not by the man she wanted.

Simon Mortimer's probing about her inheritance meant she had to remain vigilant. He'd obviously made it his business to know her business. Alex had been captured by the beautiful Sophia, who made matters worse by competing with Adelaide for the attention of all the men present. Alex sent her a smile or two but he didn't seem to mind being singled out for attention by most of the women present.

Freddie was his outrageous self and acting the fool, but sometimes his wit had an edge to it and the expression in his eyes told Vivienne he wasn't as silly as he made out.

Simon singled her out when they were packing up the picnic and preparing to return home. Obviously he preferred to believe in the rumour, and as he'd said, he had professional sources for the information.

He took her by the arm, firmly enough so she couldn't jerk away without making a fuss. 'Walk with me for a minute or two.' After a few seconds had passed, he said, 'Will you allow me to call on you tomorrow, Miss Fox?'

'You may . . . but I would prefer it if you didn't because everything that needs to be said, has been,' she added quickly.

She realized she'd only agreed because Alex had withdrawn his attention when the exquisite Sophia had appeared on the scene. She was miffed with him, unreasonably so. What was the use of hoping Alex would love her for herself? Today had proved to her that superficiality, good looks and fortune were more attractive to men than true love.

Simon said, 'Perhaps I'll approach you again when your mood has improved. I should tell you that my sister has set her sights on the earl.'

She feigned indifference. 'What of it?'

'They are saying he seems to be attached to you.'

'They?'

'Stop playing the innocent . . . you know as well as I how the marital system works. There must be something stronger than your physical appearance to keep our country gentleman so firmly by your side.'

That stung, but only because she allowed it to. 'It's called trust and friendship. We have been friends since childhood.' After all, he wasn't to know the truth of their earlier acquaintance.

'I understand you routed Lord Statham earlier. He's wallowing in money, I believe. All the same, I feel sorry for him.'

'Then you marry him.'

He gave a high-pitched laugh. 'Very droll, Miss Fox.'

Exasperated, she said, 'By any chance, did you have your ear pressed to the keyhole when he offered for me?'

'It's all over town.'

'And stinks to high heaven, like horse dung.'

He laughed again. 'You've got quite a wit. Sophia has the means to set LéSayres' estate to rights, you know.'

So do I, she almost blurted out, before she saw the trap in his words and bit her tongue. Hooking Sophia's eyes out of their sockets with a pickle fork and feeding them to the ducks would give her enormous satisfaction. 'That's hardly my business, Mr Mortimer.'

He gave a faint smile. 'Isn't it? I could have sworn you had an eye for the handsome LéSayres yourself.'

'He's an old family friend and we have just become reacquainted. I doubt if we'll run into each other again for years.' She closed her eyes and felt a memory of Alex's mouth, firm and loving against hers. Her heart began to pound, so she quickly opened them again.

'Your uncle wouldn't happen to be John Howard the financier, would he?'

'Wouldn't he?'

'Are you being deliberately irritating, Miss Fox? Or can it be that you can't manage a straight answer to a straight question? Odd, when I've been told how intelligent you are.'

'Yes . . . I suppose it might appear odd to you. The thing is, Mr Mortimer, I have just visited my uncle in Dorset. I haven't seen him since childhood, and couldn't really remember him . . .

therefore I don't presume on the relationship between us. He and the earl are neighbours . . . not that it really concerns you.'

'Quite.' He adroitly changed the subject. 'Freddie intends to officially propose to your cousin. Will he succeed, do you think? She seemed enamoured by the earl.'

'Oh, Adelaide was flirting with him to catch the attention of Freddie. I imagine she will accept him. It will please my aunt if her daughter marries a title, especially if there are no money problems. Adelaide likes him and they appear to suit each other.'

'Yes, they should . . . what about you?'

'Me?'

'You're intelligent. Surely you want to marry and have children of your own. I have property and wealth enough to keep us in comfort. I know you disapprove of me now, but I'd treat you well and if we grew tired of each other we could overlook certain intimacies with others outside of the marriage bed.'

'Are you proposing marriage to me?'

'Unofficially, it sounds like it.'

She was thrown off guard by the shock of what she'd just heard. 'But we've only just met . . .' Her face flooded with colour. 'You have a reputation, Mr Mortimer, and it's not a good one. If I ever marry it will not be to you, and I will never allow my marriage to become the travesty you are describing.'

'LéSayres would be a fool to commit himself to marriage unless money is part of the deal. No man in his position would.'

'Except for Simon Mortimer, it seems, for you've just approached me with marriage in mind.'

He smiled. 'Is anything ever what it seems? From where I'm standing I'd wager my fortune on the fact that my little goose is sitting on a nest of golden eggs that are about to hatch. I might open a book on it. Does she or doesn't she?'

'I wouldn't if I were you, Mr Mortimer. I think you've been reading too many of Aesop's fables. Your party is waiting for you to join them.' She turned and stalked off, certain her buttocks twitched with the affront she felt.

Aunt Edwina and Adelaide were heading for the carriage. She hadn't known Alex was within earshot until he came out from behind the tree and took her by the arm, turning her to face him. 'You look flustered . . . did Simon Mortimer upset you?'

'A little.'

'Tell me about it.' He tucked her arm into his and they began to stroll after the others.

'I'd rather forget it, Alex.'

'Then we won't discuss it. Tell me . . . what do you think of Mortimer's sister?'

'I didn't get a chance to talk to her and form an opinion. She's certainly attractive.'

'Yes she is . . . and wealthy with it.'

'On the other hand, her brother has a bad reputation.'

He slid a grin her way. 'I've heard he's a bit of a thug, and a rogue where ladies are concerned. But then, most men are. You can't judge a person by their relatives, I suppose. All the same, I wouldn't advise you to encourage her brother, he's nowhere near good enough for you.'

She scraped out a laugh. 'Simon told me his sister had set her heart on you. He said she has good looks to attract you, and money enough to support your estate – he also said you would be a fool to reject her.'

'I must say I found Miss Mortimer quite fascinating. Although it's not gentlemanly to say so, she's the most empty-headed female I've ever met, and she prattles incessantly about herself.'

A murderous urge had slid through her when Alex had first mentioned the Mortimer woman. Now it left her, and she was light-headed with relief. Jealousy was an ugly emotion that seemed to bring out the worst in her.

You'd be envious of any woman he singled out for attention. Try to remember he's only being sociable . . . playing the game.

Oh pish! Now she'd developed an invisible advisor. Still, it seemed to be on the sensible side. She asked it: why can't I giggle, flirt and simper, and attract the attention of the men like Miss Mortimer and my cousin?

You can . . . please go ahead.

She fluttered her eyelashes.

He didn't seem to notice, and she felt like kicking him on the ankle. Then her spirits took a sudden lift. At least she didn't prattle. Well . . . not often. Reassured, she smiled, trying not to be petty. 'That was not a very kind thing to say about Miss Mortimer.'

'I'm not feeling kindly disposed towards her. What was obvious was that she targeted me so her brother could have a clear run at you. I couldn't get away from her. Every time I tried to catch your eye so you could rescue me she moved into my line of vision. She flapped her eyelashes so hard I'm surprised her head didn't take flight. When I did manage to see you, you were enjoying a tête-à-tête with Simon and I wanted to plant my boot in his rear and kick him into the lake.'

'Why didn't you?'

'I didn't want to ruin my new boots.'

Laughter filled her. 'Thank you, Alex, you're the most wonderful fake brother I've ever had. You've quite cheered me up. I thought your neglect of me today was because you'd fallen instantly in love with Miss Mortimer.'

He slid her a glance. 'Would that bother you much?'

'No . . . well, just a little perhaps. No, more than that. I'd kick the lady into the same lake and kick you in afterwards. I realize you must marry for the sake of your estate, but I'd like you to have a wife who made you happy as well.'

'I'm of the mind it will be one or the other.'

What was he saying . . . that he'd marry for love? 'But both would be better, surely?'

'Yes . . . except a man's pride is involved where money is concerned. The button on your glove is undone.' In the shadow of the next tree he stooped and slid the tip of his tongue over the little pulse beating on the inside of her wrist.

The initial thrill brought on by the action went skittering off in all directions through her body, and was followed by shock. She whispered, 'Alex, stop that.'

He secured the loop over the button. 'You have graceful hands, my dove. I just couldn't resist. I've received an invitation to the afternoon dance at Almack's on the Wednesday of next week. Will you come as my guest? I'm told that invitations are rare and restricted to the aristocracy. Frederick will escort your cousin if her aunt allows. Sometimes the Regent puts in an appearance.'

Thank goodness he hadn't thought to invite Sophia, and her mood lifted once again. She would buy herself a new gown. There were plenty of dressmakers in London who would outfit her, and Maria would know the best one.

'Vivienne!' her aunt called out. 'Stop dawdling this minute.

Surely there's nothing you need to say to the earl in private that is so shocking that the rest of us can't be party to it.'

Alex gazed into her eyes. 'Is there, Vivienne?'

When her heart raced every time she saw him, when she lived for his glance, his smile, the touch of his hand and the sound of his voice – couldn't he see how she adored every beautiful hair on his beautiful head? She was falling apart over him and had never felt such need in her.

I love you most desperately, Alex, and I don't know what to do about it, she almost blurted out, only just managing to draw her shattered feelings together. She smiled. 'I value your friendship highly.'

'And I will value yours always.'

'Vivienne . . . do come, and at once!' her aunt called.

His mouth twisted into a wry grin and he offered her his arm. 'I'd like to spend time alone with you, and without you being at the beck and call of your aunt and cousin. You and your father might like to visit King's Acres one day.'

'As you know, we have recently visited my uncle, John Howard, to consult with him about . . . well, about some investments, I believe. It was only a short visit.'

'And you ran away from me.'

She laughed. 'Like a rabbit. One day perhaps I'll be able to arrange another visit, since I would love to see your home in Dorset. My uncle described it as . . . comfortable. I was on my way to see if I could catch a glimpse of it when you waylaid me.'

'I'm quite sure you'd love it there, and my family would welcome you. My stepmother is a little starved of female company and it would give my brother a chance to catch up on his manners . . . and the dogs.'

'Tell me about your brother . . . are you alike?'

'Not so much as we were in childhood. You might remember him from then. He remembers you.'

'You have spoken of me together?'

'He admired you and considered you to be in fine fettle when you routed me.' He grinned. 'But we can talk of him another day.'

They had reached the carriage and he handed her in before climbing in beside her.

Edwina gazed from one to the other. 'Now . . . what was

going on between the pair of you that was so interesting it kept everyone waiting.'

'My pardon, Mrs Goodman, it was my fault entirely so you should reprimand me rather than Miss Fox, perhaps. We were discussing my home and my brother.'

'And the earl's dogs, as well,' Vivienne said lightly. 'Apparently they lack manners.'

'One can forgive dogs since they have no sense. Young ladies should know better than to keep her elders and betters waiting.'

'I'm sorry, Aunt.'

'Well, since the earl has confessed to being at fault I will forgive you this time.' She poked the driver's shoulder with her parasol. 'We're all present so you may depart.'

'Tell them, Mama,' Adelaide said, almost breathless with excitement.

Her aunt smiled smugly. 'Lord Frederick is calling on Adelaide tomorrow afternoon and strongly hinted there might be a proposal in the offing, since they get along so well. Frederick is such a dear boy.'

Alex's eyebrow raised a fraction at that. 'Congratulations, Miss Goodman.'

'That's wonderful, Adelaide. I hope it comes off as you expect.' Vivienne turned to her aunt. 'I'm going shopping in the morning. Lord LéSayres has invited me to the Wednesday afternoon dance at Almack's. I thought I might buy a new ball gown, since I only have the one with me.'

'It will have to wait because Adelaide is expecting Lord Frederick. And I'm holding a tea party afterwards to celebrate. I need you to supervise the staff. They work better for you than for me.'

'That's not until the afternoon. I can take the maid with me.'

'Maria will be occupied with Adelaide, who will need to rest so she can look her best when Frederick calls.' Her aunt didn't notice that one contradicted the other.

'Then I'll go alone. It will not take me long.'

'As you will, but don't blame me if you're attacked by the footpads, felons and other unsavoury creatures who rove the streets looking for women to take advantage of. You'd better keep a tight hold on your pocket.'

'Perhaps you'd allow me to escort Miss Fox, since it was my invitation that prompted the need in her for a new gown.'

'So kind,' Aunt Edwina gushed. 'Girls are such a responsibility. I'll be glad to see Adelaide settled at long last. As for you, Vivienne . . . I despair. If only you'd inherited that fortune everyone is talking about. All that silly talk about true love has got you nowhere at all, has it?'

'If a man wants to wed me it must be for myself and not for any material gain. You do see that, don't you, Aunt?'

Her aunt sighed, and then said, 'How can anyone love you for your material gain when you have no material for him to gain? What about that legal gentleman, the handsome Mr Mortimer? He paid you a lot of attention, and would be a perfect match for you. I've heard he earns a good living from practising the law. I thought you were too hard on him when he was only teasing you.'

Obviously her aunt didn't see past the end of her nose. 'Too hard? My dearest Aunt Edwina, that man nearly goaded me into violence. If he approaches me again, especially with marriage on his mind . . .' She offered Alex an apologetic glance. 'I'll upend him and bury him head first in a heap of horse dung.'

'He proposed marriage and you turned him down?' Edwina almost shrieked. 'Why didn't you tell me?'

'I just have.'

'Vivienne. I will definitely write to your father and inform him about your odd behaviour . . . and just when I was feeling so happy. What was it you said about horses; something vulgar, I believe?'

'I said—'

'No, don't bother repeating it. I heard it well enough to get your meaning, and you the daughter of a cleric. Jesus will be turning in his grave . . . if he has a grave; I can never remember because somebody said it was empty when he walks abroad. I must ask your father to explain that to me when I next see him. As for you . . . well, I can only say you should be ashamed of yourself.'

Rebellion surged through her. 'Should I? Well, I'm not.'

Adelaide had collapsed in a heap of giggles. 'Wait till I tell Freddie what you said about Simon, Vivienne.'

'And in front of the earl, too,' her aunt said, looking horrified. 'Adelaide, stop that caterwauling at once. It's unseemly. What on earth will Lord LéSayres think?'

'I don't know, Mama, but since he's sitting next to Vivienne, you can ask him.'

'I declare . . . your cousin is having a bad influence on you.' Looking as if she was on the verge of tearing her hair out, her aunt's attention turned to Alex. 'Do you have an opinion to offer, My Lord?'

'If I dare voice one, far from being offended, I have to say it's the most amusing thing I've heard this week, and I couldn't think of a better way to get rid of an unwanted suitor. In fact, I should like to be there to see it.' Alex's laughter told them exactly what he thought and they all began to laugh with him.

Thanks to Alex the day ended on a friendly note.

After the earl had taken his leave Vivienne went upstairs and entered in her London journal:

Simon Mortimer – Attorney at law. Handsome. Wealthy. She ticked the positive words off, then reached: *Comments: This man is mercenary, persistent and unlikeable. He indicated that he'd be interested in a marriage with me, and I've turned him down. He's thinking of taking bets on whether I have a fortune or not. I understand he's been making enquiries about me, and he indicated he'd heard rumours about my inheritance through his colleagues. I formed the impression he was fishing, and his conversation seemed designed to trick me into giving him the answer he wanted. Surprisingly, Alex seemed to be attentive to Simon's sister, Sophia. It was tedious to find myself seething with envy. I must stop acting like a spoiled brat.*

Notes: Alex is taking me shopping tomorrow. I'm going to find the best ball gown in London, to wear for when he escorts me to Almack's.

Eleven

The gown was the prettiest Vivienne had ever seen. The colour of the silk reminded her of Alex's blue eyes, the diaphanous overskirt slithered smoothly over her figure and the bodice was decorated with small crystals. She'd never worn a gown so low at the front or so wide at the shoulders. Far from being flagrant, the beaded fichu that kept that area secure was also a subtle tease, for it attracted the eye while drawing a curtain over the mystery that lay underneath.

She wondered if her bosom would escape when she danced. Other women seemed to manage without disaster, including Adelaide, who was fuller of figure than her. A new respect for the art of dressmaking grew in her and she thought it might be fun to dress up now she could afford the best fabrics and designs.

Maria, who'd recommended this establishment in Piccadilly, had told her the trick was to make sure the drawstrings in her stays were tight enough to contain her and keep control.

She turned her back to the mirror, inspecting the gathers where they joined the bodice to allow the skirt ease of movement. She said to the assistant, 'It's lovely.'

'And it fits you perfectly. We must measure the length before we turn the hem up.'

There were accessories, dancing slippers created in the same material, a feathered headband and a small bag covered in crystals.

'I know I'm not giving you much time, but can you have it finished and delivered to me on Wednesday?' If she were not at home her aunt would pay what was owed from the amount she had given her towards her daily expenses. As usual the accounts would be reconciled at the end of the season.

'Certainly, Miss Fox. If you stand on the podium I'll mark the length. It won't take long to hem it.'

Half-an-hour later she paid a deposit and gave instructions of where to deliver the gown. Her father would likely have a mild conniption when he learned how much she'd spent on one ball-gown, and she smiled. She doubted he'd ever get used to her spending money at all without careful consideration, even though he'd indicated he'd be quite happy for her to spend what she wished.

She joined Alex, who was inspecting books on a stall across the street. 'I'm sorry I took so long, Alex. You could have waited in the antechamber, where there's a chair or two for superfluous men.'

He smiled. 'I did for a short while, but I'm not used to being superfluous. Women kept smiling at me. I felt rather . . . noticeable. Women have a way of examining you without it being obvious.'

'That's what you get for offering to take a female shopping. I must admit that males seem more comfortable when they're in herds.'

He laughed. 'That's not a bad observation. You were quicker than I thought you'd be. The last time I took a woman shopping it took her an hour to buy a hat that was little more than a couple of large feathers sewed to a pleated satin object that resembled half a pumpkin. I never saw her wear it.'

A hole appeared where her heart should be. 'What woman was that?'

'My stepmother. You'd like her, I think. She raised me and my brother and we both adore her.'

Relief was a swift rush. If she wanted this man – and she did – she'd have to set her cap at him, she thought. Wednesday would be a good time to tell him of her fortune . . . to tell him of her warm feelings towards him . . . to propose, if she could summon up the nerve. Saying she would was one thing, actually doing it was another. Just thinking about it brought a surge of butterflies into her stomach.

She slid her arm through his. 'I haven't got to be back yet. Shall we stroll in the park a little and I'll buy us something to eat?'

They ate some hot muffins and bought a large apple to share, then sat on the grass to watch a Punch and Judy show.

Alex polished the apple to a soft ruby glow on the sleeve of his coat. She imagined him doing the same as a small child, sharing it with his younger brother. 'We have a tree at King's Acres that produces apples just like this,' he said, an ocean of wistful longing in his voice.

'You miss being there, don't you?'

'Yes, I do . . . I like having the countryside outside my door, and the bounty nature brings with it.' He twisted the buffed apple, and it snapped into two even halves. He handed her one. The juice was sharp and cleansing against her tongue when she bit into it.

They wandered through the various stalls, set up by opportunists trying to make a living. That the stallholders were chased off now and again didn't seem to bother them, for they sprung up again like mushrooms an hour later, with plenty of clients lining up to buy their wares. Alex bought her a gift from a trinket stall, a silver brooch shaped like a star. It was not new but it sparkled with faceted garnets, peridots and amethysts, all set around a centre moonstone.

'I wish they were diamonds,' he said, pinning the brooch to the collar of her pelisse.

His fingertips were a cool but sweet caress against the skin on her neck. She gazed up at him, her heart aching. 'The value is in the giving, and I shall treasure it.'

'I know you will.' The parkland surrounding them became a muffled kaleidoscope of noise, bustle and colour while the space between them enclosed the beat of a hundred drums to replace the heartbeats. It was a warm day . . . indeed the whole of summer had been warm.

'Were we alone I'd request a kiss as a thank you,' he murmured, and then grinned. 'Or perhaps I'd just help myself to one.'

She took a step back, reminding herself how public they were. 'If you will allow it I'll owe you one. Tell me, is it your intention to seduce me, Alex?'

His eyes widened a fraction and he laughed. 'How honest do you want me to be, woman? It crosses my mind from time to time. Your lack of guile is attractive, and I'm drawn to you physically . . . you must have sensed it else you wouldn't be asking. However, it would be wrong of me to take advantage of you without clear intention, which isn't to say I wouldn't if circumstance allowed. After all, I'm only a man.'

A warm glow ran through her and she gave a shaky little laugh. 'I don't know much about men. I just know I feel comfortable with you, and . . . safe.'

'Safe?' Laughter huffed from him, and it was threaded with disbelief. 'That statement is a *coup de grâce* on a relationship if ever I heard one. I shall have to try harder.' He ran a finger down her nose, saying regretfully, 'I must get you home otherwise you'll miss the Baron's visit and that will upset your aunt.'

'Yes it would. Are you able to stay for the event?'

'I'm afraid not. Besides . . . I'm of the belief that a man should do his proposing in private. I've accepted another invitation for this evening – Charles Cresswell is an acquaintance of mine from university, and he has asked me to join his family party at the theatre. Please pass on my congratulations should the event go as planned.'

'You sound doubtful. Have you heard anything to the contrary . . . it's not one of Freddie's inane japes, is it? I'd hate for Adelaide to be disappointed . . . she'd be heartbroken. You would tell me, wouldn't you?'

He lifted her hand to his mouth and kissed her knuckles. 'I'm sure it's nothing to worry about. I just thought it came about rather quickly, but then I'm not used to the swift London ways of courtship.'

'You sound disillusioned by it.'

He shrugged, said tersely, 'Of course I am. You can't fairly judge a man or woman by their looks, their pedigree or their wealth. Being part of it has shifted my comfortable perspective somewhat. I'm trying to reconcile myself with the thought of taking a stranger home as my wife and pretending to love her, all the while relieving her of her wealth. It strikes me as being hypocritical and shallow.'

'Then why did you bother to become part of it? There's more to it than you describe. There is fun and dancing and the theatre and socializing. If you hate it so much, go home and marry the farmer's daughter.'

'He hasn't got one.' He gave a rueful smile. 'Remind me not to argue with you again. I forgot you're as without means as I am. We can only scratch in the ashes and hope we turn up a gem for ourselves.'

Her heart softened. 'Let's not argue, Alex. We can at least agree that we're better off than many.'

'Yes, we can do that. It's just a pity that someone as young and beautiful as Adelaide is so desperate to become a chattel to a man who is almost a stranger.'

'I must correct you on that. Adelaide has known Frederick since she came out, three years ago,' she said. 'It's not the first time he's shown more than a passing interest in her, but Aunt Edwina thought Adelaide could do better. Frederick appears to be frivolous, but he is good-natured and constant. He has waited all this time for Adelaide, and now has a title to commend him to Aunt Edwina. Believe it or not, he does have a brain as well as family honour.'

'I stand corrected.'

'And what of you when you find a woman to fit your purpose . . . one you care for? Will you say it's too soon, or regard her as your chattel, when she will bring you so much in the way of fortune, children and affection? Remember, you only have a month or so to achieve your purpose here in London.'

He stabbed the point of his stick into the grass. 'Like most men I will do what society expects of me when the time comes. I don't obey another's rules blindly. Neither do you, otherwise you'd be planning your step up in the world . . . marriage to Lord Statham for title and fortune, or to the wealthy Simon Mortimer, whose character is motivated by greed which he hides under a thin veneer of gentlemanly behaviour, or so I'm reliably informed.'

'No information can be claimed as reliable during the London season.'

'Then you should not be taking me to task about my imagined shortcomings and should be able to understand why I must put my estate before my own happiness.'

She sighed. 'I confess, I do not understand men. It is you who is doing that. You cannot blame me because I didn't invent the season, and you are a free agent.'

He shrugged, visibly nettled. 'To answer your question, whether I wed for fortune, pedigree or both . . . or for neither of those desirable elements . . . the woman I choose will never be regarded as a chattel and will be treated with the utmost respect and affection. First, because she is a woman; second, because she will be my wife; and third, because I value the LéSayres name and will put her above all others.'

'Then you'd better choose carefully to find one who suits your exacting requirements.'

He now looked uncomfortable, eager to be rid of her. Vivienne wanted to cry so badly that a lump formed in her throat, one she almost choked on. She shouldn't have been so outspoken. 'I do understand . . . I'm sorry I was disrespectful . . . I'm ashamed,' she said, and began to walk rapidly away from him.

He caught up to her, taking her by the hand to still her flight. Gently he turned her round and gazed at her. The depths of his eyes displayed a small, dark kernel of hurt – one she'd inflicted by her abrupt departure. 'I was enjoying our time together alone. What has happened between us to change our friendship?'

What had happened? Love! Cupid had fired his damned stupid arrow right into her heart. Couldn't he see she was head-over-heels in love with him? She couldn't even think straight when she was with him.

Her emotions churned. She'd goaded him, blamed him for all that was male, when of course she was aware of what the London season was all about.

A solitary tear slid down her cheek and he collected it on his finger. 'I've made you cry . . . forgive me.'

'Forgive you for what?'

'Being a man, perhaps?'

Laughter trickled from her and she hiccupped. 'Next to my father you're the nicest man I know . . . did I sound like a shrew?'

'The shrews that live on King's Acres estate are sweet, quiet little creatures, but they bite if they're cornered. Does that sound like you?'

She gave a cautious, 'Well . . . possibly.'

He laughed. 'Then you've answered your own question. I'm quite sure that the shrews living there would adore you.'

'You don't have to humour me,' she grumbled.

Gruffly, he answered, 'Not another word, Vivienne Fox, else I'll throw you over my knee and smack your backside.'

She gave an outraged gasp and placed her hands on her rear. 'You wouldn't.'

'Try me.'

She flicked him a look and caught the fading moment of his wry grin.

'Here, take my arm and I'll escort you home. Perhaps I'll stay for an hour to observe any hopefuls who may call on you. You see, I'm learning to play the game.'

In the next few minutes she contemplated the punishment of her behind being smacked. How absolutely embarrassing . . . well, in public at least. He had big hands. What if she smacked his behind, how would he like it?

She stifled her laughter. He'd probably enjoy it.

Stop having disgusting thoughts, Miss Fox.

Easier said than done since my mind has developed a mind of its own.

Very droll!

She grimaced and said nothing for the next five minutes. When they turned a corner into her street she saw several carriages lined up outside the house. Feeling safer she looked up at him. 'You didn't really mean that, did you? What happened to your utmost respect for women?'

He slid her a grin. 'You pushed it to its limit.'

Alex stayed at the house long enough to be polite and then stood to leave, citing a business meeting and his theatre invitation as an excuse.

'I'll see you out,' she said, hoping they'd find a private moment where she could offer him the kiss she owed him.

To her disappointment they almost collided with Simon Mortimer, who was coming in.

'Good day, My Lord. I hear you're part of Lord Cresswell's party tonight.'

'Yes. We studied at university together, so I'm eager to resume my friendship with him.'

'Sophia is also a guest of the earl and his sisters. She's looking forward to seeing you again.'

The corner of Alex's mouth twitched and Vivienne wondered why he hadn't told her there would be eligible women in the theatre party. But then, she didn't own him and it was none of her business. All the same there was a yawning sense of despair inside her. She'd heard that if you really loved someone you'd put their happiness before your own. So was it selfish of her to want to keep Alex for herself?

He'd already made his thoughts on Sophia Mortimer clear . . . but Lord Cresswell's sisters? Goodness . . . one was sixteen and the other seventeen, and they were reputed to be so superior, eligible and delightful that Alex was bound to fall in love with one . . . or even both of them.

If Alex was surprised by the news that he'd be in the company of Sophia Mortimer, he didn't show it. He just turned to her and smiled. 'Thank you for your company today, Miss Fox. It was most enjoyable . . . and illuminating too. I look forward to the dance on Wednesday.'

She gently touched a fingertip against the brooch, thinking, *traitor!* 'I hope you enjoy the opera, My Lord. I believe the heroine perishes.'

'I'm sure I shall, and in true heroine fashion, no doubt she will be resurrected in time for her next performance.' He placed his hat on his head and nodded to Matthew, who opened the door for him as he strode off.

'Well . . . well,' Simon drawled. 'So he managed to cut the knot from your apron strings. What were you arguing about in the park?'

'I don't know what you mean.'

'Yes you do. I was seated on a bench not far from where you stood. The man is rapidly making inroads into society now and his calendar will be full enough for him to drop you soon. Just remember, I'll be waiting to pick you up.' He took a grip on her arm to detain her when she went to pass him. It was too tight for her to break free and she winced when he rolled his thumb joint over the bone at her wrist.

At least there had been enough distance between them so her conversation with Alex couldn't have been overheard. 'You'll have a long wait, Mr Mortimer. Let go of my arm. I need to go to my room and tidy myself.'

Matthew stepped forward. 'I suggest it would be in your interest to release Miss Fox's arm and join the other guests in the drawing room for the celebration, Mr Mortimer.'

'Would you, be damned! Who asked you?' Simon tensed, then allowed his glance to graze over Matthew's stocky, muscular form.

The servant said quietly, 'Now sir, if you please. We don't want a scene, do we?'

Simon released her and turned towards the drawing room. He hesitated, and then turned back, sneering, 'You're just a bloody servant, not fit to clean the shit from my boots. I know the person who runs the agency you were hired from, and could make sure you never found employment through them again. Miss Fox is a witness to your incivility.'

'Me?' Though shocked by Simon's language, Vivienne made her eyes as round and innocent as she could. 'I don't know what you're talking about. I haven't seen anything untoward take place . . . yet.'

'Very funny,' and his gaze went to the hovering Matthew. 'Some other time, bird-wit?'

'I'll look forward to it . . . *sir.*'

When Vivienne heard the servant crack his knuckles, she hoped they were not going to come to blows.

When Matthew took a step towards him, Simon hastily slipped through the drawing room door and disappeared into the hubbub coming from inside.

She exchanged a grin with the servant. 'Thank you, Matthew. I do hope you don't get into trouble.'

He shrugged. 'Mr Mortimer is a nasty bit of work and you should take care if he has set his sights on you. He was two seconds away from finding himself upended on the road outside. If you don't mind me saying, Miss Fox, that's the best place for trash like him.'

'Let me know if anything comes of his threat. I'll stand up for you. Lord . . . I hope Aunt Edwina doesn't get to hear of it.'

'Thank you, Miss. I doubt if it will since Mr Mortimer will not want to embarrass himself.'

Freddie and Adelaide disappeared into the conservatory an hour later. Adelaide was rosy cheeked, dimpled and bubbling with happiness. The proposal was made and accepted. They came back glowing with the excitement of the moment and the festivities went on into the evening.

Vivienne and Adelaide went upstairs to tidy their hair and found a private place to talk.

Vivienne gave her cousin a hug. 'I'm glad you accepted Freddie, he's such a good match for you.'

'I've always loved him. He's so sweet and funny. A pity you

didn't accept Simon. He and Freddie are such good friends and we could see each other often.'

'He told you about that?'

'He told Freddie, who told me. He said he'd take you with or without fortune, since he has enough.'

Vivienne didn't believe that for a moment. 'I don't like Simon . . . not even a little bit. What type of man will take bets on whether I have a fortune or not? As for his wealth, I'm given to understand that he gambles recklessly, so I doubt if he'll have his fortune for long.'

She laughed. 'Don't be so serious about things. It's just some fun. Most people who've placed money on the outcome think you haven't got a brass bean. Simon is convinced that you have. He thinks he stands to win a lot of money, and won't listen to me when I tell him you only inherited a small amount. I told him that I think you have designs on Lord LéSayres. Then Simon said he saw you arguing in the park, so it couldn't be true.'

The colour rose to Vivienne's cheeks. 'What he thought he saw and what actually happened are two different things. The earl is my friend. We move in different social circles and he will probably marry someone of title. He's going to the theatre with Lord Cresswell's party tonight, and Cresswell has two unmarried sisters who have everything Alex wants.'

'Alex . . . the earl's name is Alexander . . .' Adelaide swooped in a sudden breath. 'You have feelings towards Lord LéSayres, don't you? He's just the type of man you'd fall in love with.'

She shrugged. 'I . . . I do like him a lot, but it's no good being in love with a man you can't have.'

Adelaide hugged her. 'Oh, Vivienne, I've been so mean to you, when all the time your heart was breaking in two.'

She felt like crying at this cousinly act of affection, though being depicted as a lovesick heroine seemed rather ludicrous when Romeo and Juliet came into her thoughts. They'd been hardly more than children, and she and Alex were adults. Surely they could control their emotions a little easier? 'I'm sure my heart will recover . . . it will have to. He hasn't abandoned me entirely though, since I'm partnering him at the Almack's afternoon dance, remember? He would have made some excuse if he'd changed his mind.'

She would tell him the truth then. Perhaps that would turn the tide in her favour. She felt a need to confide in her cousin. 'I do love him. But you must promise you won't tell anyone of my feelings towards the earl. It would be crushing for me and embarrassing for him.'

Vivienne immediately regretted telling her cousin for Adelaide cooed, her voice oozing insincerity, 'Of course I won't tell anyone. Poor you . . . such a sad mope. Finally, you fall in love with the man of your dreams and that man can't be bought, even if you did have the fortune Simon cites you as being the possessor of.'

Vivienne hoped the sigh she gave was believable . . . if just to thwart Simon Mortimer in his quest to make money out of her state of mind.

'Come, let's go down, Vivienne. This is the happiest day of my life and I don't want to spend it crying over your lost love. So boring.'

Simon behaved himself throughout the celebration tea and apologized to her in a rather smarmy manner when he got the chance, but his eyes said the apology wasn't genuine. They were as hard as stones, and Vivienne couldn't bring herself to trust him.

Twelve

Vivienne's aunt and cousin were out visiting. They would be going on to a recital afterwards, and would take supper at the theatre before arriving home about ten.

Despite her aunt's urging, Vivienne had used a genuine headache to decline the engagement, and she had slept until late afternoon.

Now Maria gently shook her awake. 'There's an urgent message for you, Miss Fox.'

'Urgent!' Her heart quickened in alarm and she scrambled out from under the sheets, tossing her hair from her face and relieved that her headache had disappeared.

Beyond the window early evening was being delivered by a sky painted with yellow, pink and grey stripes, but the grey suggested rain was not far away.

The message informed her that her father had suffered an accident and he needed her to return home. The signature was a wiry scribble and she couldn't make out the name. It was certainly not her father's signature. Was he so badly injured he couldn't write a note or sign his name to one? He must be, else why would he need to call her home?

Panicking a little, she slid out of bed and scrabbled in one of her trunks to find her travelling clothes, a plain green skirt and bodice with a short cape. 'My father has suffered an accident, I must go to him immediately.'

Maria became a pillar of calm good sense and took over, removing the clothing from her hands. 'Let's do things in order, Miss Fox. We have an hour or so before the afternoon coach leaves, and you've had a shock.'

'My head's spinning.'

'You stood up too quickly, you're breathing too fast and your face is pale. Take in a deep breath . . . hold it . . . let it out slowly. Now another . . . hold it . . . breathe out . . .'

'I'm all right now.'

'Good. Now sit down and drink your tea while I fetch you some water to wash in. Matthew will bring up some refreshment by the by. While you're eating I'll run a flat iron over your travelling clothes, since the skirt and cape are crumpled. Then you can write your notes while I pack your travelling bag.'

Maria meant well, but Vivienne was not used to being instructed in what to do. However, although annoyed by it she realized it was out of concern for her, so she let it pass on this occasion.

'You shouldn't be travelling alone, Miss Fox, and it will be dusk by the time you get there. Perhaps I should come with you.'

'But you'll lose your job.'

'I'll be finishing anyway in a week or so. I don't mind not being paid, and at least I'll have a roof over my head and something to eat while I'm with you. I can help you if your father is confined to his bed, as I looked after my own father. It won't take much time to gather my things together.'

Vivienne was about to tell Maria she couldn't afford her wages when she remembered that she could – easily. There was no reason why she shouldn't have a maid. She calculated that she'd be able to afford two coach fares with the money she had left. Aunt Edwina and Adelaide would be furious, of course.

A sense of adventure tickled inside her. 'All right, Maria, you're hired. The roads are dry so it should be a fast journey, and we can hire a cab at the other end. Perhaps Matthew can go and buy the tickets, and he can escort us to the coach terminal.'

'He wouldn't allow you to leave the house without an escort, and at least he can see you safely on to the coach. What about the rest of your wardrobe?'

'I'll have to leave it here. Perhaps Matthew will arrange for it to be sent on.' Her hand flew to her mouth. 'There's a new gown being delivered in the morning. I must leave a note asking my aunt to pay for it, and I will reimburse her when I next see her. Oh dear . . . I must write to Lord LéSayres and tell him I'm unable to attend Almack's with him. My cousin will explain the situation, I expect.'

And thinking of the earl led Vivienne's mind to the violets she'd pressed inside a book. They wouldn't be dried yet. Carefully she removed the blotting paper containing the tokens and placed

them in her London journal, on the page she'd reserved for Alex
. . . though he'd run into two pages.

She couldn't leave it in full view for anybody to read. Her
travel bag had no room left for the journal. She wrapped it in a
shawl and placed it in the bottom of one of her trunks. Nobody
would come across it there.

Matthew came back with the coach tickets and the news that
unless there were cancellations they would have to take the later
coach.

Despite the scramble, she was ready on time, and Maria quickly
threw her own belongings into a smaller bag.

They were booked on the later coach, a rather shabby affair
that had seen better days and looked as though it had been brought
out of retirement to cope with an extra crowd. They arrived at
the coach station in good time. Vivienne had paid the inside fare
of seventeen shillings and five pence each, and made sure she had
money in her pocket for refreshments, and enough small coins
for tips along the way. The horses were large, strong creatures.
They stamped sparks from the cobbles, swished the flies from
their rumps with leisurely flicks of their tails, and snorted and
whuffled, as if they were talking to each other.

She was relieved to find the other two inside seats occupied
by a man and his wife, and a child, a sweet little girl of about
five, who clung to her mother's skirt and smiled shyly.

Vivienne occupied the seats facing the horses.

The coach dipped as the outside passengers climbed aloft. She
didn't envy them . . . or the horses, having to drag this big heavy
coach behind them. The driver cracked his whip over the horses'
heads. Soon they were wheeling through the dirty streets, scat-
tering animals and people alike as they barged through the crowds.
Gradually, town gave way to countryside.

It started to rain, a persistent patter against the coach. Five
minutes later it became a deluge. Vivienne felt like swearing,
because when the road churned with mud it would slow them
right down.

The child fell asleep, her head leaning against her mother's
body and snuggled into the safety of her arms. Her father followed
her example not long after. Maria succumbed, her head lolling
in the corner.

Vivienne watched the countryside trundle past. Her mind kept going to her father. He'd been well just a few days ago. Now he seemed to be at death's door.

The rain lessened and her mind flicked to Alex. What was he doing now, she wondered? Despite his poor opinion of Sophia, would he marry her . . . or one of Lord Cresswell's sisters perhaps? Their breeding would send them to the top of the list, unlike herself, who was the daughter of a country parson. She consoled herself. Even if he'd never once considered her to be a fitting mistress of King's Acres estate she would be left with her memories of him, of his mouth claiming the pleasure of her first real kiss, and of hers accepting that gift of pleasure.

The slow, wallowing movement of the swaying coach was relaxing and Vivienne slept for a short time. They stopped for a change of horses and a pie-in-hand supper. Someone came from the inn and inspected the wheels and began banging nails into the metal. Grease was applied to the hub.

Eventually they boarded it again and resumed the journey. It was still raining, a thin drizzle that had turned the road surface into slippery mud. Sometimes the men had to help push the coach up the inclines, while the coachman cracked his whip over the horses' heads.

The spinning wheels of the coach flicked up clumps of sticky mud that caked both men and vehicle and they were obliged to slow down. The last ten miles went almost at walking pace, and it was nearly midnight when they reached their destination.

Blessedly, the rain had ceased, but the sky was overcast and the darkness beyond the lights of the inn was dense.

Maidstone was not as populated or as busy as London. The streets were empty and quiet, apart from the rise and fall of voices coming from the inn. At this time of night there were no cabs for hire. The fresh smell of the sea was a welcome change after London. They waited a while in case someone had thought she might be on the coach.

The horses were changed again and two passengers took their places, while two of the males climbed down from the top, stretched, and then walked off in different directions.

'We'll have to walk,' she said. 'My home is about two miles.'

Maria said nervously, 'But it's dark, Miss.'

'It won't get any lighter for several hours, and we can't stay here because the ticket office is closed. We'd be more noticeable were we to go to the inn, and some of the men will be influenced by drink, so will be overly familiar if given the chance. We won't get lost, I promise. If we walk briskly it should take us about an hour.'

Twenty minutes later they'd cleared the town and started out along the country lane that led past the church and into the village of Chausworth. They heard the sound of a carriage coming up slowly behind them. Perhaps someone had come to meet them after all – or at least they could beg a lift, since there was nothing between here and the village.

The carriage had its lanterns lit and the coachman stopped a little way past them. 'Miss Fox?' The rather gruff voice came from the interior, and when a man descended she thought him a slightly sinister figure in a black cloak and floppy hat. But then, anyone would seem sinister at that time of morning. All the same, she was wary.

There was something about the man's voice she recognized, and she said uneasily, 'Did my father send you to meet me . . . is he all right?'

'I'll take you to him. Get in.' He took her by the arm and a gust of brandy fumes enveloped her when he opened the door and almost threw her inside. Instinctively she launched herself from the seat when he tried to follow her in. Her momentum knocked him to the ground and she clambered over him, her knees forcing the breath from his body. When she raked her nails down his face he uttered a loud curse and punched her a couple of times in the side of her head. Blood trickled from her nose. Dazed, she gave a little groan and the world spun around her. 'Run, Maria,' she called out with her remaining breath, then swooped in another.

He punched her in the stomach. When she gasped and dropped to the ground he lost his grip. 'Stop struggling else I'll clout you again.'

The other man cried out, 'Gracious . . . enough of the fisticuffs. You shouldn't treat a young lady so roughly.'

Maria gave a scream that would have woken the occupants of the church graveyard from their long slumber. 'Don't you hurt my mistress, you murdering swines—' The noise ended abruptly with the sound of a blow.

Vivienne struggled to her feet.

'Christ . . . there's two of them . . . a maid, I think. What have you done to her?' the driver said in alarm.

'I've given her a little tap on the head with my stick and dropped her over the wall into the churchyard. She'll wake up soon.'

'I didn't think you'd go this far. You said it was just to give the chaperone a fright—'

'Shut up, you fool! You don't want them to recognize us, do you?'

Vivienne already had. The voices told her that her assailant was Simon Mortimer, and Frederick was driving the carriage. She was so furious she was past thinking about anything except revenge, but her anger was tempered by the thought that her father might not be ill after all.

Behind the wall there was a furtive movement and a whimper from Maria. Vivienne cried out, 'You'll go to prison for this.'

'Not if there's nobody left to witness against us. Get in the carriage, my dear. Give me what I want without further trouble and I'll let you go.'

Vivienne's blood chilled. Surely they wouldn't kill her?

'I won't be involved in this anymore. Leave them here and get in the carriage,' Freddie said.

'Oh, do find some guts. Whatever she says to the contrary, I have it from a reliable source that she's worth a fortune.'

'It's stopped being funny. A fright is one thing, an elopement with the lady's consent is acceptable, but a forced abduction with such threatening behaviour is ungentlemanly as well as criminal. This is a respectable young woman and the whole prank has become too risky. I'm going back to London and you're coming with me. If you refuse I'll . . .'

'You'll what?'

'I swear I'll turn you in if you don't. I want to get back for the Almack's dance. It's my first invitation and recognition of my title. If I queer my pitch I'll never hear the last of it from—' Freddie stopped abruptly, as if aware he was about to say too much, and he began to pull the horse's head round.

Simon swore.

When he got the carriage pointed back towards town, Freddie asked politely, as though taking his leave from Aunt Edwina's social gathering, 'Are you young ladies unharmed?'

Apart from a sore head and a bloody nose. And Maria was conscious; Vivienne could hear the maid retching. Her own anger was as hot as a fire raging at her core. 'With no thanks to you . . . tell your friend to unhand me,' she thrust at him.

It became obvious that Freddie wasn't going to be much help if things got worse.

After being used to the gas lamps that illuminated the smarter parts of London, the countryside seemed sinister and saturated by the thick darkness. If she found the opportunity to escape into it, the advantage would be hers, for she knew the lie of the land.

'I'm sure he'll do as you ask if you'll just calm down. If you struggle it will inflame him.'

'*Calm down! Inflame him!* If I had a gun I'd blow your stupid heads off, you dolts.'

Frederick's voice went a notch higher, though he tried, too late, to disguise it. 'I implore you, Miss . . . nothing more should be said lest the reaction causes harm to yourself. There has been no harm done yet . . . apart from a fright. I'll make sure you receive a sum of money to compensate.' His voice was nervously reasonable, placating, as if he'd just realized the seriousness of the situation, but was too cowardly to intervene physically. He did his best.

To Simon he said, almost begging, 'Get in the carriage *at once,* sir, else our friendship is at an end. Admit we made a mull of it and the jape has become a bag of moonshine. You're too boozy to think straight.'

Simon was still reluctant to let her go; he had his arm around her neck in a firm, choking grip. Vivienne's breath came in painful rasps.

'Not boozy enough . . . pass down the bottle and I'll pour some brandy down the woman's throat, it might loosen her up a bit.'

Vivienne was wearing a stout pair of boots, and since Simon was finding it difficult to follow Freddie's instructions she made them clear to him. She kicked back with her foot and heeled him in the shin.

He yelped and hopped about on one leg, curses flying from his mouth like flies from a piece of rotting meat. It would have been laughable were she not acutely aware of the danger she was in. 'Now will you unhand me?'

She was about to run when Simon recovered enough to reach her, giving her a stinging slap across the face that cut her lip. Grabbing her by her travelling cape he jerked her back towards him when she tried to run. 'Not so fast, lady, I'm not letting you go without finding what you're made of first.'

Her temper exploded and she swung round. 'This is what I'm made of, you poor excuse for a . . . *a toad!*' She made good use of her knee, bringing it up sharp, high and hard.

Simon howled and then doubled over and began to retch, gasping out, 'You rancid little bitch . . . you'll be sorry . . . for this.'

'I doubt it.' She whacked him behind the knees with a stick she'd snatched up, and he fell to the ground. For good measure she called out to Freddie, 'Give me a minute or two to find my companion and get away, then come down and assist this lout. Be careful, sir, because I have a stout stick.'

Freddie was so frightened he almost bleated. 'You won't need to use it on me.'

She located her travelling bag and threw it over the wall into the church grounds. It would only hamper them, and she could collect it later. 'Maria,' she called out softly.

There was a frightened, warbling response. 'I'm here, Miss.'

Vivienne was relieved when her maid came creeping through the church gate. Taking her by the hand, Vivienne whispered, 'Are you able to run?'

'Like a lizard with six legs.'

'Then let's run.'

Fuelled by panic they began to run to put some space between themselves and their pursuers. After a while they were forced to slow to a walk and eventually stopped, out of breath, trembling and leaning on each other for support. Their harsh breaths and rapid heartbeats began to slow.

There was no sound or sign that the carriage was following

after them. The stars spread across the dark velvety sky, peaceful and lovely. She was glad there was no moon because if she couldn't see their assailants then they couldn't see her. Her mind sifted and identified what sound there was . . . the wind soughing in the canopy of trees, a hedgehog scratching in the leaves. An owl hooted, making them jump.

Maria whimpered. Usually calm and collected, her maid had allowed her panic to come to the fore again. Vivienne couldn't blame her, for her own nerves were almost at breaking point.

'I'm scared, Miss.'

'Shush!' Vivienne gazed into the darkness they'd left behind them, the blood pounding inside her ears as she strained for a sound. The wind was fitful and played games. Leaves rustled and there was a furtive, creeping sound in the darkness. A stick snapped and her ears pricked when a fox barked. All the sounds were familiar to her, though the night had changed them from friend into foe.

'It's all right, Maria . . . they didn't follow us.'

Maria's tension was relieved in a burst of weeping. Vivienne did her best to comfort the girl, taking her in her arms, hugging her tight and speaking soothing words. Maria's body was wracked with tremors.

She was aware that the safety of her father's house was within reach, and had it been daytime she would have glimpsed the orange chimney pots above the trees, where the road wound upwards. In the dark it now seemed so far.

When Maria's tears lessened and she took a long, shuddering sniff, Vivienne whispered, 'Have you caught your breath, Maria? We must keep moving, it's not much further.'

The realization that the immediate danger no longer existed caused the tension to drain from her so suddenly that it left her fatigued. Yet there was enough of it left to warn her – to advise her to be cautious. They were not out of danger yet, and every night sound seemed to carry menace on its back.

They began to walk, treading lightly, their arms around each other's waists in mutual support, and stopping at intervals to rest. Two miles had never seemed so far.

But blessing upon blessings, eventually they were there. The gate squeaked open and she gave a shaky smile. Her father hadn't remembered to oil the hinges yet. When she placed her eyes against the coloured glass panels set in the front door she could see a small flickering light at the back of the house. Her father was a light sleeper and would be in the kitchen helping himself to a piece of bread and butter and a glass of milk, as he often did if hunger woke him at night.

When she rapped at the door it sounded loud and made her jump.

The light moved as he came into the hall. 'Who is it? State your business at this time of morning?'

'It's me, Papa . . . Vivienne,' she said, close to tears.

'Vivienne? You're in London so how can you be on my doorstep? It is you, isn't it?' He sounded totally bewildered.

'Oh Pa . . . of course it's me. Let me in.'

The light began its wavering journey again, and stopped so the spirit lamp on the hall table could be lit. Light flared.

Her father was still fully clothed, so he must have been called out to one of the parishioners earlier. Bolts were pulled back, the door opened. They nearly fell through it.

Her father's eyes were wide with surprise. 'Vivienne . . . what is going on? Does your aunt know you are here, and who is this young lady?'

'My maid, Maria.'

'I didn't know you had a maid. You're exceedingly dishevelled, and there's blood on you.' Alarm filled his voice. 'Are you injured? What has happened? Tell me.'

Half-laughing and half-crying at the sight of his dear face, she said, 'I will if you will just take a breath and hold it long enough for me to answer. As to the first, yes . . . my aunt should know by now, since I left her a note. Secondly, this young woman has just been hired to be my maid and my companion, which is why you didn't know about her. As to what happened . . . we were attacked on the road.'

'Attacked? What on earth were you doing on the road at this time of morning? I don't understand.'

'I received a note saying you'd had an accident and I dropped everything and bought a ticket on the next coach to Maidstone. Obviously, it was somebody's idea of fun. I was so worried about you, Papa, and I'm so relieved to find you hale and hearty. But it was done for a purpose, Papa . . . and that purpose was to abduct me for my supposed fortune, or to blacken my name in the attempt.'

'Oh . . . my poor Vivienne. I knew that concealing the legacy would do you more harm than good.'

'And you were right, for it attracted the wrong men, and this is the outcome. There were no cabs available at the coach station, so we decided to walk.' She began to cry, and so did Maria.

'There, there, my dears. You must be tired out. We will all go to bed and pursue the matter in the morning when you will be less prone to stress. Here, you take the candle, Vivienne, and I'll use the lamp. Take the kettle up with you so you can wash the blood and dirt from your faces and I'll bring you some milk to help you sleep.'

Vivienne rifled through her chest of drawers and found them a nightgown apiece. The bed would be big enough for both of them.

Her father knocked and said against the door panel, 'Your milk is on the table outside. Goodnight, my dears. We will sort things out tomorrow, I promise. We have your reputation to think of, Vivienne, and must avoid a scandal at all cost.'

Her reputation . . . avoid a scandal? The only scandal from this sorry affair was attached to those two louts who'd attacked them – and she was going to make sure justice was done.

She didn't know how to bring it about, and if she hadn't been in bed she would have stamped her foot.

It would have to wait until morning, she thought, as she fell into oblivion.

Thirteen

Mrs Goodman opened the door when Alex knocked. She looked frustrated.

'Have I come at an inconvenient time?'

'Do come in, My Lord . . . we're in such a pickle. That ungrateful girl has taken the maid and left us without a word. I've sent the manservant to the agency to see if they can provide us with another maid. Do join Lord Frederick in the drawing room,' and she ushered him inside.

'Was the ungrateful girl you mentioned in reference to Miss Fox?'

'It certainly was. She left, leaving a note for me to pay her debts off.'

Unease filled him. Something like that was out of character for the Vivienne he knew. 'Without saying why?'

'She used family illness as an excuse . . . but we've all heard that convenient explanation before. She's just jealous over Adelaide's betrothal and is being spiteful. And this morning a gown arrived that hadn't been paid for and I had to make good for it. Goodness knows how Vivienne got it into her head that she could afford such an expensive gown.'

Adelaide paraded in it. 'This is the gown, My Lord, isn't it pretty?'

'It's a lovely gown,' he said, but he was thinking, what was merely pretty on Adelaide would be exquisite on Vivienne.

'I borrowed Vivienne's pearl and jade necklace and earrings. They used to belong to her mother.'

There was nothing admirable about Adelaide Goodman; she was as shallow and tedious as her mother. He felt a sneaking pity for Frederick, who looked a bit down in the mouth.

But Mrs Goodman had taken the floor again. 'I was shocked by the cost of the gown. Luckily it fits Adelaide so she shall have it. All that money spent to impress the doyens of Almack's . . . as if Vivienne could with her unremarkable looks. One could almost suppose she absconded on purpose, and out of spite, taking the maid with her . . . ingrate that she is, and with no skills to speak of. She'll get no reference from me. It's so inconvenient having to train a new maid this late in the season.' She offered Freddie a fond look. 'Thank goodness Adelaide is so well matched – such a dear boy.'

Frederick looked uncomfortable, as if he had his head in a noose.

'Now . . . I must go to the landing and keep a lookout for those sly creatures in case they come skulking back.'

Adelaide picked up from where her mother finished, offering him a secretive look. 'Perhaps the gown was to impress you with, My Lord? I went into her room to look for a note and found a journal in which she'd written comments on all the men she'd met. She was terribly rude about Freddie, and scathing about poor Mr Mortimer, and after he offered her marriage, too.' Taking the journal from the table, she handed it to him. 'I imagine you'll run a mile after you read what she says about you . . . especially since she's turned her nose up at your invitation to Almack's social, and without a word of apology. Her comments are personal and unflattering, and although Mama doesn't think so, they are also funny. Freddie . . . you thought them funny, even though she was rude calling you a lap dog that would turn into a terrier once the novelty of being married had worn thin.'

Alex tried not to grin at the aptness of the description. Vivienne would have had a good reason for making personal comments, no doubt, but they were private to her. For that reason he would not read them. He imagined they were a comment on the situation she found herself in. 'I find myself appalled that you should publish her comments.'

Adelaide flushed. 'Oh . . . it's just a bit of fun, and you're such a fuddy-duddy, My Lord.' She offered her fiancé a possessive smile. 'Freddie thought you might like to take Sophia Mortimer to Almack's instead of Miss Fox, and so you won't be inconvenienced he's sent a message for her to ready herself.'

Had he indeed? 'That was presumptuous of him.'

'And here's a note for you from Vivienne.'

Freddie avoided his eyes when Adelaide handed over the note. It stated that Vivienne's father had suffered an accident and she must go home as quickly as possible. The last paragraph touched his heart.

Alex, I've been so looking forward to your company at Almack's, and I'm sorry our friendship has been cut short so abruptly. Enjoy the rest of your stay in London. Perhaps we will meet again in your beautiful Dorset.

My good and true friend, I will miss you.

Vivienne.

There came a tap on the door and Sophia entered, wearing something pink and diaphanous that nearly robbed Alex of breath. She might as well have been naked. Frederick's mouth fell open. She smiled at him, totally aware of her impact. 'Good afternoon, Freddie.' For Alex she reserved a curtsey, her shoulders artfully positioned to offer a tantalizing view of her bosom. 'Good afternoon, My Lord.'

'Miss Mortimer.'

Frederick stood. 'Where is Simon, Sophia? I rather wanted to talk to him.'

'He can hardly walk, and he doesn't want anyone to see the scratches on his face. He said he fell from his horse into a bramble patch, though I don't know where he'd find a bramble patch in London. He looks as though a savage cat had scratched him. What did you and he get up to on Monday night, Freddie, you rascals? You both arrived back late last night and my brother has been in a foul mood ever since.'

Frederick looked uneasy. 'Nothing of much consequence.'

Sophia seemed to notice Adelaide for the first time. 'Good heavens, your toilette doesn't seem to be complete yet.'

'I no longer have a maid, she has run off with my cousin,' Adelaide said sulkily, then she smiled, and it was pure malice. 'Sophia . . . do you remember telling me that you were a maid before you and your brother came into your money? You can arrange it for me.'

Sophia glared at Adelaide and said, 'I told you no such thing. I used to design gowns. However, I daresay I can arrange a simple style for your hair.'

Alex wouldn't like to wager on the outcome of that hairstyle when it was obvious that the two women disliked the sight of each other. Something was not quite right here and he was beginning to put two-and-two together. He didn't like the answers.

He was pleased when the two women left the room, and he turned to Freddie. 'Has Simon Mortimer been bothering Miss Fox?'

'How did you find out? Oh, I see,' he exclaimed when Alex frowned, 'it was a guess.'

'Actually, it's more of a deduction. Facts: Miss Fox isn't here. Mrs Goodman is in a flap and Simon Mortimer won't show his face. Do you want me to repeat the question?'

'I'm sure she wasn't badly hurt.'

'What do you mean by that . . . where is Miss Fox?'

'No harm was intended, and though she was roughed up a little, none was done – at least, I don't think so. Simon was angry because she'd dismissed his petition out of hand.'

Alex fisted him by the jacket and drew him close. 'Miss Fox said she received a note to attend her father in Maidstone because he'd been taken ill, I understand. Was that a genuine note?'

Colour flooded the other man's face and his voice squeaked. 'Simon wrote it. He was convinced Miss Fox had inherited a fortune, and was determined to have it. You know Simon is running a book on it? He'd been drinking blood and thunder all night and the effect was to bring his temper to the surface.'

'That's no excuse. What have you and Simon Mortimer been up to? You can tell me now, or you can explain what's been going on to a magistrate.'

'Unhand me, sir, you're crushing my cravat,' he bleated.

Alex dropped him into a chair. 'Who else knows what's happened?'

'Nobody, I swear, and neither Simon nor I used our names, and it was too dark for us to be recognized, so Miss Fox is unaware of who her assailants actually are.'

Freddie must be stupid if he thought Vivienne wouldn't have recognized them . . . and now he'd confessed. Had Freddie told Adelaide what had occurred, he wondered? If so, half of London would know by now.

'You know, if this gets out Miss Fox's reputation will be ruined, for nobody would believe she wasn't a party to a lover's tryst that went horribly wrong. What sort of men would carry out such a despicable action? You should be ashamed of yourself.'

'Oh, believe me, sir, I'm totally ashamed. It started out as a prank. We'd been drinking, and Simon got it into his head that if he waylaid her she would have to wed him or suffer the scandal.'

'Wed him . . . is Mortimer in love with Miss Fox to go to such lengths to capture her interest? Surely a man in love would seek to protect the lady of his heart.'

'It's more that he's in love with her supposed legacy. Simon doesn't like to be thwarted or proved wrong.'

'He attacked her for money? The girl only has a few pounds from a legacy to enjoy.'

'Simon is convinced she has a fortune stashed away, and he's been investing heavily and looking to recoup his losses by marriage. Plus his sister, Sophia, isn't quite . . . *tidy*. He wants to get her off his hands at any cost. Nothing will convince him that Miss Fox is anything less than the fatted calf.

'I went along with him considering that he might sober up on the way to Maidstone and think better of it. He had no intention of harming Miss Fox . . . at least, I didn't think so. We hired a carriage and followed the stagecoach, and then we got in front of them and waylaid her. It was easy to nab her because she and the maid were on foot. But things got confused and out of hand. Stephen planted a facer on her when she refused to get in the carriage and that's when I intervened. I managed to restrain Simon and told Miss Fox to run.'

'Very laudable,' he said caustically. 'You suffered no injuries yourself in your heroic rescue of her, I see.'

Freddie looked miserable. 'I was turning the carriage round while the struggle was going on. By the time I got down from the driver's seat it was all over and Simon was on the ground, doubled up in pain and protecting a pair of crushed acorns.'

The thought of that instilled an enormous sense of pleasure into Alex's growing anger. Vivienne Fox was no shrinking violet, but no amount of pluck would help her weather the storm that would beat around her ears once this affair got out. It would be intolerable. Because she was innocent, her instinct would be to brave it out, but if she came back to London it would be with her reputation soiled beyond redemption.

'I want this affair bottled up, Frederick, and I'm holding you responsible for doing that. I'm going to Maidstone to see Miss Fox and get her side of the story. In the meantime, tell your friend to close his book and call off the wolf pack. I'll call on him when I get back, and if I hear anything derogatory said about Miss Fox in the meantime then he'd better start running, for I'll follow him to the ends of the earth and strangle him with my bare hands. Understood?'

'Yes, My Lord . . . what about Almack's?'

'Sod Almack's! If you think I'm going to prance around a dance floor dressed like a turkey cock while your friend conspires to ruin the reputation of an innocent young woman, think again.'

'But what of Miss Mortimer . . . she will never forgive you if she misses the appearance of the Regent?'

'Miss Mortimer is not my responsibility, and I'm sure she'll get over her disappointment. She'll have to, especially since I had no intention of escorting her in the first place.'

The young ladies had begun to descend the stairs. Adelaide displayed a frizzled fringe on her forehead. 'Mama has developed a headache.'

Looking smug, Sophia said rather imperiously, 'We are ready, My Lord.'

'Since my chosen and named partner is unable to accompany me I have no desire to dance, so I must change my plans. I hope this hasn't inconvenienced you, Miss Mortimer. Perhaps the baron will be allowed two partners if he explains the situation.' He gave a short bow, then turned on his heel and left them to it. He knew he was being rude but he didn't want the company of any of them after the way they'd treated Vivienne.

Alex made plans as he strode rapidly to his boarding house. He took Mrs Crawford into his confidence over Vivienne's plight, since the woman had a tight mouth about personal matters. 'I doubt if her relative will welcome her back into her home, and other than yourself there is nobody I can trust with it.'

Mrs Crawford took it all in her stride. 'I can offer refuge to the young lady should the need arise. Would you allow me to inform John Howard of the affair, since Miss Fox is his niece?'

'I'd rather you waited until I've got to the bottom of it. I want to see her injuries for myself, and her father must take precedence over her uncle.'

'Of course.'

'It's up to him if he wishes to take John Howard into his confidence. I'd be obliged if you kept your ears open though. I don't need to tell you how urgent this is. I need to hire a horse, but have very little money left.' He took the family ring from his finger. 'Can you recommend a stable? I can offer this ring as security for the horse.'

'There's no need, My Lord. I know a man who has a stable and Mr Howard instructed me to provide you with anything you need, should you ask. He's a very generous man. I'll send my Ned with a note and he'll bring a horse to the door before you've had time to change out of those fancy clothes. It will probably be the nag Mr Howard uses when he's here.'

Alex paused on the bottom stair. 'You speak of John Howard with affection. Excuse my curiosity, Mrs Crawford, but may I ask what your relationship is?'

She gave a faint smile. 'Not what you imagine, My Lord. John Howard is my half-brother. I didn't know I possessed one until ten years ago when he sought me out. I'd just been widowed and he purchased this house for me, so I'd have a living as well as a home to raise my stepson in. John usually resides here when he visits the city, unless he has business, or wishes to impress a new client, for which he will use his office or his club.'

John Howard rose in his estimation, and although Alex didn't like owing the man money he accepted the purse Mrs Crawford offered him. 'In case you have need of it,' she said.

On impulse he kissed her cheek. 'Thank you.'

She chuckled. 'Thank John Howard, and save your kisses for the younger women, where they'll make more impression.'

He managed a grin. 'I would if I could find a suitable one.'

'Perfection has always been hard to come across. If you stop looking, a suitable woman might find you. Do you have a pistol? You might need one if you're on the road alone.'

He nodded. 'I'm pleased to say I haven't needed to kill anyone yet. Excuse me now if you would. I must hurry if I'm to stop this turning into a scandal.'

'You'd have a better chance of stopping a forest fire. There's only one way of stopping it, My Lord . . . marry the young woman.'

He laughed so hard on his way upstairs that he didn't notice that Mrs Crawford had been serious.

He placed Vivienne's journal on the table. He was tempted to read it, but it wouldn't be fair to her, and it would embarrass her if she found out. Before he left he hid it under his pillow.

His mount was saddled and waiting for him fifteen minutes later. A former army officer's horse, the sturdy grey gelding had been named Boots, because the bottom halves of his forelegs were black. The horse eyed him with a certain amount of suspicion.

Alex took him by the bridle and spoke to him for a few moments. 'We're going to Maidstone, but I promise not to push you too hard.'

Once the horse had familiarized himself with his smell and voice, Alex mounted. The saddle moulded to his behind like a second skin.

He gazed down at Ned from his superior height. 'Has he got any quirks I should know about?'

Ned grinned. 'He has a tendency to high-step if he hears an army band, but you won't find any of those on the way to Maidstone. Other than that, he should give you a comfortable ride, My Lord.'

And that proved to be the case.

The journey was without incident, the road crowded with travellers looking to make their journey while it was still light. It was just gone nine and the air was a soft and misty twilight when he reached Maidstone. It was too late to go on since he wanted to clearly see the place where Vivienne and her maid were attacked.

Boots was stabled for the night while Alex took a room at the inn. He ate a hearty dinner, washed it down with a tankard of ale and went to bed. The rumbling blend of mostly male voices, laughter and colourful curses coming from the bar downstairs kept him awake for only a short time. But no wonder Vivienne had chosen to push on. This establishment was certainly no place for a lady.

All the same, he needed to speak to the landlord for he'd left London in so much haste he hadn't found out where Vivienne lived.

'Reverend Fox?' The man scratched his head, and then gave Alex a gap-toothed smile. 'You be the second gentleman who asked after the good reverend's whereabouts . . . two day ago it were, come to think of it. It were a pair of them, and they went off without a thank you : . . didn't drink ale, but bought a bottle of brandy and port. Not that they needed it because the bigger man reeked of it. A nasty bit of work, he were.'

Alex took a shilling from his waistcoat pocket and handed it over.

'Thank you kindly, sir, though there weren't any need for it since I thought they might be up to some jiggery pokery and I didn't tell them nuthin'. Someone else may have though. Then the London coach came in and I was busy changing the horses for the return journey.'

'Did you see any young women get off the coach?'

'May I ask why you're making this your business, sir?'

'You may. One of the passengers was a young woman who is a particular friend of mine. I believe she was travelling with her maid. I need to speak to her father, to satisfy myself she got home safely.'

He nodded. 'Normally I would tell you to mind your own business, sir, but I can see you're a gentleman, and I reckon you don't mean them any harm, at that.' He drew in a deep breath. 'Apart from a woman with her family, there were two of them. Trim little duchesses, they were, but I couldn't see their faces. They didn't have much baggage, just a piece each.' He slid the coin into his pocket. 'Reverend Fox, you said . . . he lives over Chausworth way. Take the south road out of town for a mile or so past the church and he lives in the old manor house. It's called Rose Cottage. You can't miss it.'

'Tell me of the men you spoke of. Can you describe them?'

'The one driving spoke like gentry and his voice was high-pitched and twitchy. He was a bit of a showy gentleman. He was arguing with his companion and was pushed in the chest and told to shut up for his trouble. The other . . . well, I know a bad 'un when I see one,' and he spit into the sawdust. 'Fact is he had a sly look and his eyes were mean. I wouldn't turn my back on him in the dark. I recognized the carriage he was driving though. It were hired from Adams and Son.'

The man had become loquacious and Alex let him ramble, though he filed that piece of information in his mind and slid another shilling his way.

The man slid it back. 'I reckon you be looking into what happened to them two young women.'

'Could be.'

'I heard a whisper they had been set upon. Would that be right?'

'I heard the same whisper.'

'A downright shame if you ask me. That pair of felons need a good flogging. Later in the night they came back and pounded on my door, demanding a room. The drunk's face was all scratched and bloody and he was doubled over and ready to cast his accounts up on the doorstep my missus had just scrubbed. When I gave him a talking-to he threatened to come back and burn the inn down. The other one kept apologizing for him. You should keep better company, I says, and I sent them both packing. Likely they ended up sleeping in a haystack, and serve them right, though it's more than they deserved.

'I'll send my lad to fetch Boots for you. He's eaten his breakfast and is looking forward to a bit of a gallop. He's a good horse with a strong heart.'

Alex shook his hand. 'Thank you, landlord, you've been most helpful.'

The man doffed his hat. 'Pleased to make your acquaintance, My Lord.'

Fourteen

'We look as if we've been to war.'

The doleful face of Maria was reflected in the mirror behind Vivienne, who managed to drown her sob in a watery huff of laughter. 'The cat hid under the dresser and hissed at me this morning.'

'You came off far the worse, Miss Fox. Your face is all swollen up and the skin around your eyes is bruised. Then there are the bruises and welts on your body. My only injury was a crack on my head and some scratches from the holly bush I was thrown into. At least we can be thankful they didn't . . . well, you know . . . do something worse, otherwise you might have been obliged to wed Simon Mortimer.'

Simon Mortimer would have violated her if she hadn't fought back, she knew. Vivienne shuddered at the thought of becoming his wife. 'I would rather kill him first.'

In the cold light of day the assault of two nights ago would have seemed far-fetched and unbelievable, were it not for their injuries. On the odd moments when reality set in, Vivienne had bouts of weeping that she couldn't seem to control, and Maria sometimes joined in.

'Perhaps I should call the doctor,' her father had said, helpless in the face of these flooding tears from the usually most calm and sensible of his three daughters.

'No . . . you mustn't, Papa. I don't want anyone to know, since you know what the gossip will be like.'

'I could send a message to your sisters.'

'That would worry them needlessly, since by the time they get here I'll be back to normal. The injuries aren't serious and will heal and I'll just stay indoors until they do. I'm just a bit shaken.'

'Do you know who did this to you? We could take them before a magistrate.'

'No . . .' she'd lied. 'Let it be, Papa. The fewer people who know, the less gossip there will be. It was my own fault for believing the note was from you. I was so worried I didn't stop to think it may have been a hoax and somebody had set a trap for me.'

He'd gently patted her cheek, and then kissed her. 'You're a good daughter, Vivienne, but you're being evasive and that makes me sad. I understand you have to be careful of your reputation, but no blame can be laid on you for what happened.'

'You don't understand, Papa. People will always believe the worst.'

'You will be letting your aunt down if you don't return to London.'

'Aunt Edwina will no longer have any need of me since Adelaide has made a match that she approves of.' And God help her for accepting the proposal from a man as weak as Frederick, she thought.

'The men who attacked you . . . you know who they are, don't you?'

She hung her head at that. 'It was dark and I have no proof. I don't want to unjustly accuse people of wrongdoing when they may be innocent, and when there is the possibility of disruption to the lives of others. I need to think about what the point of this attack might be – and then decide what to do about it. The whole episode has been a shock, so allow me a day or two to find my strength and recover.'

'Of course you must. When you do decide you must come to me for guidance, because your happiness means much to me and I don't want you martyred. I'm going to the church for a while. I'll pray for a solution to this problem and I'll bring your bags back.'

A mixture of the mystical and the practical, of which the latter would be of more use to her right at this moment, she thought. Overnight her bruises had worsened, and her body was now stiff and sore. Maria had got over her fright, but she'd been unconscious for most of the struggle.

As for herself . . . well, it could have been worse, she conceded. She'd been unfair in branding Freddie as weak because if it hadn't been for his intervention she might not have got off so lightly.

'I was supposed to go to Almack's afternoon dance yesterday.

I wonder if the earl went without me, or found himself another partner. Sophia Mortimer, perhaps.'

Maria snorted. 'Had Lord LéSayres intended to take anyone else he wouldn't have asked you in the first place. That woman throws herself at him, and he knows it. He's only got eyes for you, Miss. You should tell him.'

'Tell him what?'

'That you do have the fortune everybody is talking about. I heard your father say so.'

'You don't understand, Maria. I promised myself that I'd only marry a man who loves me for myself. Telling him about the fortune is the last thing I can do now. He has pride in himself and his family, and he is an honest man. He'll never forgive me for lying to him when he has taken my side at every turn. He regards me as a sister.'

'If he doesn't forgive you, he doesn't deserve to have you and you'd be better off without him. I must go through your gowns here. That one you're wearing is so shabby.'

'They're old. I must write to my aunt and ask her to send my trunks on as soon as possible. I doubt if I'll return to London now. I'm thinking I might buy a cottage and settle down. I'll compensate you for what you went through because of me, Maria. I'll also pay you a year's wages if you'd prefer to look for another position. Think about what you want to do and let me know. My aunt might take you back for the rest of the season.'

'Begging your pardon, Miss Fox, but I'd rather starve than work for Mrs Goodman and her daughter ever again.'

Vivienne crossed to the window and gazed down the verdant sloping hillside to where the broad expanse of the Medway sparkled in the morning sunshine. It was so peaceful here after London. Yet she felt lonely. She'd failed to navigate another season successfully and her future stretched before her like an empty road leading to nowhere. She would buy her cottage, tend her garden and do charitable works, and she would grow old without noticing it, still referred to as *Poor Miss Fox*, only with 'old' added to it. Her poverty would come from being unloved, unmarried and childless, and not from lack of funds. '*Poor old Miss Fox* was disappointed in love,' they would say about her, 'but she's the benefactor of some worthy charity or another, so has a good heart.' That same heart began to ache and she felt like weeping again.

You're such a bore when you indulge in self-pity.

She nearly answered her inner voice out loud but didn't bother, since her self-confidence had been so eroded that she didn't need any more of her faults pointing out. She would have the brooch Alex gave her to remind her of what might have been.

Her hand suddenly went to her bodice. The brooch wasn't there. Had she left it in London? No, she'd been wearing it when she'd left. She scrabbled through the necessary bits and pieces on her dresser. 'Maria, have you seen my brooch, the one Lord LéSayres gave me?'

'No, Miss Fox.'

'I seem to have lost it.'

'When you were attacked, I expect. Shall I go and look for it?'

'No . . . if someone finds it they'll hand it to my father. That's the usual method for lost and found goods hereabouts.'

Dorset came into her mind. The little she'd seen of it had resembled Kent, with green rolling hills, rivers and the sea all within reach. But Dorset was veined with small rivulets and streams that meandered through the countryside to empty into the sea. The coast was more rugged, the heaths wilder and the woodlands dense. Alex had told her his home was large, that it would swallow the cottage she lived in with her father, and every spare coin that came into the household was spent on its maintenance – this said with a nostalgic smile on his face, as if he could picture it.

Alex had also told her about his stepmother, Eugenie, the present Countess LéSayres. Vivienne had been shocked to discover that Alex's household was more informal than most, for the countess had been his late father's mistress, and she'd refused to marry him until his life was nearly at an end, even though she'd loved him and had brought up his children.

'How romantic,' she'd said, but in a rather uncertain way as she wondered what her father would have to say about such an arrangement.

'It wasn't romantic when we couldn't afford a fire in the grate or the seed for a crop or the wages to pay the field workers,' he'd said. 'Sometimes we didn't have enough to eat, although we grow as many vegetables as we can. We have one servant who cooks and does what she can, and she hasn't been paid since God-knows-when. We have a few farm rents as income. My brother Dominic works. Eugenie has a little money of her own coming in, and we've just learned that she used it to feed and clothe us when we were growing up. We've never been able to entertain, though a king regularly visited one of the countesses on occasion, when the family coffers had more substance than a bag of buttons.'

She'd tried to keep her guilty blush under control and sidetracked. 'No wonder you all love the countess; Eugenie sounds like a wonderful woman.'

'We owe her a great deal. Now you know the reason why I must wed a woman with a fortune. If it hadn't been for my father's excesses . . .' The rest of his sentence had been left unspoken, in case he inadvertently committed himself to something he shouldn't have, perhaps.

Only a fool would fail to realize that Alex enjoyed her company and found her attractive in many ways. But he obviously had doubts, and would he consider their easy friendship to be strong enough for a marriage partnership? It had sounded as though he was trying to convince himself that it would not.'

As for herself . . . she loved Alex but she'd deceived him. What could she do about it? Nothing, but did it matter when she'd probably never see him again?

There was no answer forthcoming.

A mile away Alex was astride Boots, who was travelling at an easy canter. Ahead was the church – built of stone, ivy clad and with a square Norman tower. The burial ground surrounding it had an air of comfortable neglect, with the long grass needing the attention of a scythe. Many of the tablets shouldered against each other, resembling mossy old friends or family members reunited in death. The whole was wrapped in a well-seasoned dry-stone wall peppered with various coloured lichens and mosses.

He stopped to gaze at it. His own family attended a church just like it, and the coffins of the LéSayres ancestors were grandly entombed in a mausoleum with their coat of arms over the door.

How are the mighty fallen, Alex thought wryly. He still owed the undertaker for his father's burial.

In the darkness of the porch the church doors were open. A saddled horse and three sheep grazed amongst the graves. One way of keeping the grass under control, he supposed.

There came the sound of someone playing the organ. He recognized it as a Bach prelude that Eugenie played on their dusty old piano. The prelude became a fugue that made the organ roar into a wheezy, clunking life of rattles and squeaks.

There was something almost defiant and angry about the organ, like an old man struggling for breath on his deathbed. Alex felt sorry for it. The sheep took fright, huddling together in a corner for comfort when the tune changed, becoming a lively march.

Boots' ears pricked forward, his muscles bunched and he gave a soft little whinny and began to high-step on the spot, giving a vigorous and showy spring now and again.

It was one of those springs that got Alex. Airborne, the horse did a tricky manoeuvre as he came down to earth, rearing on his hind legs and pawing the air. Unseated, Alex fell backwards, doing half a back flip to land on his belly. He managed to roll out of the way in case the horse decided to sit on him.

Something sparkled in the long grass at the bottom of the wall, just a nose length away. He shortened his gaze, bringing it into focus. It was the star brooch he'd bought Vivienne. This was the place where she'd been attacked. Picking up the trinket, he stood and examined it. The pin was closed and had a small piece of cloth attached. It had been twisted out of shape. He straightened the pin and placed the brooch safely in his waistcoat pocket.

The music stopped suddenly, leaving the air full of oddly fading notes that didn't quite meet their promised pitch before they became a wheeze and were quickly absorbed into quietude.

Boots gazed at him, appearing somewhat surprised to find that his rider was no longer on his back. The whinny he gave was almost like laughter.

'Very funny,' Alex said, brushing his clothes off. He gazed at the wall and detected some spots of blood, broken twigs and scuffing on the stone. There were wheel marks in the soft mud on the other side where a carriage had turned – and a spot where someone had emptied his stomach. His nose wrinkled.

Alex rarely gave in to impulse, but he'd learned enough in London to give him the urge to fly to Vivienne's side. The eagerness of her relatives to replace her with Sophia in his affections disgusted him.

He'd left London with the zeal of Saint George with the scent of the dragon in his nostrils, and the rescue of his fair maiden burning a hole in the back of his brain. Now he was here, and he couldn't barge into her father's home and demand to see her. She was wounded and had earthed herself like a wounded animal in order to heal.

This must be the church that her clergyman father, the Reverend Fox, presided over. It wouldn't take long to find out. He took Boots into the church grounds, where he could dance the hornpipe without hurting anyone should he feel the urge. Boots joined the other gelding as though they were old friends.

The interior of the church was dark after the sunshine and his footsteps echoed. The windows behind the altar shone like jewels. The small organ with its array of pipes was to the left – opposite were the choir stalls. A Mozart sonata, the melody as light and pretty as raindrops, carried him to the pew near the front.

The music stopped abruptly. A little while later there came a patter of footsteps. Two lads hurried past, unwilling calcants freed from the tyranny of operating the ancient organ bellows no doubt. They touched their caps, leaving behind them an image of rosy faces and mischievous smiles.

There was a heavier tread at the back of the church. A door opened and quietly closed. A chair scraped noisily. Alex seated himself while his eyes adjusted to the change in light. It was peaceful here. The air had a musty smell and echoed with every click and crack of the timber beams in the vaulted roof.

He thought about Vivienne Fox. Didn't he always think about Vivienne Fox? She'd been raised here with her sisters, loved and tutored by her father. She would have been a lively child with a thirst for knowledge and had grown up to be virtuous. But being virtuous didn't mean she was pious. How far would he have to push her before nature advised her of the course she would take? Not very far, he imagined.

He could sense the child she'd been, safe in her father's love. Being of help to him and to the grandmother who had helped raise her and her two stepsisters. She would have taken her duties seriously. Now the nature of her love had changed, and she needed to be a woman with a husband and children to expend her affection on.

She had reached a point where her early training was being eroded by the visits from Mother Nature to remind her of her own needs. He would like to kill Simon Mortimer for attempting to ruin Vivienne's reputation for his own ends. He sat there, surrounded by peace, and deep in thought, musing on what he could do to ease the situation for her. He thought of his estate and sighed. He was thinking too much and a nap wouldn't go amiss.

He closed his eyes, and after a short while the day faded into a quiet buzz. He dreamed . . . pleasantly . . . of a woman in a drifting white gown and with flowers in her wild hair. Her feet were bare and she was dancing in a meadow of long grass sprinkled with poppies, forget-me-nots and yellow toadflax. He couldn't see her face but thought it might be Vivienne.

'Don't leave me,' he said when she began to fade, and she laughed. 'A man shouldn't have such problems,' he said.

A gentle cough raised him from his reverie and his eyes flew open. A man of middle years with greying hair had slid unseen into the pew in front of him.

Alex jumped. 'Have I been asleep?'

'It seems so. I saw you half-an-hour ago and thought you'd stopped to rest and might wake up and go on your way. Then it occurred to me that you might be a felon planning on stealing the candlesticks and cross from the altar. If so, I must warn you that they're silver plated, and rubbed silver plate at that . . . not really worth the effort of melting down. Then I recognized you clearly as a man with a problem on his mind since you talked in your sleep.'

'What did I say?'

'That a man shouldn't have such problems. You also asked someone not to leave you. Were you conversing with God?'

'I'm not that close to the throne. I was talking to myself, I'm afraid.'

'And you have problems?'

Alex smiled at him, recognizing his daughter in his manner of speaking. 'Compared to most people, no, but there is a problem I need to resolve. A church is a good place to clear the mind.'

'As you say. Allow me to introduce myself. I'm Reverend Ambrose Fox. And you are . . .?'

'Alexander LéSayres. I have a letter of introduction from John Howard, who is my neighbour in Dorset.'

'Ah yes . . . my esteemed, and very successful relative. You and I have met before in Dorset, I recall. I must write and thank John for his recent hospitality, if I haven't already.' The reverend's forehead wrinkled.

'You also knew my father, I understand. I'm named after him.'

The frown stayed in place. 'There was a Lord LéSayres who attended the same university as me. He was from Dorset. There was some talk . . .'

Before the reverend tripped over his tongue, Alex advised him, 'My father passed away just a few months ago and I'd be obliged if you spoke no ill of him, for he was a good family man and a loving father to his sons.'

The reverend shook his head as if to clear it. 'I was about to mention that I'd heard he had two strong sons . . . something to envy him for. I'm sorry to hear he has passed on. And your mother?'

'Gone too. She died when I was an infant. I have a younger brother. We were raised by our stepmother, Lady LéSayres, who is held in great respect by us all.'

The reverend's eyes glinted as he recognized the warning in Alex's voice. 'Quite, and what are you doing in Kent, young man?'

'I'm here to enquire after the welfare of your daughter, Vivienne . . . Miss Fox.'

His eyes flew open. 'Vivienne . . . *my* Vivienne. May I ask why? Surely you are not going to dump her in the pig wallow again? Such a large indignity for such a small thruppenny piece.'

This was a man who was as astute as they came. 'Your daughter has already rubbed my nose in my past indiscretion. I was justly punished for that with a thrashing from my father, though it hurt him more than it hurt me. I heard that Vivienne . . . Miss Fox that is, had been attacked on the road.'

'What do you know about the affair? If you were part of it you'd better return from where you came. My poor daughter is severely indisposed at the moment. She won't see anyone and she won't confide in me, but mostly she sits in her room and weeps.'

'She'll see me.'

'You sound confident about that. Exactly what is your relationship with my daughter, My Lord?'

'Our relationship is quite circumspect.' Alex's conscience gave him a tweak when he remembered the occasional kiss, but not hard enough to think of abandoning the delightful exercise altogether. 'I like her and we're good friends and easy together. I hold her high in my affection.'

The reverend hadn't removed his scrutiny of him. The man's eyes were fierce and unfriendly, so Alex felt like a trapped fly being contemplated by a spider. Beginning to perspire, he continued with caution. After all, this man was Vivienne's father, and he didn't look amicable, especially with that thick bible grasped in his hands, top heavy with good works.

He said hurriedly, 'We advise and support each other. Your daughter does you credit at every turn. She is intelligent and we converse well, debate even, and without any displays of temper except a little foot-stamping on her part, and on the rare occasion.'

'I schooled her myself,' the reverend said with some pride, placing the book down beside him. 'What has Vivienne told you of her circumstances?'

'That she is the eldest of three sisters, and her father . . . that's you, sir . . . is a reverend and a scholar.' Alex ignored the faint smile. Fronting a young woman's father was more difficult than he'd expected. 'Also, she recently came into a small legacy that is proving to be troublesome to her, because rumour has enlarged its sum vastly. I believe that to be the cause of the attack on her.'

'Did you offer her any advice on the subject of that legacy?'

'I'd be the last person to advise her on that since my estate is practically bankrupt due to imprudent gambling.'

'Not your own, one hopes.'

'As you say. I came to London to find myself a suitable wife with a fortune so I could reverse the situation.'

'What does Vivienne think of that?'

'Your daughter has a good head for commerce. She advises me on any candidates for the position, and I advise her. In fact, she has taught me that the qualifications of womanly perfection I had in mind were totally unrealistic. That's exactly what a friend would do, don't you think?'

Reverend Fox gave a sigh that was considerably less than pious and growled, 'No, I certainly don't think . . . in fact, it's an insult to even suggest to me that you might be using my daughter as a companion, supporter and advisor. You are a grown man. Vivienne is neither your sister nor your nursemaid. It seems that my daughter has grown to trust you in the short time she's known you, but I suspect you have a way with women, young man. Men are ever the deceiver and her belief in men has been sadly eroded by what has taken place. She needs to heal both in body and mind. She is my daughter, and I love her dearly.'

All at once it seemed as though they were combatants. Fiercely, Alex thrust at him, 'So do I, Reverend . . . so do I!'

Head cocked to one side, the reverend gazed at him for several seconds, a smile dawning on his face. 'Of course you do, Lord LéSayres, else you wouldn't be here to meddle in her life, would you? Allow me to just say this, My Lord. If any man deliberately breaks my daughter's heart, I will forget I'm a servant of the Lord and will join the opposition for as long as it takes to deal with him.'

Alex believed him.

'She would make you a good wife, and your lack of fortune wouldn't bother her a twit, you know.'

Alex gave an uncertain huff of laughter. He'd been outwitted, it seemed.

'Good,' the reverend said. 'Now we understand each other. Perhaps you would like to return home with me for some refreshment, or perhaps turn your horse around and return from whence you came. The choice is yours.'

Fifteen

The French doors leading from the drawing room opened on to a small paved area. A yellow rose – heavily blossomed and drooping under the weight of bees – clung to a lattice hung over the terrace. The rose needed pruning, but Vivienne was loath to spoil its glory.

She was seated on a chaise longue just inside the doors. She'd slipped off her shoes and her stocking-clad feet rested in a patch of sunlight on the faded pink rug. Her aching body enjoyed the warmth the sun provided. Having got over his fright at her changed appearance, the cat was now curled up on her lap, the warm breath from his purr stirring the fabric of her faded and patched gown. She would be glad when her trunks were returned to her.

A beam of sunshine shifted and danced around the room, reaching into every corner in turn. Every tired thread on the chairs, every scratch on the furniture and every dust mote dancing in the air were familiar to Vivienne. She had played with her two sisters on the worn rug as a child, keeping them occupied so as not to annoy Grandmother Fox who used to recline on the same chaise Vivienne rested on now.

Closing her eyes, she listened to the familiar hum of silence and separated the sounds. The drone of bees was close, busy at their work of collecting the pollen for honey. There was a faint bleat or two from the sheep munching on summer grass and the cluck of chickens. A fitful breeze rattled the leaves now and again. Horses clopped by . . . two perhaps, unhurried, as befitted such a fine, warm day.

Vivienne's mind drifted off, back to London. She felt frail. All the confidence her legacy had brought with it had deserted her. She wished she'd never heard of it . . . wished she'd never fallen in love. It would be another disappointment to take with her into old age.

A knock came at the door. It was Maria. 'I've brought you some tea and muffins, Miss Fox.'

'I'm not hungry.'

Maria busied herself pouring tea into the cup and scolded, 'You haven't eaten anything since we arrived here.'

Tears filled Vivienne's eyes. 'I keep thinking of what might have happened to us. We could have been killed. How is your head feeling now?'

'I've had worse cracks. My pa used to call me a bonehead, and he set out to prove it.'

'Poor you?'

Maria shrugged. 'We left him when I was fifteen. My mother became a housekeeper to the exclusive couturier, Madam Parisian. Madam taught me how to be a maid. She entertained many lovers before she died.'

'We should not talk of such matters.'

'Sorry, Miss Fox.'

Spinster she might be, but Vivienne was old enough to know the facts of life, even though she hadn't experienced them. She reacted to the suggestion of pandering to a man's appetite with a tremor that spread desire racing through her body like a tidal wave of warm honey. Alex had threatened to put her over his knee, which she'd regarded as teasing. But what if he hadn't been teasing? What if he treated a woman in the same bullying manner as Simon Mortimer?

She gave a whimper that sounded pathetic even to her own ears. Simon had been strong, and he'd been rough, and it was only by luck and by Freddie's intervention that she'd escaped from his clutches. She must remember to thank Freddie. As for Alex, he was a gentleman. Of course he'd been teasing.

'Please remember my father is a clergyman. He brought me up to meet certain standards of behaviour. I know he'd be shocked to learn of your former employer's way of entertaining herself, so please don't tell anyone. He taught me, and endowed me with the skills to become a governess if I needed to. I won't need to now I have the legacy, but still, I'd like to do something useful and worthwhile. I doubt I'll be a wife now, since Simon's actions would have placed a stain on my character.'

'Goodness, Miss Fox, with that legacy at your disposal you shouldn't have any trouble finding a suitable husband. I don't know why you've been keeping it to yourself. As for stains on characters, money has a way of making the worst of them disappear. You should face these gossips who seek to bring you down . . . pretend you don't care.'

Maria was talking about her aunt and cousin. Was it too hard for people to understand that she needed to marry for love? 'But I do care, Maria . . . I care very much. They're my relatives.'

'Well all I can say to that, and I hope you will forgive me, is they've been getting the best of that particular bargain. Now, don't forget to eat those muffins, Miss. I'll be in the laundry room if you need me.' The door closed behind her.

Vivienne ate a muffin without thinking . . . then she picked up the second and took a bite from it. There were voices in the hall. One belonged to her father.

'Wait in the drawing room, would you, My Lord. I'll go upstairs and ask Vivienne if she will receive you.'

My Lord?

'Thank you, Reverend.'

Alex's voice!

She dropped the muffin back on the plate and scrambled behind a lacquered screen decorated with inlaid mother-of-pearl flowers. The cat shot out through the open windows with a yowl when the door opened to admit a stranger.

Vivienne sat in the dusty corner of the drawing room with her arms grasped around her knees, making herself as small as possible. Her heart began an erratic thump that seemed loud enough for half the village to hear.

There was a moment of quiet when she imagined him looking around the room and taking his bearings. Then there were footsteps. He seated himself on the chaise. If she lowered her head to one side she would be able to see the heels of his hessians in the gap under the screen.

'Ah . . . a muffin, though it looks as though a mouse has been at it . . . and some tea. It's been a long time since breakfast.'

There was a slurping sound and she had a job holding on to her laughter, for it was obvious he knew she was there.

There came the clink of a cup against a saucer. 'Hmmm . . . there's a pair of empty shoes on the rug . . . come out from behind that screen, Vivienne Fox.'

'Go away, Alex . . . I don't want you to see me,' she said.

'Why not?'

'You know why not.'

'That's not a good enough answer. I came all this way to see you, and see you I will, even if I have to dig you out of that corner with a shovel. You'll have to come out eventually . . . you might as well put in an appearance sooner than later.'

'It will be later then. You can't stay there all night, my father would have you forcibly removed by . . . well . . . by *God* himself if necessary.'

'I can't argue with God, but the reverend has given me permission to use all reasonable means to jerk you out of your self-pity.' The exasperated sigh he gave was genuine. 'Let's put an end to this play-acting, Vivienne.'

She pushed the flimsy screen aside and stood, stung beyond measure, though aware he was goading her merely to get his own way. 'Does this look like play-acting to you!'

'No, it doesn't, my love.'

She couldn't bear to see the expression of pity on his face, or hear the tenderness in his voice. Her hands flew to cover the injuries. 'I'm so ashamed.'

'You have nothing to be ashamed of.' Gently he pulled her hands away and he led her to the chaise, his eyes a stormy blue. 'Did he inflict any other injuries or indignities on you?'

She knew what he was asking and tried not to blush. What if Simon had forced himself on her, would it matter to him, would the friendship he so generously offered be killed by disgust? She was not going to risk it by putting it to the test. 'There are some bruises on my body and I ache, but it's nothing serious.'

He folded her into his arms. 'I'd like to kill Simon Mortimer.'

'No . . . you mustn't kill anyone, Alex . . . how did you know what had happened, and that it was Simon?'

'When I called to escort you to the afternoon dance, your aunt said you'd received a message from your father and had left for Maidstone. Then Sophia Mortimer arrived and said Simon wouldn't come in because his face was scratched. Freddie looked so uneasy that I put two and two together. I gave him a gentle shake and he confessed all. He was worried I might crush his cravat.'

She managed a grin, imagining just how gentle Alex had been, especially since he'd grown up with a brother! 'Freddie did try to stop Simon Mortimer. How did my aunt take it?'

'I didn't wait to find out. She and your cousin were complaining about domestic matters, and were peeved that they'd lost the maid. I left Freddie to explain and also left a message for his friend to leave town. After that I immediately hired a horse. I slept at the inn last night.'

'Why did you come?'

One eyebrow rose. 'Do you need to ask? I thought you might need me.' His mouth tightened as his scrutiny touched on her blackened eyes, then her swollen mouth.

'Please don't look at me like that, Alex,' she pleaded.

His gaze narrowed in on her. 'I was wondering if there was a space to place a comforting kiss on. It might help in the healing process.'

She offered him her hand and he kissed each fingertip. 'Would you marry me?' he murmured.

The breath seemed to be squeezed from her body. 'Is that a question or a proposal? Or is it simply that you feel sorry for me.'

'I don't know. Marriage is marriage however it's delivered.'

'You said you wanted a lady who is fair of face, and who can bring a fortune into the family.'

'Your face is fair enough for me . . . or it will be when it's healed. I've been working it out. I could sell the estate and buy a smaller one. I've discussed it with your father. He agrees it might be a solution; but he cautioned me not to be too hasty. And although it won't rid you of your problem – Miss Fox being the current topic of interest in the capital – it will change the nature of the gossip.'

So, he'd talked to her father, had he? She felt herself deflate and scooped up a deep breath to nourish her anger with. 'For no reason at all you have decided to be a self-sacrificing hero and salvage my reputation by becoming my husband. The trouble is, My Lord, the rumour mill will already have it by the throat by now, and they'll be tossing *my problem* around like a dog with a bone. Hah!' She picked up a cushion and threw it at him. 'No . . . I will not marry you for that reason.'

He fended it off easily. 'Vivienne, do calm down.'

Anger renewed her need to make Simon Mortimer pay for

what he'd done to her. 'I am calm! How dare you come into my home with such an insulting suggestion? I'd like to remind you that I was the victim, and Simon Mortimer the criminal. And he needn't think he's going to get away with it. As soon as I recover my strength I intend to go back to London and swear a complaint out against him.'

'Which he will instantly deny.'

'But I have Maria as a witness. You forget she was attacked too.'

'And he has Freddie. Whose word will the magistrate believe, that of a lawyer with a titled gentleman as an eyewitness, or that of a lady's maid. Mortimer will then say he offered to marry you – which he probably will, if just to prove to everyone how sincere he is.'

'If he does, I'll take a horsewhip to him.'

'Talk sense, Vivienne.'

'Very well, My Lord. Make sense of this, it shouldn't be too taxing. Go away. *Goodbye.*'

'That's too final a word, my love.' As she moved to stand he took her by the wrist and kept her there. 'Wait! I have your brooch. I found it in the long grass by the church wall.' He leaned forward and pinned it to her bodice. His long fingers briefly caressed the hollow of her collarbone.

'Thank you, Alex, you may release my wrist now.'

He didn't. He leaned in a little further and then nipped the lobe of her ear. His breath sent quivering little echoes through her body, so each individual hair on her head seemed to prickle and dance, and she curled her toes into the rug like a bird in a thunderstorm holding tight to a branch.

When the brooch was secure his gaze moved upwards, so they were looking into each other's eyes. On an outgoing breath he said one word – so tender and pleading that it vibrated inside her ear like the stroke of a velvet brush, and was almost a plea. '*Vivienne.*'

A sigh left her mouth. If she stayed he would win her round, make love to her with pretty gestures. She wanted to stay angry with him. It energized her. She was tempted to slap him, so she tore her eyes away from his, stood, and headed for the door before she found a reason to do so.

'The proposal still stands. When you recover from your anger and begin to reason things out and trust to your instincts instead of your emotions, you will come to the conclusion that marriage between us was inevitable from the first moment we met.'

He was the earl of calm, and she felt like a tempest of contradictions. A soft but heartfelt scream left her mouth like a spout of steam. There was nothing wrong with her emotions. They were first class. She could love intensely and hate with equal passion – and all at the same time where the earl was concerned. He was infuriatingly practical and impossibly irresistible! When she was with him she felt as though her body had woken from a long slumber and had become powerfully vibrant.

Too vibrant, since he'd put her in a tangle! Dissolving into sobs, she closed the drawing room door behind her with a quiet but definite thud.

Her father was about to come down the stairs as she rushed up them. They met in the middle. 'Ah, Vivienne, I was just looking for you. Did you see the earl? He came down from London especially to see you and it would be rude not to receive him.'

'I've already seen him, he gave me no choice,' she snuffled. 'You're wearing your innocent look, Pa, but you don't fool me. You manipulated Lord LéSayres into proposing marriage to me, didn't you? How could you?'

'Quite easily, since I could see he wanted to be manipulated . . . did you accept?'

'Certainly not! You didn't tell him about my fortune, did you?'

'No . . . but you've got to admit that this legacy of yours has caused many problems so far. It must be the worst kept secret of the season, since everyone seems to know about it except for the earl.'

'Nobody can agree over how much I'm worth though, since I put it about that it was a trifling sum.'

'Well yes, that might confuse the issue. I'm sure John Howard will be discreet, and he will know the best legal minds and investment counsellors to consult with.'

'He is the earl's neighbour.'

'All the better then . . . it's a match made in heaven.'

'Except the earl doesn't have a halo or wings . . . and unless you didn't hear me before, my esteemed papa, I have refused his proposal.'

'Men expect refusals. They realize that women can be unpredictable and are prone to changing their minds. Men are prideful creatures though, so if you want this one – and I admit he seems to genuinely care for you – do not toy with his affections. You need to consider your options since he might think you're not interested and find someone else. Did I tell you that your mother turned me down twice before she agreed to wed me? We were happy together in the short time God allowed us to be together.'

He sounded so sad that she placed a comforting hand over his. 'That was a long time ago, Papa.'

'You never forget the people you loved the most, or the opportunities you failed to act on and lost. I was lucky in that your mother gave me a wonderful daughter as a consolation. You will see the sense of such a marriage when you recover your health.'

'Ah . . . so that's it. You're attempting to change my mind by bringing my mother in to the conversation.'

He laughed. 'It was worth the trying. By the way, the earl will be our guest for the night before he returns to London in the morning, so could you ask the housekeeper to prepare the best guest room. He's promised me a game of chess.'

She fought off her sudden plunge into dismay. 'The earl is going back to London so soon?'

'He has paid his respects to me and expressed his sympathy to you. Now he has business to discuss and engagements to keep before he returns to Dorset.'

Jealousy stabbed her in the heart when she remembered that the sole purpose he was in London was to find a wealthy wife. As her father had just reminded her of that fact, she would have very few options left open to her once the rumour mill had spat her out.

Simon Mortimer for a husband was the first one . . . ugh! So much for the true love she'd always imagined would come her way. She could kill herself, but why should she when she was blameless? She should kill Simon Mortimer instead . . . a much better proposition.

Men are fickle . . .

Not all of them, but some are.

What if your handsome lord finds somebody he likes better, or worse still, falls in love with another?

Alarm speared through her. It would be her fault if that happened.

'Papa?' she said when he reached the bottom staircase.

He turned, 'Yes, my dear?'

'Why do women have to cater to a man's pride? It seems rather a one-sided arrangement to me.'

He spluttered a bit, and then said, 'Perhaps because you're a woman and think like a woman. I will need to cogitate a little on the subject. We can discuss it tomorrow, when perhaps I can find a suitable proverb and have an answer for you. I don't want to keep our guest waiting.'

She hadn't wanted a paragraph written by a long dead stranger, and plucked conveniently from the page of a bible to fit into the present. She had wanted the originality of her father's thoughts on the subject. Then she considered: he often consulted the bible, so would he have an original thought?

'Must you consult the bible, can't we just have a conversation, like we used to?'

There was a flicker of anguish in his eyes. 'I was raised on the teachings of the good book and I live by its wisdoms. I know no other way. My dear, you are seeing me through adult eyes now, and that includes all my failings. If you must see through me, could you at least keep it to yourself?'

She felt a little crack open between them, as if he was growing away from her. She appeared less worthy in her own eyes because of it. If she never married, and if she bought her own little cottage and stayed in this village looking after her father, she might find contentment of a sort, but it would be limited. She would never grow or have children of her own to love, and would be poor old Aunt Vivienne right up to the end.

One day someone would stop to look at her grave and say, I wonder who *Vivienne Fox, spinster of this parish* was?

Then again, if she ended up married to the earl she'd be buried in Dorset and her tablet would read, *Vivienne, Countess LéSayres. Dearly beloved wife of Alexander, and loving mother to . . .* She thought for a moment, then whispered, '*to Alexander . . . Ambrose . . . and Rafe.*' She mixed in a couple of daughters. They would be named Eugenie after Alex's stepmother, because it would please him, and the second would be called Jeanne in memory of her own mother.

'Gracious! I'm not married yet and already I'm dead and buried.'

Her father looked puzzled. 'Are you sure you're all right, Vivienne? You seem to talk to yourself quite often these days. Perhaps that blow on the head did more damage than we thought.'

'Sorry, Papa . . . I was thinking out loud.'

'If I may ask . . . who are those people you mentioned?'

'Your grandchildren.'

'Ah . . . yes. Did I hear you mention a husband in this flight of fancy?'

'You might have to trust to your own flight of fancy for that.'

'The earl is such a determined gentleman, isn't he?'

She scowled at him. 'And such a nuisance.'

Her father chuckled. 'The earl is your guest, Vivienne, and you shouldn't refer to him in derogatory terms.'

'No, Papa . . . the earl is *your* guest,' she reminded him.

When the drawing room door closed behind him she felt guilty, and murmured on a defeated note, as she continued up the stairs, 'Men! It's a pity they're so indispensable.'

Sixteen

Vivienne rose when Maria brought her some warm water to wash in. The maid braided her hair in a simple country style with some ringlets on her forehead.

'Has the earl been offered water to wash in?' she asked.

'I gave him some soap and towels last night, and he washed himself early this morning under the garden pump, hair and all. It was quite a sight.'

Vivienne felt a quiver of shock. 'What do you mean by *all?*'

'He kept his trousers and boots on. He had a lovely chest, nicely muscled and proportioned, and without an inch of fat on him.'

Vivienne was sorry she'd missed the sight, but thought she should caution Maria, since she seemed to have picked up some bad habits from her former mistress, and besides, it wasn't Maria's place to make comments, good or bad, about their guests. 'We must allow the earl privacy at such times.'

'Sorry, Miss Fox. The earl was already in the middle of his ablutions when I came down. You can tell he's a countryman since he rises with the dawn.'

There was no sign of her father at breakfast – an indication that she might have upset him the day before, because he sometimes became introspective and avoided her after they'd argued.

Alex offered her a smile when she went into the dining room. His face was dark with a day's growth of beard, and his hair sprang damply against his face.

Her heart wrenched at the sight of him.

'I think the swelling on your mouth is less noticeable this morning. Are you feeling any better?' he said.

She didn't want to encourage his sympathy so nodded. 'Have you seen my father this morning?'

'He said he'd promised to take a lady friend to the market place and has already left.'

'Jane Bessant, I imagine. I think they'll marry eventually.' When his last unmarried daughter was safely off his hands. For the first time in her life Vivienne felt like an intruder in her own home. She shook the feeling off.

'He said to tell you he'll bring Mrs Bessant home about eleven since she will want to see you.'

'I expect he thinks I need some female counsel.'

'And do you?'

'Sometimes I think it would be nice to have an older woman to talk to, but Jane is too young for the purpose, and it would be unfair of him to place her in the position of *in loco parentis*, since it could cause dissent. As it is, Jane and I get on well together, and besides, counsel of any kind is tedious when you're my age. My father tends to treat me as a child still. Sometimes I wish I were a man, then I need only follow my own wisdoms and dictates.'

'It's not that easy. Men have responsibilities too.'

They seated themselves at the table in front of windows that framed a garden of quilted summer flowers. The cat had taken possession of a beam of sunshine piercing a windowpane. Spread out on the sill he resembled the furry trim from a winter shawl, casually tossed there at the end of winter − if one didn't notice the yellow slit of an eye left on watch.

The moment was so timeless it quivered like a heat mirage of water on a hot day, reflected to tease the tongue of the thirsty. Everything slowed down so she was left behind while the world moved on.

She drew in a deep breath and caught up with it.

'Are you all right, Vivienne?'

Everything was all right when she was with him, even when everything was wrong. She would tell him she loved him as soon as the opportunity presented itself. She wanted to be his wife, because convention would find a way to keep them apart otherwise.

All she need do was agree to his proposal. He already had it in his head that he could sell off some of his estate, and it would be easy to continue to keep him in ignorance for the time being. She would tell him the truth after they were married. That was soon enough, because he'd have to take part in those tedious meetings that men had about wealth, what to do with it and how to invest it.

All she would need for herself was an allowance, and she wouldn't need anyone to tell her how to spend it!

The housekeeper came in and served them some eggs, bacon and tomatoes, and bread fried in the juices. They ate without conversing, the atmosphere filled with unspoken words that buzzed in the air like invisible wasps.

Maria brought the tea in and hovered, trying to be unnoticeable.

'You needn't stay, Maria. I don't need a chaperone in my own home and I'm certain the earl wouldn't have the bad manners to attack me over breakfast. Tell the housekeeper I'll clear the dishes away afterwards.'

After the door shut behind the maid, Vivienne asked, 'What time are you leaving?'

'After breakfast . . . did you want to get rid of me sooner?'

The opposite was true, a reluctance in her heart to see him go. A new feeling towards him had grown in her overnight and had emerged this morning when she saw him again. It was one of possession – or was it one of being possessed? But she wasn't possessed . . . not yet.

'Not in particular, Alex. I thought it might be a good time to set things straight between us, but can we please not argue over breakfast.'

'I'm sorry. That was rude of me.'

'Would you do something for me, Alex?'

'Anything at all.'

'I left London owing a seamstress for a gown, and my aunt would have had to pay for it, would you deliver the money to her?' She handed over the purse and he slipped it into the deep pocket in his waistcoat. 'And could you tell her I've decided to return to London once my injuries are healed. Then there are my trunks. I left a note asking Matthew to send them on. Would you check with him on my behalf? I can leave them there now I've decided to return.'

'Why have you decided to return to London?'

'I don't feel the need to skulk here. I've done nothing wrong. I want to make sure that Simon Mortimer knows he's not getting away with what he did.'

'I wouldn't count on Mrs Goodman offering you shelter. I

believe the lease is almost up. The atmosphere was frosty as it was, and most of the angst was directed towards you. Anything I said at the time would only have exacerbated the situation. I will try and set your aunt straight about what occurred, though she may choose not to believe it, since she has the future of her daughter to think of. It would be better if you waited until the situation settles before you return. I need to discover what tale Simon Mortimer and Freddie Lamington have cooked up between them in my absence.'

'You're not intending to take Simon Mortimer to account, are you?'

He touched a bruise on her face. 'For that bruise alone I could strangle him with my bare hands. You need someone to take up your cause else you'll be hiding for the rest of your life. Like it or not, the role of hero seems to have fallen my way.'

Contrition filled her. 'I'm sorry . . . it was unintentional.'

'I'd rather you left the matter in my hands. You may not have invited trouble but it found you nevertheless. Events are being chewed over like dogs with a bone. Mortimer created this situation for his own ends, and if he doesn't recant it I'll tie him to a horse and drag him through the dung of the London streets until he does.'

She wouldn't be able to stop him, so she took his hand in hers and laid her face against it. 'I will wait to hear from you, of course. Be careful, Alex.' When she reminded herself the gesture was not seemly, she quickly withdrew it. The grin on his face made her blush and she laughed. 'I should like to be there to see that.'

After breakfast they strolled together to the stable. Boots snorted a greeting as if eager to be off when Alex led him from the stall and began to saddle him. He was a horse who enjoyed company, she thought.

After tugging at the straps to make sure they were tight enough he turned to her. 'So what do you need to say to set things straight with me?'

It was now or never and she murmured, 'It's about that other business you mentioned yesterday.'

'If you mean marriage . . . what of it?'

'I didn't want you to think . . . I appreciate that yesterday you acted from the goodness of your heart to a certain amount of pressure from my father, and to save my reputation from ruin.'

Apart from a faint smile that disappeared as soon as it arrived, there was no hint from Alex that he was even listening. Instead of answering, he said, 'The reverend plays a tricky game of chess. He had me on the defensive right from the start.'

Now Alex had put her on the defensive. 'I want you to know I won't hold you to any obligation—'

'I'm glad you've reached a decision.' He slid an arm around her waist and pulled her close. His mouth touched against hers, as gentle and tender as a butterfly alighting on the nectar. Releasing her, he led the horse out of the cozy thatched stable block, where he mounted. 'I'll be back in a few days.'

'You didn't listen to one word I said, Alex LéSayres.'

He smiled. 'Ah yes . . . words. I listened to every one, even the ones you didn't say. To play the London game I will politely bow over your perfumed hand and suggest I want us to part as the friends we've always been, so consider the lie as said and done.'

Did he really consider the courtship ritual a lie? Well yes, she supposed it was to a man who confessed he was little more than a farmer, and therefore must be closer to the earth and the mating rituals of nature than fancy drawing rooms, dancing and pretty words.

'Now, if you can allow me a moment of honesty, at this moment I'd rather kiss you senseless than talk. After that I'd drag you upstairs to bed, strip us both naked, let down your hair and play with you a little, so you're all rumpled, blushing and eager to experience what you've imagined. And then . . .' and his voice dropped to a whisper. 'Then, my foxy lady, I'd leave you trembling on the edge of release, so you will almost go out of your mind with the frustration of wondering what the act of love is going to be like between us.'

'And what if that never happens?'

He ran his finger down her nose. 'My intention is that it shall. I'll leave that thought with you as something to look forward to, or not, whichever is your fancy. Make what you will of these words, Vivienne. I want you, and I intend to have you, one way or another. And I think your feelings equal mine and you are looking forward to such an intimate encounter between us.'

The gasp she gave was loud enough to have been heard in London.

He chuckled, and clicking his tongue he moved off at a walk, leaving her feeling stunned.

She stood at the gate and watched him go. How domestic of her when he'd left an image in her mind so vivid it had placed her body in a turmoil that she didn't think would ever calm down. All the same, she wanted to laugh. Lord, he was so straightforward. He hadn't stopped to spare her feelings, and had almost robbed her of her senses.

Alex looked at home on a horse. His balance was perfect, his body relaxed and his thigh muscles adjusted by instinct to the movement of the mount he straddled. She grinned, trying not to imagine that movement in different circumstances. Her mind wouldn't let it go and she fanned her heated face with the white linen table napkin she still held in her hand.

Just before the bend in the road that would carry him out of sight, he turned and blew her a kiss. His smile told her he knew exactly how she was feeling and although she was too old to giggle, she did. He knew her too well, and without even trying.

She stayed there until she could no longer hear the clop of his horse's hooves, and then she went indoors to clear away the breakfast dishes.

On her side plate lay a blood red rose. She bore the fragrant bloom to her nose and discovered his signature ring on the stem. She stroked a fingertip over the seal. Alex was proud of his family, and here was a pledge to allow her to become part of it. Or was it just a token?

She was humbled to think he was willing to sell his estate on her behalf, and pleased he wouldn't have to.

'Damn you, Alexander LéSayres, you always manage to outguess me,' she said, and she slipped the ring on to her middle finger to keep it safe until she could find a chain to secure it on.

Humming to herself, she donned her apron, cleared the table and set the kitchen in order. There was plenty of work to do in the house and garden, and, as usual, she enjoyed doing it.

Shredding the lamb left over from the day before, she combined it with onions and lentils to use for a pie filling, and placed it in the larder with a damp cloth over it. With peas and potatoes fresh from the garden, it would make a tasty dinner, and there were stewed apples and custard for a pudding.

Her father enjoyed eating simply, and after the fancy tidbits served at the London supper tables – usually late at night and with more garnish than substance – Vivienne appreciated an earlier dinner. Especially so in the summer, when the light evening could be put to good use with her father in his study composing his sermon, or employed in the garden weeding the vegetable patch. Sometimes they walked the country lanes together, just talking or enjoying the other's company.

She had never stopped to consider that he might need more than she, his daughter, could provide. It wasn't as if he was an elderly man.

She went upstairs to remove the bedding from the guest room. There was a faint smell of Alex in the air as she pulled off the bed linen. It was lost when she tried to recapture the faint, ghostly essence he'd left behind on the sheets. Alex wouldn't be caught that easily . . . only if he wanted to be. His options were still open; she'd made that clear to him.

You should grab him while you can. What if he challenges Simon Mortimer to a duel and dies? Or what if Simon Mortimer has returned and is waiting for the opportunity to attack again.

They were both big men. Goodness knows what lies Simon had spread about her. Prickles crept up her spine. Before, it had just been words. Now, since she'd inherited some money, priorities had changed. She'd experienced violence from the same person, a man she knew barely anything about, except this – he was willing to commit a crime against her to get his hands on her fortune, even though he represented the law of the land. He might even kill for it, arrange a convenient accident to befall her if she married him. The world suddenly felt very dangerous.

The sun went behind a cloud and she shivered and gazed out of the window. He might even be hidden behind the shrubbery, watching her. It was Mrs Tilly's day off and, except for Maria, who was in the laundry at the back of the house, Vivienne felt isolated and alone.

There was a sudden gust of wind, the house creaked, a door slammed downstairs and a draught moaned softly up the stairs and along the corridor. It carried her name on its breath and the hairs on her neck stood on end. Footsteps crept up the stairs and she froze to the spot. 'Who is it?' she tried to say, but the words strangled in her throat. When the door creaked open she felt dizzy and held on to the bedpost, trembling. 'Maria!'

'Miss Fox, there you are. I called you twice.'

'You crept up the stairs and that scared me.'

'I thought you might be asleep . . . I'm sorry, Miss.'

'It wasn't your fault. I was just having one of those moments.' She could have died from the relief she felt. 'Thank goodness it's you.'

'Who else would it be? You look as pale as a ghost. Here, come and sit in this chair for a moment, Miss. I'll make the bed and then we'll go down to the kitchen and have a nice cup of tea before Reverend Fox gets home. Mrs Tilly made a fruit cake yesterday, and we can have a slice of that to go with it.'

'You won't tell my father, will you, Maria. I thought . . . with the earl no longer here I didn't feel safe in case someone had managed to climb into the house. I left the window in the dining room open, you see. I suppose you think that's silly.'

'No . . . I don't think that, Miss. It's only a couple of days since we were attacked, and you got the worst of it. I overheard the earl tell your father how courageous you were to fight back in the way you did.'

She gave a faint smile. 'He said that? I don't feel very courageous now.'

Maria nodded and busied herself spreading the clean sheets on the bed. 'There's bound to be a reaction when you let your imagination run riot. Besides, if anyone climbed in that window he'd have to get through the rose bushes first, and he'd collect a few thorns in his . . . rear end for his trouble.' Maria thrust a fierce face at her. 'And serve him right, that's what I say!'

Even though it wasn't a laughing matter, Vivienne chuckled at the thought of Simon Mortimer impaled thus.

They went downstairs together. It was a pretty kitchen with curtains of patterned cream lace, geraniums flaming in pots on one windowsill and herbs on the other. The china didn't match, but it didn't bother them. They had a best dinner service with gold rims and pink roses decorating it for guests.

'To use when royalty visits,' she remembered her grandmother saying.

The kitchen was the hub of the house. In the winter it was warm and cosy, in the summer it was bathed in sunshine for most of the afternoon.

The cat joined them and lapped up some milk, his ears flattening against his head with pleasure, and then he coiled into his basket. He liked company. She couldn't remember never having a cat in the house.

There was a sudden recollection of her grandmother sitting at the opposite end of the table. She was carefully peeling an apple, using the sharp point to create a corkscrew peel as thin as she could manage. Vivienne couldn't see her grandmother's face; it was fading from her memory as she grew older, but she knew she was smiling. The peel grew too heavy for its width, tore apart and dropped to the table, where it tried to coil back into its original shape.

Her grandmother looked up at her and laughed. The sound was sharp and clear, like the ring of the little crystal vase on Vivienne's dressing table if she flicked her nail against it. She gazed at Maria, wondering if she'd heard it too, but the maid was bustling about getting the cups and saucers out.

Vivienne smiled. Lord LéSayres was the closest thing to royalty they'd ever entertained. Her mother would have liked him. There was nothing superior about him. He sat comfortably in the shabby armchairs of their drawing room as though he'd grown up in them, and he didn't seem to notice that they'd served his meals on chipped china, because they'd forgotten to get the good service out.

Maria made the tea and cut them a slice of cake.

They heard the gate creak open and a knock at the door.

They gazed at each other with nervous grins, and then they rose together and approached the door.

'Who is it?' Maria said, while Vivienne moved into the drawing room and gazed out of the window. She recognized the man.

'Letter carrier with mail for Reverend Fox.'

Vivienne nodded to Maria.

Seventeen

When he returned to London Alex was surprised to find John Howard waiting for him in his rooms. He admitted that his earlier opinion of the man may have been flawed, and since people who knew him painted Howard in a generally favourable light, on that recommendation he was pleased to see him. They shook hands.

Howard came straight to the point. 'I'm on my way to Maidstone and I thought I'd stop in and see how you're managing.'

Alex raised an eyebrow. 'How I'm managing . . . what an extraordinary thing to do.'

An embarrassed expression crossed the man's face. 'Yes . . . I suppose it is. I beg your pardon, My Lord. I put that very badly, and I apologize for that. I wasn't prying . . . just interested, since your brother, Dominic, mentioned that you hadn't often been in London.'

Alex allowed it to pass. 'London is much like any other city, except it's bigger and more crowded. Thanks to you and a small win at cards, I'm managing quite well. You must keep account in case I'm in the position to repay you someday, though by now you might think the LéSayres family a lost cause.'

'More a waste of paper,' the man said drily. 'I understand from Mrs Crawford that there's talk about my niece and I gather you've just returned from Maidstone. Perhaps you'd oblige me by giving me a first-hand account of what's going on, My Lord.'

Alex would rather have rested and taken some refreshment first. 'Have you spoken to her aunt, Mrs Goodman?'

John made an impatient sound in his throat. 'Not yet, as I recall the woman is an irritation who is prone to hysterics. So is her daughter, I have heard. I'd rather hear your version of the affair without the hard-done-by accusations, breathless embellishments and tit-for-tat of the women. If Vivienne Fox is about to marry some mountebank who passes himself off as a wealthy attorney, then he will need to be investigated.'

That was something that sounded like a fair observation to Alex. 'Vivienne has no intention of marrying Simon Mortimer, believe me. How did you hear of it?'

'I dropped in on my club before I came here. The gossip was rife. What on earth was Vivienne's father thinking of, allowing her to chaperone her scatterbrained cousin? And why did she run off with a lawyer . . . what on earth was her aunt about by allowing it?'

'Allow me to put you straight about that. Miss Fox received a letter informing her that her father was at death's door. What else could she do but rush to his side? Mortimer hid in the darkness waiting for her, and laid about her when she refused his advances.'

'Mrs Goodman is a fool if she allows the girl free rein to run about the countryside.'

'Her aunt is inept, but it wasn't her fault because on this occasion she wasn't informed of the situation until after Miss Fox had left. I should also remind you that Miss Fox is not a girl, but an adult woman. Chaperonage of her cousin is a task Vivienne has grown used to doing by all accounts. The young woman is also a romantic and has vowed not to wed until she finds true love, or so her father tells me. As for the reverend, he was upset by his daughter's injuries but not unduly disturbed, since she played them down to assuage his worry over the affair. According to her maid, she cries at the least provocation and is scared of her own shadow, and has worse bruises concealed under her garments.'

'What is the Reverend Fox doing about it?'

'There's nothing he can do except keep her at home and allow it to blow over. Vivienne has sworn she'll confront the perpetrator of this crime against her. I intend to confront him first.'

John examined his fingernails, then said hesitantly, 'How far did the assault on my niece go?'

'I didn't ask her, but judging by her state of mind, not as far as you fear. She was embarrassed, but only because she'd fallen into the trap that was set for her and frightened by the violence. Her reaction stemmed from anger rather than shame, though I think she understands that the outcome could have been worse had she not received assistance from Lord Lamington.'

'That nincompoop!'

Alex gave a faint smile at the scorn in his voice. 'Without him she would have come out of this with more serious injuries. She managed to damage her assailant apparently, and with the help of Lamington, she and her companion made her escape.'

'Hmmm . . . the best way to avoid a scandal is to marry Miss Fox off as soon as is possible. What of the man who attacked her? I heard he was a wealthy lawyer.'

'Simon Mortimer has been losing money hand over fist to the card sharps from what I hear.' Alex laughed. 'The lady in question is a tigress when she's angered. She will tear his eyes from his skull if she sees him again . . . and if she doesn't, I will. I sent him a message suggesting he leave town before I returned. However, he may not have, since he's running a book on the amount of Vivienne's legacy, and he doesn't scare easily. He has it in his head that she has inherited considerably more than she's let on.'

John scrutinized him intently for a moment. 'And what do you make of that, My Lord?'

Alex laughed. 'To be honest, I don't know what to make of it. I've never known Vivienne to be any less than straightforward and truthful. A young woman who appreciates a humble posy of violets must be as poor as she says she is. Surely a woman with an independent fortune would let it be known, for it would give her an advantage when it came to marriage. Vivienne wouldn't know what to do with a fortune, and neither would her father.'

John Howard's eyes gleamed. 'What about Mortimer's companion? He's a baron, is he not?'

'Lamington?' Alex burned at the cold-blooded way John was going about arranging Vivienne's future. 'The baron is promised to her cousin, Adelaide. Besides, I have a better plan.'

'Which is?'

'To put it about that I intend to marry Vivienne Fox myself. From what I hear, some people already think we're involved.'

'Are you involved?'

Alex conveniently forgot his parting words to her. 'We have become good friends, which is why I'm interfering in her life. It's for her own good, though she doesn't see it that way at the moment.'

Howard's eyes probed the depths of his, and then he chuckled.

'That might work, but didn't you state that she intends to wed only for love.'

Alex shrugged, then he grinned. 'I've discovered that love is a state of mind, and I'm working on it. We are well matched and I think I can convince her to fall in love with me. Vivienne might not have much to her name, but then neither do I so we'll be on an equal footing.'

'You might do better to allow the girl to imagine you're in love with her.'

'That goes without saying. I've been thinking I might consider selling you two acres of land to give us a start. Not King's Acres, of course, but the strip on the east side. That will provide me with enough money to plant a corn crop, and more besides.'

'It's poor soil, nothing grows there and the beach is inaccessible. Besides, there's a boggy patch in the middle.'

'You've inspected it without considering my permission?'

'I didn't need your permission since your father was with me. He had the same idea as you. He was going to give up his wild ways and work the land. It was a month before he died, and just before his unexpected marriage.'

'My father's marriage is not a topic for conversation. I'm surprised he didn't tell me about the meeting though, since he wanted to pass over the state intact.'

'He was considering possibilities, as we are now doing, My Lord. I have reached the same one as I did then.'

'Were you to build there you would need water, and since the bog is fed by fresh water from somewhere it could be dug out. The estate plans suggest the bog was once a gravel pit. It may have been dammed upstream. A house could be built halfway up the slope and would allow a view of the sea.'

'I will reconsider that option, but I shouldn't be too confident about the outcome since the sea has undermined the cliff and it's unstable, having collapsed on a couple of occasions. By the way, I have offered employment to your brother, Dominic.'

The statement surprised Alex. 'Did he accept?'

'He intends to discuss the matter with you first.'

'It's not up to me. I thought Dominic was contented in his present position.'

'He's too ambitious to be contented for long. I've offered him a more responsible position and his salary will be commensurate with that. Whatever your feelings towards me, and I admit I'm not a man to suffer fools gladly, if you have any influence over Dominic you should advise him to secure his future by taking me up on this offer.'

While Alex was wondering what was in it for John Howard, a knock came at the door.

'Come in,' they both said together, and exchanged a chuckle.

Mrs Crawford entered. She carried a platter bearing slices of pie, a crispy loaf of bread, and some plums and a couple of apples.

Ned followed with two bowls of steaming chicken broth on a tray. He broke into a wide grin when John said, 'You've grown two feet since last I saw you. You'll be tall in a year or so.'

Alex's stomach rattled and Mrs Crawford laughed. 'I thought you'd be hungry after your journey, My Lord.'

'Thank you, Mrs Crawford, I'm quite ravenous, and it was thoughtful of you.'

She looked pleased by the compliment. 'How did you find your young lady, My Lord?'

As usual word had preceded him. 'Miss Fox will recover, but she's rattled, and as angry as a nest of hornets.'

'The whole town is waiting to see what happens. The season is almost exhausted, and this affair has livened things up. They can talk of nothing else. They are saying she will have no choice but to wed him, if he asks her.'

Alex's appetite fled at the thought. 'She will not wed him, this I promise.'

'There, I've upset you, My Lord. I thought you might like to know what has been going on in your absence.' In a more motherly fashion she said, 'Eat your food before it gets cold . . . you too, John. You can't conduct business on an empty stomach.'

She left Alex a pile of invitations that had arrived during his absence, which he placed to one side for later perusal. London was fast losing its glitter and he was longing to go home.

But he wouldn't go unless Vivienne Fox went with him, and she would – even if he had to tie her hand and foot and throw her over his shoulder. That would set the tongues of the gossips wagging.

With that thought affording him a huge amount of satisfaction,

Alex picked up his spoon and scooped some chicken broth into his mouth. His appetite returned with a vengeance. Mrs Crawford had been right about conducting business on an empty stomach. As for Vivienne, it had been bravado on his part, since he wouldn't harm a hair on her head.

There was a reluctance in him to get rid of the land – any land, not just the King's Mile. He lifted his gaze to his unexpected but not entirely unwelcome guest. Howard had made no mention of a visit to London, so what was he doing here?

'The problem with carving up an estate is that you can never retrieve the slices you've made in it.'

'Ah . . . but I see no real problem with that now, and I doubt if you will either after you hear me out.'

'We'll talk over dinner tonight, John, but I'm not such a bad businessman that I'll commit to anything without Dominic's advice. And I do need to visit Mrs Goodman and her daughter before the day is out.' He patted his waistcoat pocket to reassure himself that the purse for her aunt was still there.

'Then I will pay her a courtesy visit with you, if you don't mind.'

'If you do it will probably be the only courtesy you'll hear there today.'

A wry thought found its way into his mind. Once he'd been adamant that the estate would never be carved up or sold off. Now – tempted by the wiggle of a pert backside and urged on by his own needs – he was prepared to sell his soul for just one glance from Vivienne's pretty green eyes, contrary creature that she was. He was well and truly hooked and had no doubt that Vivienne would make a perfect mistress for King's Acres. All he had to do was convince her.

John Howard had been right about the boggy patch. It had been undermined for its gravel in the past, and what was left was washed down by rainwater to cover the small strip of beach at the bottom on the cliff. Fissures appeared now and again when the chalky soil dried out in the summer. It would collapse into the sea eventually.

Idly, he wondered, how much would the man be willing to pay for the strip of land called King's Mile?

Eighteen

It was mid-afternoon by the time Alex and John Howard arrived at the Goodmans' house in Portman Square.

When Matthew presented their cards, Mrs Goodman gave a screech.

'Goodness, it's Mr John Howard and Lord LéSayres. I hope they've brought that ungrateful creature with them so she can be confronted with her lies. Not that I'll offer any clemency. I will not allow her to set one foot over my doorstep again.'

The door was slightly open and there was a whispered conversation. Alex heard Freddie Lamington's voice, and he sounded panicky.

'Ask them to wait in the morning room until I'm ready to see them,' Mrs Goodman said dismissively, obviously on her high horse and just as obviously forgetful as to whom the message was meant for. She caught herself quickly. 'With my apologies for the delay, of course.'

Matthew delivered the message. 'Would you like some refreshment . . . a brandy perhaps?'

Quietly, Alex said, 'Thank you, Matthew, but no, we'll wait here, though you might want to disappear. If you stay, perhaps you would be kind enough to guard the front door to prevent anyone going out, though if a *gentleman* called Simon Mortimer should arrive, then by all means allow him entrance, since he needs teaching a lesson.'

Matthew's lip curled. 'I'll stay, sir.'

Alex turned to John. 'Mrs Goodman should be pleased that your niece is not present, since she was of a mind to take a horsewhip to someone when I left her this morning.'

'My niece is inclined to violence? I'm surprised, when my observations have shown her to be such a calm and reasonable young woman. But then, perhaps she's just realized the gravity of the situation she's been placed in.'

'Perhaps I exaggerated a little. I would describe her as

quick-minded and spirited, but she has been sorely tried. Vivienne is scared and is doing her best to overcome it. Even so, she feels vulnerable, and with good cause. The rest is bravado.'

Alex heard Freddie Lamington saying a hurried farewell. 'You must excuse me, ladies, but I have just remembered an urgent appointment.'

'But Freddie,' Adelaide wailed, 'you were going to take me to the summer solstice fair in the park. We are to meet Simon, his sister and Viscount Statham there, remember.'

'Tomorrow perhaps.' The drawing room door opened and Freddie strode out.

Alex planted a hand in the middle of Freddie's chest and pushed him back into the drawing room, where he tripped backwards over the rug and fell in a heap. He scrambled to his feet, brushing fluff from his trousers and then moved swiftly behind the couch. 'Do be careful what you're about, My Lord, you are ruining my clothing,' he squeaked.

'I don't give a tinker's cuss about your clothing.'

Mrs Goodman and her daughter clung to each other, eyes wide, and displaying unease at the drama unfolding in their own drawing room. They were twittering with nerves, like a pair of sparrows.

Alex smiled reassuringly at them. 'Good afternoon, ladies, I do hope you are enjoying your day.' Though they wouldn't be enjoying it for much longer. 'May I introduce Mr John Howard. He is here on a courtesy call, but whether or not he will find any courtesy is debatable.'

Mrs Goodman drew her frazzled edges together with a conscious effort and a stiff smile. 'You must forgive me for keeping you waiting, My Lord. John Howard? The name sounds familiar. Have we met before, sir?'

Adelaide said, 'Mr Howard is Vivienne's uncle from Dorset, Mama.'

'Ah yes . . . how lovely to meet you, sir.' Mrs Goodman sent a quick, ingratiating smile his way and Adelaide bobbed a curtsey.

John offered them a courtly bow. 'Ladies.'

Adelaide recovered first and went into the attack, like a terrier pup that had just found its adult teeth. 'Will you explain the reason you are handling the baron so roughly, My Lord?'

Alex smiled at the man. 'You're a wonderful storyteller, Freddie, so I'll allow you to relate the tale to them. I will correct you if it differs too widely from the account related to me by Miss Fox – if that becomes necessary, of course.'

Freddie looked sick. 'Surely this is not the time and place.'

'It's exactly the time and place. Unless you wish me to drag you in front of a magistrate by the length of your tongue, tell them . . . and right now. I must inform you that, as evidence, I have the original note addressed to Miss Fox in Simon Mortimer's handwriting. I also have a statement from the innkeeper, including a description of the carriage you hired, and a statement from the hire company.'

He'd stretched things a little, but it would be easy to collect such evidence.

Freddie shrugged and turned to Adelaide. 'It started off as just a lark, you understand. It was Simon's fault, he was drunk and it all got out of hand.' He stopped to gaze at the floor and mumbled, 'If it hadn't been for me, things would have been much worse for your cousin.'

'Vivienne? What on earth has my cousin got to do with this?' Adelaide's bewildered expression was artless enough to be believed as she gazed from one to the other. 'What have you been up to, Freddie? Surely she hasn't eloped with Simon Mortimer? There has been talk, of course, but I didn't take much notice of it since she loves . . . but then, I promised her I wouldn't reveal his name.'

'Perhaps you should have thought of that earlier rather than help spread unfounded gossip and lies about Miss Fox,' Alex offered her. 'The man you intend to wed, and his constant companion Simon Mortimer, collaborated to rob a decent young woman of her reputation, her health, her peace of mind, and of any fortune she may possess.'

The Goodman females exchanged a glance. As if a message was being passed from one to the other. 'Less said, soonest mended,' Adelaide said.

Mrs Goodman opened her mouth, and then clapped her hand over it, squeaking something unintelligible. Pressing her fingers to her forehead she emitted a martyred sigh and groaned, 'This is too much to bear.'

'Yes, isn't it. I imagine Miss Fox holds the same sentiment, since she was badly injured in the process.' Alex turned back to Freddie. 'Tell them, Lamington – tell your future wife and her mother what you have stooped to.'

Freddie resembled a trapped rat as he gazed from one to the other. 'It was all in jest, you understand . . . a lark.'

'Watching a young woman being beaten by a man twice her size was a lark? Mortimer used his fists. Miss Fox was lucky not to have been killed.'

Mrs Goodman gave a shuddering cry. 'Oh, my poor Vivienne.'

'I didn't mean . . .' Freddie looked desperately from one to the other. 'Simon wrote a letter to Miss Fox suggesting her father was ill. Then he . . . we . . . Simon waylaid her on the road. He thought he might put her in a position where she would have to accept his marriage proposal. He was certain she was wealthy and keeping it quiet.'

'Why should he think that?' John Howard asked.

'He had a colleague who knew someone who knew someone else who was signatory witness to her deceased relative's will. I told him it was more than likely a game of Twisted Whispers someone had started, but he didn't believe me. Things got out of hand when she resisted. Simon didn't expect that. As I said, he'd been drinking, and he was rougher with her than I expected . . . though I couldn't see much of what was going on in the darkness.' He looked stricken. 'Was she badly injured? I told her to run, because I knew I couldn't hold Simon for long . . . and she did.'

'Miss Fox had blackened eyes, a swollen face and lip, choke marks on her neck, and other injuries and bruises that were covered by her clothing. She is shattered by the experience,' Alex informed them. 'Also, her maid was rendered unconscious by a blow to the head during the attack.'

'That's when I stepped in,' Freddie said lamely. 'I thought Simon was just going to kiss Miss Fox and that would be that. Then things got out of hand.'

'Are you stupid or totally naïve? You know perfectly well what a man is capable of when his blood is up.'

'I beg you to remember that ladies are present, sir,' Frederick bleated.

Adelaide took up the attack and hurled at Freddie, 'You waited long enough to tell me, you coward. How could you, Freddie? Poor Vivienne. I don't think I'll ever forgive you . . . I don't even think I can bring myself to wed you now.'

Mrs Goodman groaned and sank into the nearest chair. She fanned herself rapidly. 'You don't mean that, Adelaide. I'll never be able to hold my head up in public again.'

Freddie protested, 'I didn't lay a finger on Miss Fox. I was turning the carriage around.'

'How could you have agreed to help that horrible man hurt my cousin in the first place? And how could you have kept quiet about the affair? I thought you were a gentleman, but you're despicable. What did poor Vivienne do to deserve such treatment? She will never find herself a husband now.'

Alex dropped his pebble into the gossip pond and hoped the ripples would travel far and wide. He wished them a safe journey and prayed his lady love would look kindly on the effort he'd made to save her reputation from ruin. She would probably give him a tongue-lashing for his trouble, and it would be his pleasure to kiss the words from her mouth.

'Oh . . . I wouldn't say *never*, Mrs Goodman.' He sent a wink in John's direction and received a faint smile in return. Like Dominic, John Howard was content to listen, absorb, and cue in on appropriate clues.

Mrs Goodman's gaze latched on to John Howard. 'The girl was under my care, and her flight caused me considerable distress. If she is suited then I demand to know to whom she is promised?'

John Howard had a long nose that contributed to his overall haughty expression. He gazed down the length of it at her. '*Demand?* I'm afraid not, madam. Miss Fox is now in her family home in the company of her father . . . where one presumes she is recovering from her injuries. You have no authority there, and neither do you have any with me. I do not discuss the business of my clients with anyone but them, and those closest to them.'

A knowing smile touched the woman's mouth as she turned back to him. Alex watched the terrier emerge in her when she wagged a finger archly at him. 'It's entirely obvious you've offered for her yourself, My Lord, and that Mr Howard has come to settle the details. I must then presume that Vivienne inherited a fortune after all.'

Alex sighed, and suddenly realized what pressure Vivienne had been under. 'My dear Mrs Goodman, must you keep harping back to that rumour? If you're so convinced, there would be no purpose in confirming or denying it. I must say though, that your presumption that you have the right to meddle in Miss Fox's affairs, or indeed my own, is extremely tedious. I must ask you to desist, and at once.'

Much to Alex's satisfaction she looked stunned by the put down as she stuttered, 'You must forgive me, My Lord . . . It was . . . out of concern for my niece.'

'Who has seen precious little of that care to date. As for Mr Howard, if I may speak for you, John?'

Howard nodded. 'By all means, My Lord.'

'Mr Howard is in London on another matter altogether, one concerning his business dealings. As for who has offered for Miss Fox and who has not . . . and whether she has accepted that proposal or not . . . well, I must ask you not to mention the matter outside of these four walls.'

Mrs Goodman nodded her head several times. 'And to think we blamed that poor girl. I'm so thrilled. Who would have thought that our little Vivienne would have plucked the prize of the season out from under our nose. Ah well . . . they say money talks, and no amount of you telling me otherwise will change my mind, My Lord. Vivienne has fallen into the ways of the *nouveau riche*. And that's given her away. She has been spending money freely, flaunting new gowns from the most prestigious of dressmakers, and hiring a maid for herself, and at the expense of myself and her cousin. What else are we to do but believe the rumours?'

Alex winced and loosened his cravat with a finger as he offered, 'Perhaps the subject should be avoided altogether, since nothing is settled between us as yet.'

Her voice grew stronger, more purposeful. 'Nonsense! I must write to congratulate my niece on her engagement, and at once, and offer to support her through her *indisposition,* dear child that she is. Blood is thicker than water, after all.'

He imagined Vivienne stamping her foot and throwing a

frustrated yowl into the air when she got that letter, and he almost chuckled. The best it would achieve would be to stop her from feeling sorry for herself. 'As you wish. I must warn you though, Miss Fox was in a confrontational mood when I left her, and may not appreciate your kind support.'

Freddie, who'd been inching his way towards the door, was brought to a sudden halt when Adelaide said, 'Where do you think you're going, Freddie Lamington? We have something to discuss.'

'As I said, I have urgent—'

'Your other business can wait. You've ruined my life and I have something to say to you. Sit, and at once!'

Freddie perched himself on the edge of a seat near the door, as frozen as a threatened hare. Escape was only one leap away but he obviously didn't have the guts to get up and take it. Alex's twinge of pity for him quickly evaporated when he remembered Vivienne's injuries.

John Howard fussed with the buckle on his satchel for a moment or two. 'Before Lord LéSayres and I depart, may I mention that I'll be urging Miss Fox and her maid to seek compensation from all parties for their injuries – the amounts to be determined once I have consulted with the two young women concerned.'

A look of consternation crossed Freddie's face.

It was a master stroke and something Alex wouldn't even have thought of, which was one of the reasons Howard was wealthy and he wasn't, he supposed. He fished in his pocket and came out with a purse, which he placed gently on the table in front of Mrs Goodman. 'Miss Fox asked me to give you this. It's payment for the gown she had on order. As for her trunks, which she left in your care, she has asked me to deal with them. Perhaps you would send Matthew to my accommodations with them later in the day.

'There was a message from Miss Fox too . . . now what was it? Ah yes . . . she asks that you inspect her dressing table as she can't remember seeing the necklace and eardrops when she and the maid packed her trunks. Vivienne values the gems highly, and I noticed you were wearing them just a couple of days ago, Miss Goodman, along with her new gown. I remember thinking how pretty they were.'

Adelaide blushed. 'My cousin must have forgotten she allowed me to make use of her wardrobe.'

'The blow she received to her head would have befuddled her.'

Adelaide grabbed at the excuse. 'No doubt it has. I have kept the jewellery safe and will, of course, place anything I have of hers in her trunk. I will pack it myself, since my cousin took the maid with her. Mama is going to ask for a refund of the rent, since Maria's services were not set to expire for two more weeks.'

Alex nodded. 'We will take our leave now. I've got an urgent matter to attend to before I return to Maidstone. Where will I find Simon Mortimer, My Lord?'

'He'll be at his club.' Freddie stood, suddenly eager to be helpful. 'I'll show you if you like, My Lord.'

When Adelaide folded her arms on her chest and glared at her hapless Lord, Alex couldn't do anything but grin. 'I would suggest you stay where you are and make peace with your future wife, Freddie. I do know where Mortimer's club is, but I understood you were to meet in the park, so I will try there first.'

Freddie's sigh was one of defeat and imminent doom.

They collected their hats and canes from Matthew. 'Your pardon, My Lord, but may I ask how Maria is?' he said.

'She collected a thump on the head from Simon Mortimer that knocked her unconscious for a while. She's a brave young woman and was in good spirits when I saw her this morning. I understand Miss Fox has offered her a permanent position.'

Matthew looked a bit down in the mouth.

'Do I sense an attraction between you and Maria, Matthew?'

'I was working on it, sir. I hoped we'd find work together.'

'I don't think the Reverend Fox's household is big enough to support a manservant. Leave it with me for the time being. Where's the best place for me to confront Mortimer?'

'He would have learned you were back in town and would have gone to ground by now. May I ask what your intentions towards him are?'

'I intend to make him publicly apologize, and then . . . and then . . .' He shrugged. 'Were we in the country I'd flatten him with my fists and upend him into the pig wallow.' He groaned silently. That was what he'd done to Vivienne as a child. She'd been so teasible, and he'd been so mean to her.

John Howard sighed. 'You are not thinking of challenging him to a duel, are you, LéSayres?'

'Someone has to act on the young lady's behalf.'

'Even so, it would be expected that someone of your rank would have had access to duelling skills since childhood and therefore the duel would not be a fair one. He is too far beneath you, and the honour of your family would be discredited. Swords are messy, so it would have to be pistols. I must also warn you that, although a blind eye may be turned from time to time over these matters, duelling is illegal . . . and however it starts the outcome is usually fatal. Are you prepared to kill a man in cold blood?'

Alex had never killed anything except a few rabbits or pigeons for the cooking pot. He shrugged. 'There's always a first time.'

'How do you think Miss Fox would feel if you were mortally injured on her behalf?'

'Peeved to an inch I would hope, but before I expired she would box my ears and tell me I deserved it. What say you, Matthew?'

Matthew spread his hands and smiled. 'Who am I to argue with a peer of the realm? Miss Fox can certainly be quite spirited when the mood takes her. Perhaps you'd wait at the corner for a few moments, then allow me to walk a little way with you, sirs? There is another way to sort this matter out.'

'A boxing match!' Alex said five minutes later. 'I don't know a damned thing about boxing. The closest I get to it is wrestling with my brother – and he usually wins.'

Matthew cracked his knuckles and grinned. 'You don't need to know anything. I've seen Mortimer fight a couple of times. He's not a bad pugilist, but I'm far better. With your permission I'll be your stand-in since I do have an interest vested in this affair. I can arrange a grudge match at Hyde Park within two weeks, and it will attract heavy betting.'

Viscount Statham appeared from a tavern across the lane. He nodded to Alex and then dodged between the horses and carts to reach them.

Introduced to John Howard, Statham smiled widely and handed John his card. 'How do you do, sir, your fame has gone before you.' His bristly gaze fell on Matthew. 'Tell me, laddie, is your employer in residence? We'd arranged to meet in the park with that Mortimer fellow, so I could look his sister over. I can't see hide nor hair of any of them there.'

Matthew said, 'I was just on my way to advise you. Unfortunately there has been an upset in the household, My Lord. The young lady of the house . . .'

'What of her, Man? Quickly, speak up.'

Matthew didn't even flicker an eyelash. 'I understand there has been an accident, My Lord.'

'Accident? Which young lady are we talking about?'

'Miss Fox.'

'Ah yes, I believe I heard a whisper about her conduct. She was a rather argumentative young woman who considered herself to be above her station, as I recall. It seems as though I've had a lucky escape.'

'Not yet you haven't,' Alex ground out between his teeth, and he clenched his fists.

John Howard stepped between him and the Scottish peer. 'I advise you not to say any more since I claim kinship. Miss Fox is my niece and the allegations are without credibility, since it was a spiteful act perpetrated against her by another suitor. It is a man well known to us – but not a gentleman, I might add. He damaged a young woman's reputation in pursuit of her legacy, and in that he was supported by another man, who was a gentleman, but by name only.'

Alex cracked his knuckles for effect. 'When we catch up with Mortimer he will be brought to justice for his crime and will pay the price. I just hope his sister will survive the scandal.'

'I see . . . of course.' Statham pushed Matthew against the shoulder. 'You, Man . . . is anyone there to support Mrs Goodman and her daughter through their troubles?'

Matthew shrugged. 'Sir Frederick Lamington and Miss Mortimer were still there when we left, sir. I was loath to leave them together, since I formed the opinion that the Goodman betrothal might be in jeopardy. But then I'm only a servant. The business of the gentry is not my business and it's not something I'd wish to involve myself with.'

Statham's eyes began to gleam. 'She will need a wise old head to advise her.'

'As you say, sir. Especially since Lord Lamington seems fond of both ladies. Although he is recently betrothed to Miss Goodman, should she discard him he would not have to look much further to find another young lady to fill his purpose.'

Statham hurried off and Matthew turned when Alex laughed. 'If I hadn't heard you say that I wouldn't have believed it, Matthew. You hurled the cat amongst the pigeons with a vengeance.'

Matthew grinned. 'If you say so, My Lord.'

John murmured, 'I'll provide a purse of twenty guineas. My money is on the old tom cat.'

Alex disagreed. 'There is more to the pigeon named Freddie than meets the eye. If he's waited several seasons to get the flirty Adelaide into his bed, he isn't about to hand her over to Statham at this stage of the game.'

They both gazed at Matthew.

'Dare I say there is a wild card called Sophia Mortimer . . .'

Nineteen

Shocked by her appearance, Jane Bessant hugged Vivienne too warmly for comfort.

Vivienne swooped in a breath. 'Not so tight, I beg you, Jane. There are bruises you can't see.'

Jane released her. 'I'm so sorry, dear. When Ambrose told me about the attack on you I didn't expect you to look quite so . . . battered. You must allow me to treat those bruises with witch hazel.'

'There is no need, Jane. I have a maid. Her name is Maria and she tends to the bruises.'

'A maid? Why would you need a maid in the country? Surely the fortune you inherited would be better spent supporting your immediate family and charitable works. I must admit to a slight disappointment in you.'

Goodness, her father seemed to have spread the news of her financial business far and wide. Was everyone going to be allowed to have a say into how her fortune was to be managed?

Vivienne said, more curtly than she intended, 'Maria was chaperoning me, and was injured during the incident. The least I can do is offer her employment. As for my inheritance, it is in safe hands, and I have yet to take informed advice. However selfish it may seem to others, I intend to place my future and those of any children I may bear, first.'

Jane looked stricken. About forty, she'd been widowed for three years and had a grown-up son and one granddaughter. Her calm but busy demeanor hid a tender heart. She lived but an hour away in the next village.

Now her soft brown eyes flooded with tears as they took in the visible evidence of the beating. 'Oh my dear girl. I didn't mean to sound as though I was interfering . . . and of course you aren't selfish, and I didn't mean to imply that you were. Nothing could be further from the truth.'

'I know, and I've been short-tempered since this awful attack on me. The worst thing I can do is to ignore expert advice and give everything away on a spur of the moment decision.'

'Of course it is, and you must not. I cannot think of one piece of advice. In fact, words fail me. I cannot imagine what you went through . . . I don't think I really want to know.'

'Which is good because I don't want to repeat it all over again.' She was about to ring for some tea when she remembered it was Mrs Tilly's day off. 'I'll go and make us some tea and when I come back you can tell me how your baby granddaughter is getting along.'

'And you will tell me about this titled country gentleman who is championing your cause. Your dear papa is quite taken with him. Am I to understand there is a betrothal in the offing?'

She sighed. 'My dear papa should stop meddling in my life, and so should my country gentleman. He is a friend.'

'Your father considers him to be more than that. He is looking forward to reading the marriage vows over you.'

She gave an unladylike snort. 'Do I advise him it's about time he took you down the aisle? No . . . well, not very often. I simply mind my own business and hope the pair of you are old enough to know what you're doing.'

Jane coloured. 'How long have you known?'

'About a year.'

'We decided to wait until—'

'I know . . . until I'm wed and off his hands. Well, you won't have to worry about that much longer—'

'You have accepted your earl – that's absolutely wonderful!'

'I haven't accepted anybody. I was about to say that now I have some money of my own, if I don't become a wife I can purchase my own home and live independently. I might even go overseas.'

'Your father will not approve.'

He didn't have to approve since she was of an age to run her own life. 'When he asks you what I said, tell him it's about time he realized I am grown up. Now you have done your duty I'll go and make the tea, and will then show you the tapestry I'm working on.'

Vivienne had enjoyed Jane's visit on the whole, but nothing had been achieved by it except for an unspoken reminder that she was keeping her father from his true love.

That had been three days ago. Now she felt like a caged tiger. Deep down she was still scared and prone to weeping over nothing. If anything, the face that gazed back at her from the mirror earlier that morning was in a worse state than the day it had been redesigned by Simon Mortimer.

The original bruises had deepened and new ones had appeared. What's more, she was almost cross-eyed with fatigue from working on her tapestry. When finished, it would depict an intricate flower garden, and a lady on a swing being pushed by a nobleman with a couple of leaping brown dogs by his side. Goodness knows why she'd picked such a complicated pattern.

She had disliked her appearance before the attack. Her eyes were neither green nor grey, her nose was too straight to be pretty and her mouth erred a little too much on the generous side.

Alex likes your mouth.

She ignored that.

He likes your eyes, too.

She liked his. A flame grew inside her and she began to tingle. She touched her mouth and wished she were in his arms, pressed against his warm body, aware of his smell and the tiny bristles that sprouted on his chin when he needed to shave, his taut stomach, and the parts that made him a man. She had felt him harden against her and experienced a little of the desire in him – he would use that desire to excite her, and it would need only a little of his strength to fuse them together, a nudge or two.

She could hardly breathe; just thinking of it the way she did was almost indecent, yet so natural. Nature was wonderfully inventive and extremely urgent!

Not that he'd actually proposed marriage because he loved her . . . he'd just skirted around it as a way to save her reputation.

Did all spinsters walk around in a frustrated ferment of mind and body?

She pushed the tapestry aside and sighed as she crossed to the silver-framed mirror on the mantelpiece. Her pale complexion was now patched with several shades of black, grey, purple, yellow and deep red.

She would have given anything to have her much-maligned normal face back. Her eyes could see, she could hear, and her nose inhaled and exhaled the air to keep her alive. What more did she need? 'I will never complain about my appearance again,' she vowed.

Her father's face appeared beside hers and she turned.

'You never had any reason to complain before. Be thankful your teeth are still intact and no bones were broken.' He offered her a smile.

'I am thankful . . . I was just having a private moment that was all about misplaced vanity, while you were observing me through eyes filled with fatherly pain and love.' She turned and kissed him. 'The messenger has been. There were two letters for you . . . one had the bishop's seal on it. I've put them on your desk. There was nothing for me.'

Was that a twinge of self-pity in her voice?

'Were you expecting some letters . . . from the earl perhaps?'

There was no need to deny it to her father now. She was in love with the earl and he knew it. Nevertheless, she found herself sidestepping the question. 'I thought my cousin might have written to me with news of what's been going on in my absence.'

'Does it matter very much? I'm sure London society is managing the season without you, and the earl will have it all in hand.'

'As you know, Papa, I prefer to manage my own affairs. He has almost forbidden me from confronting my attackers – and we are not even connected. How dare he?'

'The earl has my permission to act on our behalf. His title gives him authority. People will think you are connected, and that will dampen down the speculation considerably.'

Or it would merely send it flying in another direction, like the spread of a summer cold from a careless cough or a sneeze that had found a new body to inhabit. She would become even more notorious when their false engagement was exposed. People would put two and two together and make six out of it.

'You are too sensitive and your feelings bruise too easily, my love. Lord LéSayres is a capable young man who appears to be a good judge of character. Trust him. He will do what he feels he must to secure your reputation.'

She touched a fingertip against the ring hanging at her throat. Yes . . . she must trust him. She had no choice. 'I'm worried he'll be injured trying to defend my reputation, and all this came about because I believed that letter. It wasn't even in your handwriting.'

'But then, if I *had* been desperately ill and you'd ignored the missive, how badly would you have felt about yourself then?'

That hadn't even entered her head. 'Have I disgraced myself so badly, Papa? I've never pushed myself forward or sought notoriety. I've been over and over it in my mind and my only crime seems to be that of having too much trust in people.'

'Without trust and love we have nothing. The disgrace is not yours, Vivienne. Money attracts the greedy. Some people will do anything to obtain it, and they don't care who they hurt in the process. If it's any consolation, I now think you were right in trying to keep the matter quiet . . . a pity someone who knew or heard of it didn't keep their counsel.'

It was too late now. Someone had let her secret out, right down to the sum of it. It was obviously one of the people who had been trusted with her deceased relative's will.

'We will not confirm the existence of the inheritance. Mr Howard has been instructed as to that. He has assured me he's not in the habit of discussing his clients' advice, else he wouldn't be in business for long. This other letter might be from him.'

Her father hadn't considered that his interference might have been part of the trouble. She hugged him, loath to condemn him, even in her thoughts. 'You always make me feel better. Shall we go for a walk?'

He extricated himself with a smile. 'Much as I'd like to, I'm going to work on my sermon for Sunday. Why don't you go and visit Mrs Owens and her new baby.'

'Oh . . . I don't feel like showing my face to the public just yet. Besides, my face would likely frighten the baby. I'll walk to the meadow and find a spot to read. Perhaps I'll ask Maria to come with me.'

'She's gone to the market with Mrs Tilly.'

'Oh . . . I shall go back to the tapestry then, though it's not my favourite occupation.'

'You haven't got the patience for it. You should find the courage to go out by yourself again, Vivienne. A young woman who was brave enough to fight off her attackers certainly has the courage to face up to her fears. Nobody can do it for you. When you've mastered that particular fear once, you'll be more confident the second time.'

Sound advice. She would start by walking around the meadow to pick a bunch of poppies. She secured a chiffon scarf over her head and face and placed her bonnet on top. She could always tuck the scarf up if anybody was about. Not that many people would be since the villagers would be gathering in the last of the hay.

She fetched a basket. In it she placed a stone bottle filled with ginger ale, a ripe, juicy pear, her drawing tablet and a book of poetry.

Summer was nearly at an end. Already the leaves on the trees were beginning to yellow, and the berries on the rowan tree were turning a cheerful red that invited the thrushes to feed. She seated herself in the long, dry grass that sloped down towards the river and flipped the book open at a random page and read a couple of verses out loud.

> *She dwelt among the untrodden ways*
> *Beside the springs of Dove,*
> *Maid whom there were none to praise*
> *And very few to love:*
>
> *A violet by a mossy stone*
> *Half hidden from the eye,*
> *Fair as a star, when only one*
> *Is shining in the sky.*

She began to laugh. It was as though Wordsworth had written it just for her. After a while, the warmth of the sun made her drowsy and she sought shade under a horse chestnut tree, her back against the trunk. She began to sketch the meadow flowers, the golden rod covered in glowing petals, delicate blue hare-bells, the daisy-flowered mayweed and the black-throated scarlet flamboyance of the remaining poppies. She kept a record of the colours in her mind and would paint them in when winter had set in, to remind her of the warmth of the previous summer.

Some of the leaves were curling and they crunched into brown dust and fluttered from her fingertips, flying on the breeze, as if set free from restraint by their destruction. Their prickly cases were plumped and ready to release nuts as polished and shining as her father's eyes.

Beyond the hedge a cart trundled slowly by. The rhythm of the wheels had a regular squeak to them. Not long after came the sound of horses and a carriage, the deep growl of men's voices and laughter passed in an instant, never to be heard again. They were like ghosts through time, though she couldn't quite make out the words.

What was this tree like a hundred years past, a sapling growing from an acorn, pushing deep into the earth to nourish its life, and thrusting its limbs to embrace the wind? How long did oak trees live? She must ask her father.

A single horse went by. There was a moment of alarm in her, a breath held tightly inside so no hunter could hear it. Deprived of a fresh breath of air her heart began to bang against her ribs like a lively frog, betraying her to those with sensitive ears.

The rumble of a cart came and went. The voices faded into the distance. Her held breath exhaled in jerks and shudders as if it didn't want to leave the safety of her body. She was left with a momentary dizziness, like a top spinning on its last pirouette.

She would not give in to fear – she would not!

Closing her eyes she thought of Alex, her lord of calm, and the nature of the day no longer threatened. She slipped into a state of drowsiness, as if the summer perfume of the flowers had drugged her senses. Now her mind had turned to Alex, so fully engaged was it that she could think of no one and nothing else.

What was he doing at that moment? Sitting in a drawing room of some beautifully groomed young lady – Miss Cresswell perhaps, upright and well trained – sipping tea and chatting politely about nothing in particular while his brain calculated the sum of her worth, both to him and to his precious King's Acres estate.

She consoled herself by thinking – hoping really – that Alex would be bored half to death. No matter, he would put his estate first. What was it he'd said . . . he would place his wife above all others.

She brushed an insect from her nose.

Would Miss Cresswell's body react like her own at the sight of him? Would she send silent messages of desire across the space between them, like arrows with honeyed tips? Perhaps Miss Cresswell was too refined to allow her hands to shake and the tips of her breasts to swell and graze against her bodice until the need to caress was intolerably uncomfortable? Vivienne doubted the young lady would yearn for his touch, like she did. Would she blush and tingle at the thought of him, at the smell and taste of him, from every hair on his head to his little toe. Did she think of the incursion of the wedding night when he would penetrate all her defences and make his bride a woman?

An insect landed gently on her cheek, danced about her face. She waved it away. Her nose was its next stop. She wrinkled it and it flew away. She'd barely relapsed back into her daydream when it landed on her nose again, and tickled its way down the length.

The bruises must have attracted it. When it crawled along the separation of her mouth she spluttered and waved her arms around her head, crying out, 'Stop that, you pest.'

A low chuckle reached her ears. 'I've never been called a pest before.'

Propelled by a stab of alarm, her eyes flew open, and she didn't know whether to scold him or smile. She did both. 'Alex! How long have you been there?'

His eyes captured the sky as he tickled her chin with the long frond of ripened oats he held. 'I've been here long enough to find the pear in your basket and eat it. It was delicious.'

'How did you know I was here?'

'Your father told me.'

Snatching the frond from his hand she threw it aside. 'I must have fallen asleep. Why didn't you wake me?'

'I liked the way your nose twitched when I tickled it, and you smiled in your sleep. I thought you might be having a pleasant dream so didn't want to disturb you.'

Her face warmed at that. 'Why are you here?'

'I've brought your luggage and I'm in company with your relative, John Howard . . . who has some business to discuss with your father, so I came in search of you.'

Rising to her feet she straightened the skirt of her gown. 'Oh . . . my goodness. I must go and find some extra food and prepare your rooms.'

'There is no need, since we are staying at the inn overnight and travelling back in the morning. We have business to take care of in London.'

'Not on my behalf, I hope.'

'What makes you think that?' He gazed at her for a moment, eyes searching her face and head cocked to one side, then he leaned forward and captured a kiss from the mouth he'd just tickled.

It was only a dab of a kiss, and it tasted deliciously of pear juice.

'Stop teasing and kiss me properly,' she said, astounding herself – and him as well, by the expression on his face.

Twenty

It was not just a kiss . . . it was a wonderful kiss . . . one she didn't want to part with. She went up on tiptoe, her arms slid round his neck and her fingers splayed through his curls.

When they came apart she gazed at him, and he laughed and pulled her down into the long flowers and grasses of the meadow. Smoothing his hands down over her buttocks he held her against him. He kissed her again, and then he rolled her over on top of him in a shockingly intimate matter.

He was hard against her, and her thighs trembled with the effort of not allowing them to take the next natural step, which was to relax and give him access. A couple of thrusts and all her questions would be answered, her frustrations laid to rest and satisfied. It was tempting . . . so very tempting. He wouldn't have noticed her blush amongst the multitude of colours on her face, thank goodness, but she could feel it.

'At this moment, here amongst the flowers, the urge to make love to you is almost unbearable,' he said.

Her imagination was on the very brink of stepping out of the fiction and allowing the incursion into the factual. 'I know, Alex. I'm not entirely ignorant of the ways of nature . . . or of men. I cannot allow it even though I might want to . . . and I do want to,' she confessed.

He loosened the crushing strength of his arms and she rolled off him. Turning on his side he propped himself up on his elbow. They gazed at each other, saying nothing. After a few agonizing moments he reached for her hand and placed a kiss on each fingertip. 'I should be sorry for allowing the male in me to take over . . . but I'm not.'

Would it matter if she allowed the intimacy he so clearly needed, especially since her own body was raging with desire for the caresses that making love would bring. When he traced a finger over the swell of her breast through her bodice she gave a little shudder of delight, and reminded him, 'I only asked for a kiss.'

The expression in his eyes changed, became almost feral. Then he took a deep breath, rolled away from her and got to his feet in one fluid motion, his smile self-deprecating as he held out his hands to her. 'I went too far. I apologize if I embarrassed you.'

'You didn't . . . it was my fault for encouraging you.'

'It was nobody's fault. This is not the time and place, that's all, Vivienne. I would be breaking your father's trust in me as well as taking advantage of you, especially since he appears to think all peers are well-mannered and honourable gentlemen.'

'My father is not so naïve. He no more thinks that of you than you would consider him to be . . . well, less than a man because he's a cleric. He wants to marry again so it's in his own interest to get me off his hands.'

'All the same, if we were observed . . .'

He didn't need to finish the sentence. Her reputation was already unfairly shredded in London, unless Alex could redeem it. It wouldn't do to be seen alone with a man now, especially exchanging passionate kisses with one.

He pulled her to her feet and kissed her on the forehead . . . and so tenderly he almost convinced her that he loved her.

But he'd never mentioned love. She kissed him in return, something light, impersonal and sisterly, to ease the growing tension between them. 'You wear your hair long,' she observed.

'My brother usually trims it for me.'

'I like it long. Thank you for being so kind, Alex. Most men would walk away from me in this situation. I won't hold you to that proposal though, so you needn't play the part of the lovesick swain.'

'Needn't I?' He grazed his knuckles across her nose. 'I quite enjoy playing the lovesick swain. I've never taken on the role before.' He laughed and picked up the scattered contents of her basket. Eyeing the ginger ale bottle he gave it an experimental shake. 'There's some left.'

'Most of it, I've only had a couple of sips. If you're thirsty please drink it. You can wash down the stolen pear with it.'

He didn't need telling twice. Pulling out the cork he upended the bottle and gulped the liquid down. He gave a gentle belch afterwards. 'Your pardon, Vivienne, I was thirsty . . . and I'm tired. There was a lot of dust on the road and most of it lodged in my throat.'

He eyed the horizon, where a line of dark cloud had appeared. The warm afternoon had gathered a sultry feel to it. 'It looks like a storm is on the way. I'll escort you home?'

'The storm will take ages to get here. This is the first time I've had the courage to leave the house and I'm enjoying the fresh air. I want to pick a bunch of meadow flowers to take home. Rest here, it shouldn't take me long.'

Twenty minutes later a low but prolonged howl of wind blew through the meadow. Petals and loose debris were plucked into the air and borne on high. Those plants with stems firmly rooted in the earth were flattened to the ground under the onslaught. Fat drops of rain scattered like a handful of liquid diamonds thrown from the sky. A rainbow arched in fragile stripes, bridging the gap of the meadow. Vivienne remembered a tale about Irish leprechauns who buried their gold at the rainbow's end. But which was the beginning of the rainbow and which was the end?

She hung on to the hem of her gown, which had plastered against the front of her body and was slowly inching up her thighs, while the back fluttered like a demented flag.

There was a lull when the world seemed to hold its breath, then the wind dropped and a low and menacing rumble of thunder took its place. She gazed in Alex's direction. He hadn't moved. It was supposed to be dangerous to shelter under the tree in a thunderstorm and alarm pricked at her.

She picked up her skirts and ran, calling out, 'Alex, wake up! The storm's almost upon us . . . we must find shelter.'

Oblivious to the storm, he was fast asleep. She fell to her knees beside him and gave him a shake, and although he mumbled something he didn't wake. He was totally relaxed.

Should she slap him? Her heart melted. He looked defenceless, like a baby in a cradle and she couldn't bring herself to. She just wanted to sit and keep watch over him.

Laughter trickled from her when she thought of something better to wake him. Leaning forward she kissed him. For a few moments nothing happened, and then she sensed a change in him. She sprang to her feet just before his eyes opened.

'I was dreaming,' he said.

'Of what?'

To which question he smiled with delight. 'I was hoping you'd ask. I was dreaming of a long pair of legs with pink ribbons securing white silk hose above the knee.'

How could he know she was wearing pink ribbons when he'd been fast asleep? He must be guessing. 'Is that why you look so smug?'

'Do I look smug?'

'You were fast asleep with your eyes closed, and you tell me you were dreaming about wearing white hose with pink ribbons. How odd.'

'You know very well they were your legs I was looking at.'

'You can't see my legs so you must be guessing.'

'It's amazing what the wind and rain uncovers. I enjoyed the kiss you gave me.'

She laughed. 'You have a vivid imagination.' The sky was darkening and she cried out, 'We must hurry, Alex, else we'll be drenched.'

'We are drenched.'

'The storm came across quicker than I expected. The church is closer than the house. Papa usually leaves the door unlatched during the day. If not, we can shelter in the porch.'

He was on his feet in a few seconds and snatched up the basket. Dumping her flowers on top he took her hand in his and they began to run.

There was something relentless about the rain. It overtook them when they reached the hedge and swallowed them whole. The wind tore her carefully styled hair into shreds and the water turned it into rats' tails. Snatched from her head, her bonnet went bowling off down the road. They didn't bother to chase after it. He took off his coat and sheltered them both under it.

They were laughing when they turned into the churchyard. The door was unlatched and the church interior had an air of gloom about it. Vivienne's gown trailed slimy mud round her ankles; thank goodness it was one of her older gowns. Panting for breath, she said, 'I must look as though I've been cleaning out a pigsty.'

His laughter echoed around the empty church. 'Yes . . . you do rather . . . luckily you don't smell as ripe.'

She shrugged, and then shivered. 'It's become quite chilly.'

'It's because you're soaked through. We'll stay until the lightning no longer poses a danger, then we must get you home before you take a chill. Does your father have an office here? He might have left a coat.'

'There's a vestry. It's behind the altar and down the steps, though it's not very big. There's a lost property box there.' Unease filled her again when every little shadow between her and the vestry seemed to take on a new meaning. She felt jumpy. What if Simon Mortimer lay in wait for her? She moved closer to Alex for comfort. 'Will you come with me, or wait here?'

He sensed her disquiet because his hand closed warmly over hers. 'I'll come with you.' He kept her hand tucked into his as they made their way down the aisle. The church was filled with noisy echoes, the rattle of rain, doors creaking in the draughts and the bang and crash of thunder. All were accompanied now and again by spectacular white snicks of lightning.

They'd just reached the top of the stairs when there came a prolonged and eerie moan.

Alex drew them to a stop and his eyes turned into blue stars with the next flash of lightning. 'Tell me . . . is this place haunted?'

'I'll tell you a story about it as long as you promise not to run away and leave me here alone.'

'I promise.'

Vivienne felt brave with Alex beside her. 'It probably is haunted, but that noise is caused by draughts in the organ pipes. The organ tries to play its own music when the wind blows off the sea.'

'Is that fact or fiction?'

'Both. Pa made up a story about it once. He said the maker of the organ was a German musician who lost his sweetheart at sea in a storm. The king of storms fell in love with her and decided to keep her, so he turned her into a mermaid. The musician created a lament for his lost love, and he whispered it into the organ pipes before he went to the grave, where it was trapped for eternity. Now, with every storm, his ghost plays a love song to her to entice her back to shore.'

'Does she ever come to him?'

'It's impossible. Her soul can only survive in the sea, and his on the land.' She lowered her voice. 'His unmarked grave is in the corner of the churchyard, and on the date of her drowning he rises from his lonely bed and wanders among the graves in the storm, singing for his lost love.'

The hairs on her neck stood on end when another moan from the organ rose and fell. She hadn't heard if for a long time and had forgotten how the noise sounded, like an animal in pain. She laughed, rather shakily. 'Pa has a vivid imagination and he made up lots of tales. Do you want me to go down first? It's only a few steps.'

'Are you saying I'm scared?'

She tossed lightly at him, 'Are you?'

'If you're not, I'm not,' and he gave her hand a little tug. 'Come on then.'

The light in the vestry was dim. Alex picked up a woollen shawl from the lost property basket and wrapped it around her shoulders. With a corner still held in each hand he pulled her by the shawl towards him and kissed her. 'That should warm you up a little,' he said, and before she had time to react he released her.

There was a black umbrella hanging on a hook. He grabbed it up. 'This should get us home.'

They locked the church door and put the key on the hook in the porch. With the umbrella in the forward position like a battering ram they butted into the bluster of the wind and rain and struggled up the slope, avoiding the potholes as best they could and stopping to laugh at each other every so often.

At last they reached the house.

Maria was coming down the stairs. 'I saw you coming, Miss Fox, and I've laid out some towels and dry clothes.'

'Thank you, Maria. Could you fetch some towels for the earl?'

'I've placed some in the kitchen. They've been warming in front of the stove. If you'd like to give me your jacket I'll hang it in front of the stove, too, sir. It's nice and warm in there.'

'Is that you, Vivienne?' her father called out. 'You must come in and greet your uncle, John Howard. Is the earl with you?'

'Yes, Papa. We're both damp, so if you'll just allow me time to dry myself.'

'A little water won't hurt. Come in at once to greet our guest. I insist.'

She sighed when he opened the door and pulled her into the

drawing room. 'Here she is at last, John.' His eyes widened. 'You are not damp, you're drenched. What do you make of her?'

She stood there dripping, her hair hanging in strands on her shoulders, her gown muddied and her face covered in bruises.

A pair of astonished eyes grazed over her, then he chuckled. 'I really don't know what to make of her on this occasion.'

Her father peered over his glasses at her. 'Good gracious . . . what have we here? That *is* you, isn't it, Vivienne? I've never seen you so bedraggled.'

Vivienne laughed at their expressions. 'How-do-you-do, Uncle? It's only been a short time since we last met, so this is a double pleasure. Forgive my appearance, you find me the worse for wear since the earl and I were caught in the open in a storm — and it was a most wonderful storm. Now, I must go and dry myself. I left the earl in the kitchen with some towels.'

'In the kitchen! What ever will he think?'

'Oh . . . he's quite intelligent, Papa. I imagine he'll think he's in the kitchen. I might ask him to peel the potatoes while he's in there.'

Her father hurried to the door. 'Don't you dare, Vivienne. I'll go and see if I can find him something dry to wear.'

John Howard chuckled after her father left and Vivienne grinned at him.

'You won't mind if I desert you too, will you, Uncle? I promise not to be too long. Then I'll fetch you some refreshment.'

He moved to where she stood and she didn't flinch when he examined her face. 'If Simon Mortimer did that to you he deserves more than a mere boxing match as punishment. Are there more bruises?'

She nodded. Vivienne had forgotten her discomfort while she was with Alex. Now, with just one reminder of her attacker's name, all the shock and physical hurt of the abuse came rushing back. Although she'd managed to escape from him, Simon had made her feel like nothing, and had reduced her to nothing in her own eyes.

Her smile faded. With it went the bubbling sense of intimate excitement she'd shared with Alex, replaced by tears she couldn't quite hold back.

She bobbed her uncle a curtsey, saying more formally, 'Excuse me, Uncle. You find me at a disadvantage, and I was so looking forward to seeing you again.'

Far from being embarrassed, he handed her a handkerchief. 'Go and compose yourself, my dear. Simon Mortimer will not get away with this. Nobody will believe you encouraged his attention by the time I've finished with him. As for the baron . . . he's already been punished.'

'In what way?'

'Your cousin, Miss Goodman, is undecided on whether she will become his wife, after all. I believe Viscount Statham is eager to step into the breach.'

Vivienne cried out, 'But she can't jilt Freddie! She loves him and he loves her. She will break his heart and break her own at the same time. You must stop her from being so foolish.'

'I'm not a marriage broker, Miss Fox.' He sighed. 'I suppose I could speak to the girl on your behalf. Perhaps you would write her a note expressing your opinion on that.'

'I would prefer to return to London with you. I've forgiven Freddie, who meant me no harm, but I definitely have something to say to Simon Mortimer.'

'Where would you stay? Your aunt thinks you've brought shame on the family and she will keep you at a distance.'

The sick feeling returned. 'I had not thought of that. Would you not offer me shelter then?'

'Do you honestly think I would compromise myself in such a manner? Besides, I'm staying at my club, and they do not allow females past the front door. As matters stand, if you put in an appearance it would make matters worse, and yourself even more conspicuous. Imagine what the tittle-tattlers would make of your appearance.'

In his high-handed way he was right, of course. 'Am I to take it that you would rather I didn't return to London?'

'Lord LéSayres suggested you might approach me with this request. He is adamant you should stay here until the matter is resolved, and in that we must take your father's feelings into consideration, which I have done. I take it you would not seriously entertain a request from Mortimer to wed you?'

An exasperated sigh left her mouth. 'Not for one second, and if that was my last second on earth I'd seek him out and kill him.'

'Allow me to speak plainly. That's one of the reasons why we don't want you in London. We have plans for retribution already in place, and they do not include murder or threats. It will be handled in the way of gentlemen, and hysterical female outbursts that have no real purpose other than to vent feelings are not part of them. Allow your protectors to handle the matter and all will turn out well, do you understand?'

Nobody had spoken to her in that sort of tone before and it was like having a pail of cold water thrown in her face. As if she wasn't wet enough.

The truth in what he said snapped her out of her temper and did what it was designed to – it stiffened her spine. 'Of course I understand. What is the plan you spoke of, are you going to tell me?'

Amusement filled his eyes. 'Not until it has reached resolution.'

She would not be able to outwit this man, and she offered him a wry smile. 'I'm quite in awe of you, Uncle. Are you as clever as reputation would have it?'

He thought about it for a second or two. 'Successful would describe me better. I should be modest and say I'm not clever, except that would be a lie, because the perception of cleverness is in the eye of the beholder. So the answer is . . . there is no answer to that. However, I'm successful in most of my dealings.'

'Very well then, Uncle John, I will allow myself to be guided by your sage advice.'

'I'll make a note of it.'

'There is no need to make a note since I'm completely trust-worthy. Ask my father.'

He chuckled at that. 'Now, off you go and make yourself presentable. You're beginning to shiver.'

She kissed his cheek. 'There, that might make you a little less . . . *serious*.'

It did, for she heard him chuckle as she closed the door.

Twenty-One

The storm passed over and the sun shone again. A fine mist floated in the floor of the valley and everything sparkled.

Their guests were invited to dinner.

'You mustn't go to such trouble on our behalf,' Alex protested at first, and rather half-heartedly because he was hungry.

She smiled at him. 'It's no trouble, Alex. You can help me if you wish.'

He made himself useful, following her back and forth with plates, and setting cutlery on the table in the small informal dining room, despite her protests.

'I don't mind. Eugenie has listed the essential tasks and Dominic and I have our tasks, such as washing the dishes, dusting the furniture and washing the floors. The housekeeper does most of the cooking and laundry.'

'So you're the butler at King's Acres as well as the master?'

'And the gardener. I just have to swap coats.'

'The LéSayres brothers seem to be talented in many ways.'

He took a dish from her hands. 'Let's just say we manage, but thank you anyway.'

'For what?'

'Making light of my lack of wealth. I'd grown used to it, but in London I'm reminded at every turn. Sometimes I feel ashamed when I haven't the coin to pay for a theatre ticket and they turn up at my lodgings. It becomes obvious that people support me one way or the other, and I never know who they are.'

'Don't be ashamed. The sum of a man can't be measured by how much money he has. If someone supports you then it means they like you and are friends you can rely on.' She changed the subject. 'Shall we play a game of chess when we've finished the dishes? I promise I'll allow you to win.'

'Allow me to win? I won't hear of it. I'm very good at the game.'

'In that case I shall give you no quarter.'

'I warn you, Vivienne, I shall demand a kiss if you lose.'

'And I shall demand one if you win.'

'It sounds as though I'm going to be the winner either way.'

They looked at each other and laughed.

The two older men spent most of the time penned up in the reverend's study. Their voices rose and fell, and there was the chink of glass against glass and laughter.

'Goodness knows what they're talking about, but I hope my father doesn't drink too much, he's not used to it. I'm pleased my uncle decided to call on us again. I like him, don't you? They haven't seen each other in years, and now two visits, one after the other.' Hands on hips she gazed at the kitchen bench, looking sweetly domestic in an enveloping white apron. 'I seem to have forgotten something?'

'Custard?'

'Ah yes . . . custard.' She tipped some cream and milk into a pan, dropped half a pod of vanilla into it and set it on the stove. 'Come and stir this while I get the rest ready.'

Eggs were cracked and adroitly separated, the right amount of cornflour and sugar measured into the bowl, and seemingly by sleight of hand rather than any real measurement. The resulting white paste was dribbled little by little into the pan he was stirring.

'Stir gently until it thickens and then set it to one side,' she instructed.

His mouth had watered with a vengeance as he'd carefully followed her instructions. He gazed proudly at the gelatinous yellow contents of the pan. 'I think it's cooked.'

She appeared at his shoulder. 'That looks perfect, Alex. Come and taste this apple tart, and bring a spoonful of that custard to sit on top . . . you can tell me if it's sweet enough.'

His custard was perfect, she'd said, and he wanted to laugh because firstly, she had complimented his effort, which he'd been stupidly proud of . . . and second, he got to eat the result of his labours. The wedge of pastry, the cinnamon and sugar crusting a sweet contrast to the sharpness of the fruit, filled the empty crater in his stomach.

He had a short, sharp image from childhood, of Eugenie asking the same thing while he and his brother stood like a pair of hungry birds on a branch, watching her cook the dinner and hoping they'd be asked to do the testing. They would stick out their tongues while she dropped a tidbit of something delicious on it.

'It's delicious . . . so is the custard. Try it.' He dipped the spoon in the custard and held it out to her. Sticking out her tongue she licked the bowl of the spoon clean, and drew the confection into her mouth. A small blob dropped to her chin. Alex lifted it with his forefinger and held it out to her. For a moment her mouth closed around his finger and she sucked it into her mouth, allowing her tongue to curl around his fingertip. That small act was blatantly sensual.

He watched the moment that awareness came over. Her greenish eyes darkened and her lashes hid her feelings from him. She drew in a breath and began to bustle about, avoiding him as she served the meal, a makeshift repast of potatoes stuffed with mushrooms, cheese and chopped chives, and baked in their jackets. It was accompanied by slices of smoked ham, roasted beetroot and pickled cabbage. The meal was both delicious and filling.

Vivienne had cooked and served it, leaving her maid free to unpack her trunks and sort out her wardrobe.

Alex's clothes had dried, and he felt more comfortable as he watched Vivienne bustle back and forth. She had changed into a cream gown embroidered with primroses. Yellow ribbons were woven into her braid, which ended in the small of her back. It was decorated with a yellow silk rose that made the braid sway as she moved.

She darted a glance his way now and again, shy and intimate. He ached every time he saw her abused face. Although he agreed with John Howard's plan, which was to hit Simon Mortimer in the pocket rather than the stomach, his own instinct was to batter the man to a pulp. He'd have to be content with watching Matthew batter him.

They departed about seven, after she'd soundly thrashed him on the chess board.

There was a small amount of time when he found himself alone with Vivienne. 'I'll be back in about ten days,' he said. 'Your face should have healed and regained its former beauty by then.'

'I've never been beautiful.'

'You are to me. Your face is a perfect oval and your skin is like silk. You have the damnedest eyes, like a lady cat we had as children.'

'What was her name?'

'She was called Griselda. One day a handsome tom cat came calling and she packed her bag and ran away with him . . . at least, that's what Eugenie told us.'

Vivienne laughed, linking arms with her father who'd just joined them, along with her uncle. 'Take care, My Lord,' she said. Then she eyed her uncle. 'Your visit has been very mysterious and my curiosity is piqued. I enjoyed the little I saw of you though. I hope we'll see you again.'

'Be sure that you will, my dear. Perhaps you could come and visit us before too long.'

'I would love to. Please give my felicitations to your wife and tell her that I hope we can meet again at some future date.'

'I'm sure she'll appreciate it.' He clicked his tongue and they set out.

There were messages waiting for John Howard at the inn, and he disappeared into his room with them.

Alex said later, 'What do you think of your niece, John?'

'Vivienne has a way with her, and is sensible on the whole, though she's still angry and doesn't know how to handle that anger.'

'I'm angry on her behalf, too.'

'Any decent man would be under the circumstances. Despite her injuries her looks are not as indifferent as I was led to believe. With her classic face and high cheekbones she will always appear elegant, even when she's old.'

'Her father said she gets her looks from her mother and the Dubois family.'

'She does.'

'And where do you fit into the family?'

'Strictly speaking, I don't have any blood tie. Clemency Howard, née Dubois, was wed to Charles Howard, a scribe and moneylender. He took me from the orphanage at the age of five to become his apprentice, and adopted me as his son. Whether

I actually was his natural son or not was never questioned. He was a hard taskmaster. A little later I discovered a half-sister born to a woman called Lily Hooper.'

'Mrs Crawford?'

He nodded. 'I have given her the means to make a living and provide her with a quarterly allowance. She has a stepson from her marriage to support, as you know. He's a good-natured lad with manners, but without any real prospects. He will inherit the house when the time comes.'

After a moment, he said, 'Clemency Dubois had a second cousin who married Ambrose Fox. Jeanne I think her name was. I only met her once. However, I always thought Vivienne resembled Clemency a great deal.'

'They are related so it stands to reason.'

After another moment of thought, John said, 'Vivienne would make you a good wife.'

'I know. Unfortunately she has no fortune to speak of and neither do I. If I didn't have the responsibility and expense of the estate, I could happily live with Vivienne in a wooden shack.' He sighed. 'As it is, every time I set eyes on her my affections . . . *surge* and I resolve to throw caution to the wind and say, "To hell with King's Acre."'

'It's always a healthy sign when a woman grabs you by the balls!' Howard said bluntly, and slid him a sideways grin. 'So, you must ask yourself, my friend, which is the more important to you: Vivienne Fox . . . or the King's Acres estate.'

'Dominic would make a better custodian for the estate.'

'Be that as it may, for Dominic to take the title you'd have to die without issue. Your brother certainly doesn't envy you the responsibility, and will be pleased when you settle down and produce a son.'

'It's an impossible choice, you know that.'

'Perhaps . . . yet it has to be made. Nothing is impossible if you want it badly enough.'

'How?'

'Sell me the King's Mile.'

Alex sighed. 'I don't see the connection. Why do you want it so badly?'

'Why do you?'

'Because it's part of the LéSayres family legacy and it's my duty to pass it on to my children intact.'

'I can understand that, but to get those children one needs a wife who is young enough to breed. If you happen to like her as well then it makes life easier, since you can enjoy the task. The alternative is to marry for money and set Miss Vivienne up as a mistress for your pleasure.'

'Ask Vivienne to become my mistress!' Alex was shocked. 'I would not insult her or her father in such a manner, and besides, she would not agree to such an arrangement. I'll take her for my wife, and nothing less.'

'Good . . . At least we know what you don't want. Then you'd best formally propose before someone else takes it into their head to follow the lead of Simon Mortimer. There are plenty of rakes out there with an eye on the main chance.'

'Not many would be foolish enough to believe Miss Fox is worth such a huge amount of money. There is nothing about her that signifies an excess of wealth.'

John Howard shrugged. 'You'd be surprised how many people do. I have heard that Simon Mortimer's book is doing exceedingly well . . . but the small timers are getting in on the act.'

'Mortimer has wagered all he has on rumour, and he will be relying on his own boxing skills. Winning a couple of sporting cups at university and bashing the daylights out of a woman in a drunken rage is one thing. Out-boxing an experienced prize fighter is another thing all together.'

'Matthew is a prize fighter?'

'Have you ever heard of a pugilist called Scarlet Fury?'

'No . . . but it's a ridiculous title to assume. Surely not Matthew?'

'When you're the recipient of his fist then the words "Scarlet Fury" will take on a new meaning. Simon Mortimer has inflated himself to the point of bursting, which is a dangerous place for him to be. Apparently, Lord Statham is acting as his manager for the affair. He could be sorely out of pocket when this is over, and it will serve him right.'

'Another ale,' Alex called out to the landlord, and then said to John, 'I still don't feel right about allowing someone else to take up my fight.'

'It's only yours because you wanted it to be.'

'Someone had to champion Vivienne. What if Matthew loses?'

'He won't. Matthew intends to open a gentlemen's academy and I've offered to invest in it after he wins this fight. I only bet on sure things, remember that. He will also have the money from the nobbins, which as you know will be a generous share of the money thrown into the collector's hat.

John slid a folded paper sealed with wax across the table. 'Now . . . on a different note, I've taken the liberty of assessing the sum of money needed to get your estate on a level footing. Inside is my offer for the King's Mile, which I consider to be generous. I will not negotiate.'

Twisting a smile at him, Alex said, 'I believe it was you who stated . . . and not so very long ago . . . that everything is open to negotiation?'

John laughed. 'In my case it depends which side of the negotiation I'm on.'

When Alex went to open it John stopped him. 'Don't read it until we've got this Simon Mortimer affair sorted out.'

According to the books, the estate had paid for itself long before they'd acquired the King's Mile. If an avenue of trees were planted between the sites, none would be the wiser if a house were situated there or not.

He couldn't choose between what was clearly his familial duty, and the woman he loved. He knew he had no choice where duty was concerned. He did with Vivienne. He could live in poverty with her if his situation dictated, as Eugenie had with his father. They'd been happy together. Then again, he could let Vivienne go and wed someone with wealth.

The thought of letting Vivienne go was too painful to contemplate. The thought of being wed to another woman was twice as painful, and the thought that Vivienne might end up married to someone like Simon Mortimer was unthinkable! When set up against King's Acres, he really had nothing to lose, just a strip of land that would still be there after they'd all gone.

He stopped thinking.

John Howard was offering him a solution of sorts, and Alex had a great deal of respect for the man, his mind and his ability to out-think all who stood in his way – but Alex wasn't going down without a murmur. What would Dom advise him to do under the circumstances? He wondered, but not for very long.

Drawing in a deep breath he took a great leap of faith, which afterwards made him wonder if he'd inherited his father's nature in the need to gamble. 'Whatever the offer might be . . . double it and we'll shake on it.'

John shrugged, and then smiled rather ruefully and held out a hand.

Twenty-Two

The morning was humid and sticky.

Crowds had gathered outside the ring in Hyde Park. The streets leading to the park were crowded and choked with carriages. Men milled about, their hats resembling bobbing chimney pots. Collective voices sent an expectant buzz into the air to join the flies.

Alex had woken with a throat that tickled and itched, and he had a slight fever. Mrs Crawford made him a concoction of willowbark, lemon and honey mixed with brandy. Combined with the atmosphere, the tincture made him perspire, and his skin prickled uncomfortably.

There were several women in the crowd, some showing their wares in more ways than one, and others dipping their fingers into unguarded waistcoat pockets as they wandered through the crowd. Some women were obviously of the upper classes, and attended with their lovers or a retinue of servants. They wore veils so they couldn't be recognized.

Alex and his party unobtrusively made their way to the organizer's tent, where Matthew stripped down to his breeches. He slipped his red satin mask over his head and a red satin cloak about his shoulders. He adjusted the loo mask over his eyes. The garment was designed to keep the flies out of his eyes as well as acting to disguise the top half of his head. The cloak was purely for show.

Simon Mortimer came into the tent a little later with Freddie trailing after him. Freddie nodded, then shrugged, seemingly reluctant to be there. He held out a hand, which Alex took. 'Good morning, My Lord. May the best man win.'

Simon looked Matthew up and down and sneered. 'What have we here, the Scarlet Fury? He looks more like a wilting poppy to me. Was that the best you could get?'

'Excuse me, My Lord,' Matthew murmured, and placed a hand on Alex's arm when he gave an involuntary twitch that would have ended up as a punch to Simon's jaw if it had not been stopped in mid-air. They moved away.

Alex remembered a ladies match was next in the program. They were popular with men, but the main attraction this day was the first fight. It was a grudge match featuring a boxer called Scarlet Fury. He was billed as being promoted by Lord LéSayres, and in defence of the honour of an unnamed lady who'd been subjected to an unprovoked attack by the opponent, Simon Mortimer, leaving her considerably disabled.

Prolonged boos and hisses came from the crowd when Simon Mortimer put in an appearance with a doleful-looking Frederick in attendance. Surprisingly, Viscount Statham joined Simon Mortimer's party and was billed as his sponsor. He paraded Simon around the ring, holding his arm aloft, piercing the crowd with fierce eyes. Alex received a long, bristling stare from under his bushy brows.

'What the devil is Statham doing, supporting Mortimer?' Alex said, before remembering Vivienne had turned down a proposal from both men. Statham was a bad loser, and being petty about it.

Matthew told him, 'In your absence the Scottish Viscount succumbed to the charms of Miss Mortimer, who is almost as desperate as he is to wed. Miss Mortimer has taken advantage of that, I feel.

'As for Miss Goodman, she has forgiven the baron for his part in the affair. He's not a bad fellow, just weak and easily led. His mother was a bit of a termagant, so he's used to being managed by a woman. Miss Goodman has taken her cousin's side, and has berated her mother over her attitude. The woman was quite taken aback. I think Miss Goodman will demand that the baron drops Simon Mortimer from their circle when they're married. She is eager to go up in the world.'

Alex grinned. 'You're a mine of information, Matthew.'

John offered the man his hand and smiled.

'I shall enjoy relieving you of your purse, Mr Howard,' Matthew said.

The atmosphere of the crowd changed. It fell quiet, except for a couple of catcalls.

'Coward,' someone called out. 'Call yourself a gentleman, Mortimer.'

John Howard patted Matthew's well-padded shoulder. 'Good luck, Scarlet Fury. Whatever the outcome, you will be looked after.'

Alex paraded him to rousing cheers. It seemed that a lady's honour was a very popular subject with the crowd.

Like Matthew, Simon wore long white breeches and his trunk was bare. Matthew was imposing in his swirling red cloak and the silk hood that ended in a mask for eyes. There was another outburst of cheering when he threw aside his cloak and shadow-boxed at the air to keep his muscles warm.

Simon's efforts brought some more name-calling and hisses. Somebody threw a dead rat at his feet. The referee threw it into the crowd and sent the opponents to their respective corners.

'Go easy on him, Matthew. I don't want his death on my hands.'

'I'll just bloody him a bit, sir.'

At first glance the men were ill-matched. Matthew was shorter and stockier than Simon, who had the longer reach to his advantage. Both were well muscled, especially across the stomach. Matthew's shoulders and arms supported more muscle, and his hands were thick, tough and callused.

The crowd parted as a closed carriage edged through and found a place to stand. It bore the royal crest. A cheer went up from the crowd when two soldiers took up duty.

The promoter drew the fighters together and related the rules. There were not many. No grabbing below the waist was allowed. No wrestling holds. If one of the contestants fell and couldn't square up – which meant being able to get up and stand upright unaided, and no more than a yard from his foe – he'd lose the match. If he stayed down he lost, whether alive or dead.

Both men bowed towards the carriage.

'Scarlet Fury! Scarlet Fury!' the crowd began to chant.

Simon stuck his fists in the air in the pose of a boxing stance.

'Very pretty,' John Howard muttered.

The referee lowered his handkerchief.

Simon had left himself wide open. Matthew drove a fist up under him. The first punch made a solid, meaty contact with Simon's stomach.

Alex winced when the air huffed from Simon's mouth and he bent over. Another punch from Matthew set him upright again.

'Scarlet Fury!' was shouted from several hundred mouths.

It was obvious who was going to win the match right from the beginning. Simon got in a few good punches to the body, but Matthew was methodical and seemed to be working to a plan. He allowed enough punches to land and bruise him a little, staggering now and again to give his opponent confidence. In his turn he inflicted real punishment on Simon, punch for punch and every one landing where it counted, so the man knew he wasn't going to get off lightly.

After an hour the crowd was crying out for blood.

Breathing heavily, Simon staggered, as if his legs were too weak to support him for much longer. Blood streamed from his nose and his eyes were puffy and swollen. He lifted his arm to ward off a blow and there was a sharp crack when a punch landed on it.

Simon screamed and staggered backwards, clutching his broken arm with the other. Colour drained from his face, leaving it waxen.

A hand shoved him back into the middle . . . Freddie's, Alex thought.

Matthew smiled at the swaying Simon. 'That one was for Miss Fox. The next one is for the maid, Maria. It might teach you not to hit women again. So far I've just tickled you.' The stomach punch had some weight behind it and sent Simon flying backwards on to the canvas. He lay there, his body doubled over his good arm, and retching. He wasn't moving and groaned loudly.

After a while the referee climbed into the ring and began to count. When he'd finished he nudged Simon with his foot, and getting no response he took Matthew's arm and held it up in the air. 'I declare this bout to have been a fair fight, and the winner is the Scarlet Fury.'

The occupant of the coach lowered the window a little. An arm clad in a dark blue sleeve with a buttoned cuff and immaculate frill slid through the gap. A purse was dropped into the palm of one of the soldiers, and then the arm withdrawn. It was passed on to Matthew. The soldier took his place on the back of the carriage.

Slick with sweat, Matthew indicated his thanks by giving a short bow before the coach made its way out of the park.

The crowd erupted into cheering.

Alex handed Matthew a towel. 'Well done, Matthew. Are you still in one piece?'

He nodded as they gazed at the body of Simon being carried off through the crowd towards the doctor's tent by Statham and Freddie. The mood of the crowd was unsympathetic, especially from those who had wagered their all on him.

Matthew shrugged. 'I hope that will be the last I see of him. I won't be so kind next time.'

The hat was passed round the crowd. John Howard took charge of the nobbins and their share of anything else they were entitled to, making sure Matthew got his. The servant had bet all he had on the fight.

Covered again in his flamboyant red satin cloak and with the hooded mask still in place, Matthew's departure was as spectacular as his appearance had been. He swaggered a little, arms flung far and wide, like a triumphant hero in an opera. The crowd screamed and shouted when he stood on the carriage step, then tore off the mask and threw it into the crowd. A scuffle for the prize began.

The program moved on with two females taking the crowd's attention. A cheer went up when a buxom woman clouted an equally buxom opponent. She screeched like a cat and then shouted some foul vulgarity as she raked long fingernails down her protagonist's face.

'This will be a no-holds-barred affair,' Alex observed.

Matthew began to scramble into his shirt and trousers in the swaying carriage. 'I'm glad to be rid of that mask. I never did like that fancy dress stuff. Besides, the colour doesn't suit me.'

Alex asked, because he knew there must be a point, 'Why wear it then?'

John laughed as he directed the carriage to Mrs Crawford's address. 'The crowd will remember the match more for its theatrical touches than the purpose of it. The Scarlet Fury will be a legend for several days . . . or even longer. The effect should be to minimize my niece's part in the affair. If we can keep her out of sight until her injuries heal, in a few days they won't even remember her name.'

Vivienne was too pretty a name to forget, and it suited her, he thought.

'The punters will dislike Mortimer, because they lost a lot of money backing him. He also lost a great deal of money on himself. He could end up in debtors' prison unless his colleagues stand to cover his debts. Statham might, now he's going to wed the sister.'

'He'll lose even more money when he learns that Vivienne isn't as well off as he imagined. I put a shilling on a negative result.'

John said with a grin, 'A whole shilling?'

'Don't mock. That's just about the extent of my fortune.'

'If you win you'll be able to buy me a tankard of ale.'

'With pleasure. Personally, I'll be glad to get home. My guess is that nothing more will come of this, and the whole pack of them will leave town with their tails between their legs, and as soon as possible. Will you be returning to your place of employment, Matthew?'

'Yes, My Lord, Mrs Goodman can't dismiss me, only the agency can, and they will if they find out about the fight. Then again, with the contract due to end in a week they probably won't bother.'

'Won't they have missed you?'

'The ladies sleep till noon, and will still be in bed, I imagine. No doubt they will have me running back and forth, and the agency will keep me on until after they've gone, if only to set the place to rights. Then I'll look around for some premises to rent, big enough to start my academy, and with some rooms to settle down in if Maria will have me.'

'I'll put the word out amongst my colleagues,' John offered.

'And I'll put in a word for you with Maria.' Alex held out a hand. 'Good luck, Matthew, and many thanks.'

'Thank you, My Lord. Miss Fox is a lovely young lady with a good heart, and it was a privilege to act as her champion on your behalf, as well as Maria's. It would be a shame to lose her to another man.'

As if he would . . . There was no doubt in Alex's mind now. He was going to marry Vivienne Fox.

The carriage dropped them off at John Howard's club. 'Join me for dinner later, My Lord. By then I will have sorted out the proceeds of today's little monetary exercise,' John said, and he handed over a purse. 'Here's an advance of your winnings today.

Would it be an insult if I suggested you buy a new suit of clothes? Those dittos are looking rather shabby. I'll deduct the amount from your share.'

At least he had that as salve for his pride.

Which reminded Alex about Howard's offer for the King's Mile. When he returned to his lodging from his shopping expedition he inserted a thumbnail under the edge of the wax seal and applied a little pressure.

He hesitated. John Howard was tricky.

It's too late! You've made a counter offer and you've shaken the man's hand on it.

I know, but what the hell have I agreed to?

There is only one way to find out.

He pushed his nail a little further and the edges of the paper sprang apart. He laughed. The man certainly had a twisted sense of humour.

Twenty-Three

The day came when Vivienne looked in the mirror and discovered the last of her bruises had disappeared.

Alex had told her she was beautiful and now she felt it, like a warm glow had spread from her heart into her body. She saw it reflected in her eyes too, something bright and shining and filled with love.

August turned. September became a riot of autumn hues that painted the landscape with the glow of warm honey. With each breeze the leaves shook free from their winter bones and the air was filled with a swirl of bronze, gold and red that danced like gypsies, and then settled to be crunched underfoot.

Vivienne's mind began to heal. She no longer jumped at shadows or feared the worst at every snap of a twig. She no longer cried without reason.

Vivienne enjoyed being with her father again. He was a calm man – a good man without being self-righteous. She was proud to be his daughter, but there was a restlessness inside her . . . a marking of time and the need to free herself of his influence.

He called her into his study one day. Jane was there and the pair looked so happy that she guessed what he wanted to tell her.

She hugged them both. 'So tell me, Papa, when is the wedding to be?'

'The weekend after next; it will be conducted by the bishop.'

She experienced a momentary shock. 'So soon?'

'Who was it that chided me not so long ago that I'd kept Jane waiting for too long? We saw no reason to wait any longer, and we want you to know that nothing will change, and it will make no difference to the household arrangements.'

'You mean you won't throw me out into the street? That's a relief.'

Alarm filled his eyes. 'Oh . . . my dear child . . . I didn't mean . . . of course we wouldn't. You will always have a home with us and I'm sure Jane will act as a wonderful mentor to you, should you need any advice.'

Us. The word hung there provocatively. Even while she understood it, the use of the word had raised a barrier. It hurt her, for it changed things. She'd been demoted into second place . . . an unmarried daughter, a guest in the home she'd grown up in. As an infant her mother had nurtured her here. As a child her grandmother had taken over. She'd been loved in this house, and had given her love in return when it had been her turn to be the carer. Now it was being taken from her.

Her inner voice was stern. *If you regard yourself as an adult then act like one, Vivienne. Your father deserves to be happy.*

Drawing in a breath, she said, 'I'm sure Jane would make a wonderful mentor had I the need for one. However, no doubt she'll be pleased to know that I'm old enough to manage my own affairs.'

She exchanged a glance with Jane and they both laughed, but there was something in the woman's eyes . . . a challenge perhaps, and they both knew that change was inevitable . . . that Jane would not expect, or accept, being placed second place to his daughter. She would take over responsibility for the household, and she would run it her way. Vivienne would have to defer to her. She conceded that it was how it should be, but she didn't have to like it.

She needed her own home – her own husband and children. So why didn't she have them now she was sitting on a fortune? Not even the ubiquitous Simon Mortimer had followed up his terrible assault with a proposal, so she could have the satisfaction of turning him down.

When the earl came she would tell him about her fortune . . . and tell him that she loved him. Yes, the next time she saw him she definitely would tell him, she promised herself. After all, how hard was it to say out loud. 'I love you,' she murmured, and she smiled. There, it wasn't hard at all.

She waited patiently for Alex to come, counting the seconds as she wove the needle in and out of her embroidery, building up the stitches like moments of her life. When she tired of that she took up a pencil and pad. When she tired of sketching the cottage that had always been her home, and tired of sketching the inside of the church when she should have been praying . . . then she sketched her father in the pulpit and the congregation in their best Sunday dresses. Next came Jane, looking demure and in training for her upcoming role as a clergyman's wife, accepting the interest of the parishioners gracefully.

The Reverend Fox was married to Jane Bessant without fuss. Half the population of the village turned up to watch them take their vows.

Vivienne cried a little, for even while she wished them much happiness there was a deep sense of loss in her. She felt abandoned and alone, and it seemed as if summer had slid into a quiet autumn and had taken her with it.

The following week, Vivienne learned that Jane disliked dust. She was efficient, almost ruthless. The house was cleaned from top to bottom and what was deemed as rubbish was thrown out to make room for Jane's things.

There was a silent struggle between the two women. Into a box went the offerings of childhood, paintings dedicated to a beloved father's various birthdays by his daughters. They were relegated to the attic.

There was a grand bonfire, as if Jane was seeking to wipe away her father's past. Vivienne was forced to rescue several items that had belonged to her mother: a small landscape she'd painted, a tortoiseshell box. The furniture was repositioned to the taste of the new mistress.

Her father and his new wife belonged together. When he came home from work his eyes sought out Jane's first, and they'd exchange a smile that spoke of an intimacy that shut her out. It was embarrassing to see him in love. He was her papa. Jane was his wife . . . his help-meet.

Vivienne had not expected her life to change. She had adored him first. Jane offered him a different kind of adoration.

Jane helped him with his sermon . . . something he'd never allowed Vivienne to do.

Vivienne began to feel like an outsider. People could no longer wander into the cottage to pass the day with him over a glass of cider. She could not argue with him over some point lest Jane frown on her. In fact, she could no longer consult with her father on a whim. She discovered something ruthless about Jane. She liked to organize people.

'Alex has forgotten about me too,' Vivienne said to her reflection one day, in a slightly surprised voice.

The cat appeared out of the point of her pencil as she quickly sketched memories before Jane changed them. He was lying on the windowsill and still following the sun, which now had a mellow September glow to it. Soon it would be winter and he'd swap his position for a human lap or the armchair, to roast in front of the fire. He was already practising his charms on the new mistress, cozying up to her with little mews. He knew where his comfort would be best served.

A dead mouse was dropped at Jane's feet as an offering. Jane didn't turn a hair, just picked the mouse up by its tail and cooed to the cat, 'There's a good boy,' before throwing it out of the window into the shrubbery.

Vivienne was dying of boredom. She felt herself beginning to dry up from doing things by habit. She dusted places that no longer needed dusting. She absorbed the uselessness of it since the dust hadn't settled from its last dusting. She fought the boredom, still waiting, for she had not yet given up. Inside her was a creature waiting to be loved . . . waiting for the demons in her body to be sated. She wanted that disorder of body and soul – needed it. Needed Alex. Why hadn't he sent word?

Jane's industriousness made her feel guilty.

Maria was tight-lipped, so she carried an atmosphere around with her like a swarm of disturbed bees. 'I'm a lady's maid not a housemaid,' she said to Jane one day, to which Jane replied, 'We don't need a lady's maid, but we do need a maid of all work. I've never seen such a dusty, unkempt house.'

Mrs Tilly was resentful, and looked magnificent with her hands planted firmly on her hips as she informed Vivienne, 'Ten years I've been working here and this is the first time anyone has said my work isn't good enough. The new mistress has wrote something called a schedule and pinned it to the wall. No good putting that there, I told her, since I can't read all them fancy words.

'Then she told me if that was the case I must attend her every morning when I arrive, so she can instruct me on my duties for the day. The mistress said I sit around drinking too much tea, and that it's expensive. She's going to put the tea in a locked box, and from now on I can only have the dregs in the pot if I care to water them down. Hrrumph!'

Vivienne agreed with Jane on that, but she wasn't going to side with either of the women since she couldn't do anything about it, and it was no longer her task.

Alex had said ten days. Two weeks had come and gone. It had been the longest two weeks of her life. She stopped watching for the messenger who brought the letters.

A week later Jane handed her a letter. Adelaide had written to say she'd married Freddie.

We have dropped Simon Mortimer from our list of friends. Sophia has married Statham. Now she's titled we're unable to drop her, though she was playing the lady to the hilt before they left for Scotland. Oh, how I wish she didn't outrank me . . . so annoying. There are some terrible rumours circulating about her now. Some say she was with child but procured a miscarriage.

It has quite laid the talk about you to rest. The boxing match helped, of course . . .

Boxing match . . . there it was again. What boxing match?

. . . Simon was so prideful but when it came down to it, his skills were no match for those of the Scarlet Fury. I do wish I'd been there. There is a rumour that it was our manservant, Matthew, dressed in a red mask and cloak. How could it be when he was at the house at the same time as Mother and me?

Simon hasn't been seen for the past week. He owed Freddie such a lot of money. The Viscount refused to pay Simon's debts and it will only be a matter of time before the debt collectors catch up with him.

Freddie is such fun. Now the little season is over we are staying in London until after Christmas. Then we are going to Bath in the spring.

Dearest Vivienne, do join us there. Freddie is so remorseful of his part in the affair and he begs your forgiveness and is determined to find you a splendid husband. Mama has gone home. It's such a relief not to be obliged to listen to her complaints.

I do hope the earl is recovering from his recent illness. Freddie called on him a week ago, but his landlady wouldn't allow him in because Lord LéSayres still had a fever and was infectious.

Alarm tore at her. Alex was ill!

The woman said he was suffering from a dose of chicken pox but he should be ready to receive visitors before too long.

Vivienne shouldn't have laughed, but she did.

Vivienne knocked at the door of her father's study and slipped inside before Jane had a chance to make it down the stairs to stop her. She didn't want to have to force her way past her new stepmother, but on this occasion she would if she had to.

Her father looked up from the paper on his desk and smiled. 'Oh it's you, Vivienne dear. I haven't seen you in here for quite a while. My brain has stopped working. How do you spell righteousness?'

When she spelled it for him he looked at the paper and then stretched. 'That's what I thought, but it didn't look correct. Perhaps I need a new nib, it's a while since it was changed.'

She changed the pen nib for him. 'There.'

'I'm glad you've paid me a visit. I always welcome a distraction, especially if it's you. Was there anything in particular you needed to consult me about?'

'I have heard from Adelaide. Lord LéSayres has been inflicted by a bout of chicken pox. I imagine he'd no longer be infectious.'

He read her mind. 'And you feel you must go to him?'

'I would like to talk to him and clear the air between us. Would you mind?'

He sat back in his chair and gazed at her. 'Where would you stay, my dear?'

She handed him Adelaide's letter. 'I would take Maria with me, of course. She will probably stay in London if I decide to return home, since she finds the country dull. I thought that after that I might pay a visit to my uncle. In Dorset. The time I spent with him here was too short, and he did invite me.'

'Wherever you travel you will always have a home here to come back to.'

'I know, but should the earl find it in his heart to respond with displeasure at my approach then I will consider buying a home of my own. Having me here will eventually cause conflict and you would be the meat in the pie, dearest Papa.'

'Don't think I haven't noticed a little frisson of atmosphere between you and Jane from time to time. It troubles me.'

'It's nothing that won't pass. I'm your daughter and Jane is your wife. It's a difficult position for her to be in, since she needs to be in charge of her own household, and she needs to be reassured that she's equal in your eyes and your heart.'

'And you're being forced to defend your position.'

She laughed. 'It's more that I have to learn to stand aside and change.'

'Women have such odd instincts at times, but you have enough sense to know I must now put Jane first and adjust accordingly.' He sighed. 'Are you sure you love the earl?'

She nodded. 'Truly I do. There can be no other man for me. I should have been truthful with him from the very beginning.'

'Yes . . . well now . . . you should have listened to me in the first place. Trying to fox the goose is always a risky course to take, but you've always been headstrong . . . just like your mother. Go then. I'll find you some coin as well as paper money and I'll arrange a letter of credit with the Bank of England, since your uncle arranged a generous allowance for you.'

Why was she always the last person to hear of such things?

'I'll take you into Maidstone in the morning. You could take the mail coach. It's rather uncomfortable, but it's fast and will get you to London in no time at all.'

The sooner she saw Alex again the better she would like it. She nodded, and was halfway to the door when a thought occurred to her. She turned. 'Papa, do you know anything about a recent boxing match that took place in London?'

Picking up his pen he gazed down at his paper, as he always did when he felt guilty. 'Hmmm. It's a common event in London, I believe. Why are you interested?'

'I shall find out, you know.'

'I daresay you will,' and he laughed. 'I know you shall . . . I shall miss you a great deal, you know?'

There was a knock at the door and Jane poked her head around the door. 'Oh . . . there you are, Vivienne. You must allow your father to finish his sermon in peace.'

He leaned back in his chair. 'I have never been a stickler for timetables, Jane. I'm here to serve the spiritual needs of my parishioners at any time, day or night. I can always find time for my daughter, as I can for my wife. As for the sermon, it can wait. Come in, my dear. Vivienne has just informed me that she's about to fly the nest.'

Jane couldn't quite hide the relief in her eyes, while Vivienne hoped she would fly more successfully this time.

Twenty-Four

Alex finally felt human again. At least he was no longer infectious and the torment of itching blemishes that had driven him crazy had gone, leaving behind little pink patches of healed skin. He hadn't been allowed to scratch them lest they leave scars.

Between them, Matthew and Mrs Crawford had nursed him through the worst of it, and put up with his bad temper.

The doctor had told him he'd been lucky. 'It was a fairly mild infection but your body was strong enough to fight it. Had it got into your lungs it would have been a different outcome altogether.'

Mrs Crawford had kept him up with the gossip. Sophia had wed Viscount Statham, it seemed. Alex didn't know which one of the pair to feel pity for. Adelaide had forgiven Freddie and they were now man and wife. That, at least, seemed a suitable match since they were alike in temperament as well as intelligence.

The vapid Cresswell sisters, still maids, had returned home with their brother, no doubt still giggling together when they weren't supposed to, which had always earned them a faint indulgent smile from their more serious brother. They were delightful and endearing girls, more like children than adults. The little season had been a training session, for Lord Cresswell intended to take them to Bath in October, where the main season lasted until July.

Then there was Vivienne . . . *his* Vivienne, his heart's ease.

As he'd hoped it would, the talk about her misadventure had been overtaken by tittle-tattle about Simon Mortimer's debt – a debt he couldn't pay. Mortimer had gone to ground. Rumour had it that he'd left London and gone to Scotland with Viscount Statham and his sister. Another rumour suggested he'd joined a religious order. Then there was the one that stated he was dead, and had been secretly buried in Potter's field . . . it all depended on who was doing the talking.

When each rumour faded, someone started another – sometimes it was Matthew. Alex didn't care where Simon was, unless he took it upon himself to harm or annoy Vivienne again. He would regard that as a personal affront.

Mrs Crawford knocked at the door and smiled at him. 'Lord Lamington has called, and he has a young lady with him.'

He supposed it was the tiresome Adelaide. Mrs Crawford had told him they were wed. At least her equally tiresome mother had left town. Adelaide might be able to tell him how Vivienne had fared while he'd been ill.

He was unprepared for his lady's appearance at the very moment he was thinking of her. It was as if a magician had produced her from his box of tricks. He shot to his feet so quickly that he forgot the low beam until the last minute. The house had not been built with tall men in mind. Ducking just in time, he stammered, 'Miss Fox . . . Vivienne . . . I was not expecting you. Are you accompanied?'

She gave a soft trill of laughter. 'Since when did you observe convention, Alex? You should have let me know of your illness.'

'I didn't want you to shed tears over me.'

'Hah . . . as if I would.'

'Had you seen me, covered in decorative pink dots and roaring like a bull from the frustration that comes from not being able to scratch an itch, you would have felt so sorry for me that you would have drowned us both in your tears. As a patient I'm quite pathetic. Ask my landlady, Mrs Crawford.' His gazed travelled over her face. 'You are quite healed now, my angel, and you look exquisite.'

A little curl had escaped from her bonnet, and he wound it around his finger. It sprang against her face when he slid his finger through it.

Then he remembered he was not fully dressed. He shrugged into his jacket too hastily and got into a tangle with the sleeve.

She laughed, and was on him in a moment, helping him into it. The smell of honeysuckle drifted around him as she cooed, 'Your landlady said you must rest.'

'I'm better now, and had intended to visit you in a day or two, when I got my strength back. Where are you staying? Your uncle, John Howard, has returned to Dorset, I understand.'

Frederick appeared in the doorway behind her, carrying a bunch of flowers. 'Miss Fox is my house guest, my Lord.'

'Yours . . . what have you done, Vivienne? The man is a friend of your enemy.'

'Nothing. Freddie has married my cousin and is a reformed character now, so it's all quite respectable. He has something he wishes to say to you.' She nudged him with her elbow.

Freddie stumbled through an apology for his part in the assault on Vivienne. After a while his stammer became worse. What the devil was the matter with the man?

'You must accept Freddie's apology, Alex. After all, it was me who was attacked in the first place . . . and I've forgiven him. Poor Freddie, you are making him nervous with that frown.'

'I'm frowning? I hadn't realized.'

'Ferociously . . . like a mad dog about to bite.'

Yes, he supposed he was. He began to smile. 'Run away then, Freddie. Go and put your flowers in water.'

'They are for you, My Lord.'

He raised an eyebrow. 'A jug of ale would have served my ills better.'

Vivienne interjected. 'The flowers are from me, Alex. Accept them with good grace else I'll leave you to your own devices . . . then you'll be sorry.'

That sounded promising and he pulled a smile to his face. 'Ah . . . flowers. How delightful. They're just what I need to cheer me up.'

Vivienne turned towards Freddie. 'I wish to have a private word with the earl. Find the kitchen and put those flowers in water, would you, then wait downstairs for half-an-hour. After that you can fetch Lord LéSayres a jug of ale from the tavern. No . . . a tankard will do. Too much ale can excite the blood.'

His was excited just looking at her.

'But Miss Fox, I promised my wife—'

She placed a forefinger over his mouth. 'Oh do shut up, Freddie. Half the fun of being a chaperone is looking in the opposite direction, as you well know. After all, I allowed you enough time to exchange more than polite smiles with my cousin when you were courting her.' Freddie backed away when she poked an accusing finger at his chest. 'And I assure you, I will not mention to Adelaide the time when I caught you flirting with another young lady when you were supposedly secretly engaged to her. Now . . . what was she called? Lettie . . . Lottie . . . Lalage?'

'It was Lillian . . . but it meant nothing.'

'There, I knew I'd remember it. You're not as foolish as you appear, and you're quite charming when you're just being yourself, Freddie. I wish you would remember that.' She closed the door in his face.

Vivienne was utterly charming in a green taffeta pelisse with embroidered panels, worn over a cream gown hemmed in lace. A straw half-bonnet covered in silk flowers adorned her head.

Laughing, he took her hands in his and kissed the palms. 'You're a sight for sore eyes. I've missed you.'

'Never mind that, Alex LéSayres. Tell me about the boxing match.'

'Oh that . . . John Howard arranged it with a promoter. It was a grudge match between myself and Simon Mortimer.'

'You fought that man over me?'

'No . . . I didn't fight him, but I would have. Apparently, it's not the done thing for a peer to fight a commoner. Matthew put himself forward on my behalf, but also to defend your maid, Maria. He won. Mortimer fled town, leaving huge debts behind him. I expect you know that. He hasn't been seen in public since. The match did what it was designed for. It served to restore your good name and shift the scandal sideways. Simon Mortimer has been promoted from a rogue into a scoundrel. It was a gentleman's resolution to a problem.'

'With me being the problem.' She touched his face. 'Why didn't you tell me?'

'You were recovering from the attack, and I . . .' There was bound to be safety in numbers . . . 'That is, John Howard, your father, Matthew and myself, decided that knowing about it would cause you unnecessary worry. Your father thought you might go haring up to London and cause a fuss, which would have defeated the object of the match. The rest of us agreed.'

'Ah . . . it was for my own good then.'

'Certainly. It didn't take long before it got around that I'd sponsored Matthew on your behalf, though nobody knew who it was under the disguise. He was billed as the Scarlet Fury and wore a satin cloak and mask.'

A little snort and a whispered, 'Men!' indicated what she thought of such male ingenuity.

'People came to the obvious conclusion. Because you and I were betrothed it wouldn't be good policy to snub you.'

'Betrothed? . . . Obvious conclusion? I can't remember a formal proposal of marriage . . . not from you, though there are at least three . . . perhaps five proposals from other men.'

He grinned, doubting she would have received any, not since word had leaked out that she was spoken for. 'I thought we had an understanding. Didn't you allow me to kiss you on several occasions? And aren't you wearing my ring with the family crest?'

She blushed. 'A gentleman wouldn't remind a lady of her weakness in certain matters.'

She hadn't yet learned what weakness was, or what those certain matters were. 'Is that so? I sold King's Mile to your uncle so I could afford to take you for a wife. I do hope that was not in vain.'

He didn't mention that John Howard intended to gift the land to Vivienne on her marriage. So, if she accepted him the land would be returned to the estate.

'You sold King's Mile? How could you? You said you'd never sell it and I so admired your stubbornness over the issue.'

'That was then. But your uncle doubled his initial offer, and I won some money betting on the outcome of the boxing match . . . enough to do the repairs and buy the seed for a corn crop and a plough horse. Luckily my wager was placed with a book-keeper other than Mortimer. I'm not exactly flushed with money, but if I'm careful and if the weather remains fair, the estate should earn enough to get us through next year's harvest with a profit. If that happens we will not need your little legacy and you can keep it for your own use.'

'You sold the King's Mile for me?' Her voice had softened and he knew he had her. 'Will I be worth more to you than a plough horse?'

He laughed. 'Only if you learn to pull a plough faster.' He pulled her against him and inched his hands down her back to cup each of her buttocks, wondering if she'd notice the liberty he was taking, or the effect it was having on him. The body gliding under his fingertips was firm and shapely, as well as giving.

How could she not notice how aroused he'd become? How could he stop the progress of what he'd started . . . or had it been Vivienne who'd started it?

His lady-love chose not to mention the position she found herself in, but she placed the flats of her hands against his chest – in case she felt the need to push him away, no doubt. He removed them and kissed her palms.

'I believe I owe you a kiss, My Lord.'

She was one big tease, but it was instinct rather than artifice. 'I believe you do.'

Their mouths met in a gloriously hungry caress. Afterwards he couldn't believe his luck when she smiled up at him through eyes like polished jade, and purred, 'Do you intend to seduce me, Alex LéSayres?'

It was unexpected. She was the daughter of a clergyman and he respected both. Her uncle was his friend and she was untouched.

'I am shocked, Vivienne.'

Her eyes widened. 'Really?'

She has to be plucked sooner or later.

For once his conscience agreed with him.

'Well perhaps not.' Removing the bonnet from her head he loosened her hair from its pins. It dropped in a glorious tumble about her shoulders when he swept her up in his arms and carried her to the bed. There he gently set her down on the edge. He seated himself next to her, giving her an opportunity to change her mind.

'Are you sure, my Vivienne?'

'Of course . . . afterwards I have something to tell you . . . something I should have told you when we first met.'

He drew the pillow down for her head to rest on and began to undo the buttons of her bodice. His signature ring lay in the shadows between her breasts. Placing the tip of his tongue against the pale rise of flesh he took a delicate lick, like a lion tasting its prey before the feast.

There was a hiss of breath, her fingers fisted in his hair and she dragged his head up. 'How dare you . . . you trickster!'

Twenty-Five

Vivienne had been about to give in to her urges – and to Alex's obvious urges too, she thought, hating the puritan streak that had suddenly taken over in an attempt to spoil her fun.

But what she was feeling had nothing to do with being prissy, since she'd been looking forward to her moment of debauchery with some eagerness. Her plan had been to allow Alex to have his way with her to soften him up for when she told him about her fortune. After all, he was a gentleman and therefore he'd honour his commitment to her, come what may.

But no! The real reason was that she'd set eyes on a book that had appeared where his pillow had formerly resided. It was her London journal – the one Maria had told her she couldn't find. She struggled to rise and pushed him from the bed. He landed on the floor with a thud.

'Stop it, and at once, Alex.'

'What the devil's the matter?' Alex said from his new position on the floor, as she fumbled to do her buttons up.

Alex loosened the laces on her boots and slid them from her feet. He reached out to straighten a wrinkle in her stocking. 'You have a sweet little pair of trotters,' he said, and gently ran his fingernail along the sole of her foot.

Who would have thought she'd experience a bolt of such unbearable pleasure through her body.

She leaned forward to gaze down at him through her hair, waving the journal in his face. 'You knew about this all the time, didn't you?'

'Knew what?'

'Knew what my journal contains. Oh do get up, Alex, you look quite ridiculous on the floor.'

He joined her on the bed in case a second chance came his way. She moved along and placed a flimsy barrier of air between them. He moved into the space.

She pursed her lips at him. He kissed them.

She nearly gave in. 'Stop that at once! I can't think straight.'

'I like a thinking woman, but I adore you when your senses are in tatters.'

She poked a finger in his chest. 'Tell me how my journal came into your possession. Have you read it?'

'I wouldn't dream of reading it! I only knew it contained a summary of people you'd met. Adelaide was amusing her mother and their guests with some of the contents when I arrived at the house, and I put a stop to it. I'd intended to escort you to the Almack's social that day, remember? That was the day you left me without a word – except for a short note – and I was all dressed up like some fancy fop on display.'

'Why didn't you take someone else to Almack's in my place?'

'How could I when I was chasing after you, and half worried to death when I learned what had happened to you?'

He was getting a little bit riled, and Vivienne knew she deserved it. Guilt surged through her and she kissed his cheek. 'I'm sorry I accused you of replacing me with another.'

'It's no good being contrite now, it's too late,' he said. 'I took the journal with me and put it under my pillow. Then I promptly forgot about it. I'm not that interested in reading female meanderings.'

'I do not meander, I write straight to the point. Are you telling me you didn't read it?'

When he twirled her hair around his finger into a ringlet, she shivered.

He said, 'I saw no reason to read it, and if I had read it, right now I can think of no reason that would be served by confessing that I had.'

That was a mouthful.

'Hah!' she said, trying to figure out the meaning behind it. It seemed unnatural that he wouldn't have wanted to read it. She was a little miffed that he could dismiss it so easily. Female meanderings. Hah twice!

What about his meandering hands? He had his finger in her ear . . . tickling it. She swooped in a breath and pushed it away, then picked up her hat and unsuccessfully tried to stuff her hair back under it. 'You weren't interested in what I'd written about you then? If I'd been you and had found your journal I'd have done you the courtesy of being interested enough in you to read it.'

'Remind me to hide my journal after we're wed. Stop twisting things . . . here, allow me to tidy your hair. I'll do something with it . . . make a rope so I can strangle you with it, perhaps. I think I'd enjoy doing that at this moment.'

She wondered if she could squeeze a tear or two out, play on his sympathy. 'What about my fortune?'

'What about it?' His big hands tugged gently through her hair, sending shivers rioting through her.

'It's worth hundreds of thousands of pounds.'

He began to laugh. 'Nobody else has got a sense of humour like you. There isn't that amount of money in the entire world.'

She grinned, triumphant. She'd told him now, was it her fault he didn't believe her? She reinforced the notion so it was in his head.

'What if it were true, Alex?'

His eyes met hers. 'Tell me it's not, otherwise I'll have to rethink my position.'

'Why should you do that?'

'Because I value your honesty. I love you and you love me. We don't need anything else and you don't have to pretend. Were it true it would give the London crowd something to talk about, even though it would make me a laughing stock. In fact, it would make me look like the biggest fool going because I wagered my last shilling on the opposite result.'

'Your last shilling? Oh Alex, were things that bad for you? And you bought me that pretty brooch, something I'll always treasure.'

'I know . . . and that just makes matters worse.'

'Why?'

'Because the gossips would say I married you for your wealth.'

'But isn't that why you came to London . . . to marry a wealthy woman so you could restore your estate?'

'Saying it and doing it are two different things. I don't like the thought of being bought.'

'Oh piffle! Does it matter where a fortune comes from? How do you think I felt when some relative I can't remember dropped a huge amount into my lap without even a by-your-leave?'

He raised an eyebrow. 'I'd have been overjoyed if he'd dropped it in my lap instead. The thing is, Vivienne my love, you've taken that chicanery as far as it will go. We shouldn't start off married life with a lie, and you didn't have to invent a fortune to make yourself more attractive to me. I love you as you are.'

She opened her mouth at that example of male logic, and then firmly closed it again. Some things were not worth the risk of arguing about just to prove a point.

She kissed his eyelids, the handsome slope of his nose and the sensuous curves of his mouth.

'Of course we shouldn't start with a lie,' she cooed, and knew it was the time to tell him. 'I do love you, Alex LéSayres.'

His eyes opened and they gazed at each other.

His grin was almost boyish as he grunted, 'I love you too, but if I hear your fortune mentioned again I'll catch the next boat to China.'

Guilt flooded through her and she ignored it. Why not let sleeping dogs lie? After we're wed will be soon enough to convince him. 'You do love me then, so why did you keep asking for an opinion on other young women?'

'It gave me an excuse to be with you . . . mainly because I didn't expect any woman to be interested in an impoverished earl. Then . . . well . . . I realized it was because of the way I felt about you.'

She accepted his kiss and smiled at him. 'How exactly do you feel about me, Alex?'

Taking her face in his hands, his thumbs caressed her chin. 'I fell in love with you the minute we met.'

'And I you.'

'Which is why we need to do something about it.' He lowered her to the bed again and kissed her until her heart beat so fast she was scared it would take wing.

'Can we get rid of the pelisse?' He'd barely finished that pleasurable task and started loosening the laces on her stays, when there came the sound of a heavy footstep on the stair.

'Freddie will think we've been up to something,' she said.

'We were just about to get up to something, I believe. He's taking his responsibility too seriously.' Alex sounded so aggrieved that she giggled nervously. 'And in answer to your earlier question . . . I didn't wonder what you'd written about me. I didn't need to. I adored you from the moment we met and I sensed that feeling was reciprocated. I'd already made up my mind to abandon the notion of marrying for money, because I needed to have you in my life.'

The latch on the door rattled and he smiled at her and called out, 'Go home, Freddie. Vivienne is quite safe in my hands and I'll bring her home later.'

'Am I safe in your hands?' she asked after Freddie had gone.

'Not at all . . . there would be no fun in that.'

He triumphantly dangled a pink ribbon he'd plucked from her stocking top. 'I knew it would be pink. I love you, my darling Vivienne.'

He left the bed, went to the door and turned the key in the lock, then came back and gazed down at her. 'You look lovely, all ready to be ravished. Are you sure, my Vivienne?'

Love for him had become a torrent of fire that pulsed through her veins.

He hopped across the room, shedding his clothes on the chair, to the floor, and joined her in the bed. Soon, the remainder of her clothes joined his.

He sank on the bed next to her and took her hands, guiding them over the muscular perfection of his body. His member nestled in her hands, silky and warm. He kissed her jutting breasts and his lips skittered down the centre of her, over her stomach and disappeared inside the opening in the silky darkness at her groin. Her body arched and she gasped when his tongue stroked along the slickness of her.

She was so ready for him and she pulled him up and gazed into his eyes. 'Do it now, Alex my love . . . do it now.'

'Not yet . . .' His mouth touched the peaks of her breasts and his fingers slipped inside her. Everything within her cried out for release and she was riding the exquisite peaks of sensation when he drove into her wetness.

The shock of it forced a little cry from her, but her pelvis arched to meet his thrusts. For several moments there was a flurry of thrusts, and she wrapped her legs around his hips and captured him as they rode the wave of loving between them.

They collapsed together and he drew her against him, her

head snuggled against his shoulder. Both of them panted for breath.

After a while Vivienne looked up at him and giggled.

He chuckled, and kissed the end of her nose, then pulled the quilt over them.

Vivienne and Alex were wed in her father's church in Chausworth early one morning, using the special licence the bishop had provided them with.

Most of the village attended, as did Adelaide and Freddie. Maria had attended her and Matthew had joined them for the service. The pair had some prospect in mind that Vivienne thought might end in marriage, as Maria had decided not to travel to Dorset with her.

Her father had smiled proudly as he conducted the service that had made them husband and wife, and had hugged her goodbye with tears in his eyes. 'I wish you much happiness, my dearest daughter. The earl is a good, caring man who deserves a good woman by his side. Where there is love there is always respect, and you will get that with him.'

Almost straightaway they boarded a boat that took them around the coast to the port of Poole. It was a less strenuous mode of travel than the stagecoach. From there they hired a cab.

The county of Dorset blazed with early October colours as they passed through the winding countryside, but there was a nip in the air that promised winter was not far away.

Vivienne watched Alex take in a deep breath of air before he turned to smile at her. 'It's not much further . . . shall we walk?'

He rapped on the cab roof when she nodded. 'Stop at the top of the hill, coachman. You can take the luggage on and we'll walk the rest of the way.'

It was early evening and a faint misty purple haze hung on the horizon. To their left was the sea. About a quarter of a mile away a house was set in a sheltered copse. It faced towards the water and was set well back on a rise. Built of stone, it shone golden and warm in the lowering sun.

Alex slid his arm around her as the carriage moved off. He rested his chin on her head, murmuring, 'Welcome to your new home, Lady LéSayres. How do you like it?'

A lump filled her throat at the naked pleasure in his eyes at the sight of his home. 'It's lovely, Alex . . . which is my piece of land?'

He pointed. 'The King's Mile is that strip along the coast, and it curves around by the gate and up to the road. What will you do with it?'

'Nothing. It looks very comfortable and happy where it is, so I'll leave it there for everyone to enjoy.'

He tipped her chin up with his cupped hand and kissed her, and then they slid their arms about each other's waists and began to walk, Alex shortening his stride to match hers.

After a while the cab passed them on its return journey. Alex put his fingers to his mouth and gave a piercing whistle. Two dogs detached from the house, cast around, then sniffed the air and gave excited yaps before finding Alex's scent and heading in their direction at a run, their tails streaming behind them like flags. They were followed by the long-legged figure of a striding man.

Alex let her go and began to run. They came together and the two men embraced, slapping each other on the back, the dogs wagging their tails and sniffing at their ankles.

Alex brought his brother to her. 'Dom, may I present Vivienne, my wife, and the love of my life.'

'Lady LéSayres. I'm so pleased to meet you again. Welcome to King's Acres. I hope you'll be happy here.'

There was something guarded about Dominic. 'Call me Vivienne.'

Dominic kissed her hand and smiled. 'I'm employed by your uncle, and with Alex's permission we'll be managing the fortune you bring into the LéSayres family to best benefit the estate.'

'Will I have a say in the matter?'

'If Alex agrees . . . it won't hurt for you to learn the farming side of things. I've arranged a meeting for the day after tomorrow, by which time you should be recovered from your journey. We must sort out how best to manage the wealth you bring with you. We also need to hire some house staff, Alex, but I daresay Vivienne can sort that out with the housekeeper. I hired some labourers to get the corn crop in the ground before it was too late.'

Alex turned to gaze at her, puzzled. 'Why didn't you tell me it was true?'

'If you recall, I said I had a fortune of thousands of pounds. You refused to believe me and laughed. I didn't like to disillusion you because you said your gentlemanly pride would prevent you from marrying a wealthy woman, and I didn't want to dent that pride. Neither did I want to lose you.'

Alex looked stunned. 'But I didn't mean you, my love, I was referring to all the other wealthy women in London.'

'As I said at the time: piffle! Don't worry, Alex, you'll grow used to the legacy, as I had to. Keeping it quiet from everyone was the worst thing . . . You know what happened when a whisper of it got out.'

He pulled her protectively against his side. 'It won't happen again.'

Dominic gazed from one to the other and grinned. 'How did you manage to fox my brother, Vivienne?'

'It was easy,' and she sent him a smile. 'He didn't want to listen so it would have been a waste of breath arguing with him.'

'That's Alex for you.'

There was a wide grin on Alex's face with the pleasure of being in his own home.

Later there was Eugenie. Vivienne remembered how she'd felt being ousted by Jane Bessant. This woman, small and neat, commanded respect from the men in the house. She had taken the place of their mother, kept the family together and had spent most of her own income to keep two needy boys alive. They loved her, and Vivienne felt the need to honour her for that.

Vivienne caught a few moments alone with her. 'Eugenie . . . may we talk a while? Alex has told me you intend to move off the estate.'

'I imagine he has told you of my circumstance.'

'Yes, he has, but please, do not feel you have to move on my account. I would be proud to acknowledge you as my stepmother, as does Alex and his brother. I would also welcome your advice on how best to manage the household as well as value your presence for the female companionship it would afford me. Men are so overwhelming at times.'

Eugenie kissed her gently on the cheek. 'I have sometimes

wished for a daughter to talk to and confide in, and it will be my pleasure to stay until next spring so we can get to know each other.'

But spring became summer, and with good reason Eugenie stayed on. Another LéSayres male had arrived for an indefinite stay. The little viscount had blue eyes and a cap of dark curls, just like Alex.